THE BLOODLINE CURSE

THE BLOODLINE CURSE

JAMIE LEE FRY

BOOK ONE OF
THE DARK MAGIC SERIES:

THE BLOODLINE CURSE

JAMIE LEE FRY

Print edition ISBN: 9781737120261
E-book edition ISBN: 9781737120278
Barnes & Noble Edition ISBN: 9781737120285

First edition: July 2023
10 9 8 7 6 5 4 3 2 1

WWW.AUTHORJAMIELEEFRY.COM

FOR MY MOM, FOR EVERYTHING

"MAGIC IS NEUTRAL, NEITHER GOOD NOR EVIL. IT'S THE PRACTITIONER WHO DECIDES HOW TO FOCUS THE ENERGY."
-UNKNOWN

CHAPTER 01
MOVING DAY

Goodbyes are always hard, but they are even more difficult when you have no choice in the matter—being seventeen sucks.

As my dad loads the last of our boxes into the back of our black SUV, his face is long and sorrowful, unaware I'm watching him from afar. Normally, he puts on a brave face for me. I love that about him—my protector. But it doesn't change the facts about today.

I sway back and forth on our porch swing one last time, letting my feet dangle toward the floor like the little girl I once was. But so much has changed since I was that little girl. Life happened, and now I have to grow up—fast.

The rain picks up and pelts off Dad's jacket while the thick Pacific Northwest fog blankets him. I'd like to believe it's trying to keep us here, telling us not to leave, keeping us wrapped in its cozy and familiar embrace. But somehow, cosmically, the weather is fit for an ending such as this. As I continue to rock with the swing, I close my eyes, soaking up the calming noises from the Puget Sound beyond our house. I take mental notes, locking them deep into my memory to take them with me: the roar of the waves crashing against the rocks, the feisty wind whipping through the salty air, the seagulls cooing in the distance. These relaxing sounds I once took for granted, but now realize I will miss dearly. How will I be able to sleep at night without it?

"Are you ready?" Dad hollers toward the house from the bottom of our driveway.

I open my eyes, wishing it were just a dream, but the car is loaded, and reality is punching me in the face.

"We need to get on the road and beat the morning traffic if we want to make it to Montana before dark," Dad replies, jetting into the garage for one last look around.

"Be there in a second!" I shout back, but he's already out of earshot. Three straight days of driving and sleeping in motels hardly sounds like the start to summer break that I had initially planned, but things changed in a blink of an eye. I must keep going, or my sadness, anger, and denial will swallow me whole.

I let a single tear slide down the length of my face before patting it dry with my jacket. I jump off the swing, taking a final loop around the wrap-around porch, bidding a farewell to my neighborhood and childhood home. I do not want this, but I have to put on a brave face for Dad. I must mirror his act. We both need to be strong. We've only got each other.

The reality of our situation sucks, and I guess it's both of our faults that we have to move. I prefer to argue it's more his fault, but that little incident I had with Sondra would be tough to argue against. It's probably for the best, but I can't imagine where we're going will be any better. There will always be girls like Sondra. I'm not sad because I'm leaving my high school and so-called friends. That would be silly. They didn't have my back. No one did, except Dad. But even he looks at me like I really did it. But I didn't—I swear. I think. No, I'm sad because I'm leaving the security of my home and the memories of a happier time. Before it all went down the crapper. Dad's words, not mine. I take my time walking down the long driveway. I'm unfazed by the rain soaking its way into my clothing. I quickly tuck my wet shoulder-length dirty blonde hair behind my ears before slinking into the passenger seat. I fasten my seatbelt with Dad coming into focus in the side mirror. He's absolutely drenched. My grayish eyes reflect at me, causing me to shudder at my appearance. I don't look much better.

"Hey, kiddo, you ready for a new beginning?" Dad asks, sliding his wet body into the car. His dampened denim screeches across the cold leather seat. He presses the ignition while I try to force a smile. The ends of my lips curl, but the emotion doesn't match.

"Sure, new beginnings," I say the words, but my act isn't convincing.

Dad knows this move will be harder on me than him. No one wants to move their senior year. If we stayed, I wonder if I could have survived the cruelty of my peers. The rumors and the judgment would have been hard. I'd like to think I could have gotten through it, though. It's only one more year. I'm strong. But none of that matters now. We're in our car, and we're moving. There is no going back at this point.

I know Dad tried to find a new job, but his talent is becoming obsolete. In the world of ever-changing technology, there was no need for his services anymore, at least not here in Seattle's highly competitive and evolving city. Everyone is looking for someone younger, smarter, and fresh out of Silicon Valley with their millennial ideas and new ways of thinking. Well, at least that's what Dad says. I'm not even sure what he did. Something with coding, maybe? But it used to pay well, until it didn't.

"I'm not going to miss the Seattle rain. That's for sure," Dad remarked, gesturing to his wet clothing, flinging water droplets from his hands like a wet dog shaking his body, not caring what's in its way.

I know this is his attempt to lighten the mood and make me laugh, but I can't find it in me to play along. I want to for his sake, but I can't. Instead, my attention is diverted to the windshield wipers, which are whooshing fast, trying to catch up to the constant downfall of rain. I let myself get hypnotized by them. The whooshing sound, the fast movement. My eyes are glued to them. It's the only thing I allow myself to focus on until we're out of our neighborhood.

I sullenly let out my delayed response. "I'm going to miss the smell right before it rains."

"I think I will miss that smell too, but I'm sure it rains in Connecticut," Dad says with a lighthearted laugh. "I'm sorry we couldn't wait out another year, but I think a fresh start is what we both need."

"I know, Dad. It's not all your fault. And you might be right."

Guilt snakes its way through my gut. But both of us know it's fifty/fifty. We share the fault, but thankfully he doesn't bring up that fact.

Dad's face contorts to a frown and then quickly back to a forced smile. I don't think he knows how much his features give away. He'd be a horrible poker player.

"I'm sure glad I didn't sell old Gran-gran's house. You know I almost put it on the market a little over a year ago. Thank goodness I didn't. Something inside me told me to hold off. You can't argue with that gut feeling, you know," Dad says, stroking his clean-shaven chin with his non-driving hand. "I really don't know what state we'll find it in. I've let it sit for over five years. I can't believe it's been that long since we've visited East Gate."

I offer Dad a soft smile. "I wish I remembered Gran-gran more. I don't remember much from the last time I saw her."

"Gosh, you must have been twelve the last time we were there. She passed away the month after we visited, and we couldn't afford to go back again. I'll always regret missing her funeral, especially after finding out she left everything to us, including her house."

"That was very nice of her."

Now, I feel worse for not remembering more. Sadly, all I can recall from East Gate is a boy named Riley. My first real crush. The cute boy with kind eyes and a playful smile. The two of us always got into trouble together. Other than that, I don't remember East Gate much, nor my last time with Gran-gran. The memories simply aren't there. I give Dad a thoughtful grin and allow him to recall stories of his time with her. Dad loves talking about the good ol' days. Sometimes I think he hung out with old people too much as a child, because he talks more like someone in a nursing home than a man in his forties.

"She was a special gal—that one. As you know, I used to spend summers with her when I was little, but my mom and your Gran-gran always seemed to fight, and our trip would be cut short. I hated leaving her. We had a special relationship, and she was actually fun for someone of her age. She would get down on the floor and play with me. We even made forts out in the woods behind her house. I always felt closer to her than my own mother. I really miss Gran-gran." He pauses, and a sadness flushes through his words.

We don't talk much about his mom, Anna. I'm surprised he even brought her up. I've only met her a few times. I don't even call her grandma. She's just Anna to me. My Dad never knew his dad, and he was an only child, so with a challenging relationship and very little family, there wasn't anyone else pulling us together. I don't mind. Anna was never nice to me. It's amazing that my dad turned out so kind with a mother like Anna. I don't think she even likes me. Who dislikes their own granddaughter?

Dad takes a left onto the 405. The windshield wipers are whooshing quickly as heavier rain tings against the windshield.

"I remember the day you were born," Dad says while accelerating to merge with the eager traffic. "Gran-gran, well, she was just Gran to me, called before I had a chance to let her know you arrived into the world. She said you were perfect, as if she had already met you. She always had good timing, that old broad." Dad chuckles at his fond memory. "I couldn't think of a better person to name you after. When I got off the phone with her, and I glanced at your mother—all pink in the face—I said, 'how about Isobel?' Your mother studied me and wrinkled her nose. I could tell she didn't like that name for a little girl, but when she saw your tiny little body and called you Izzy, we knew the name had stuck. Our little Izzy."

"Ah, Dad, stop getting all mushy."

The corner of his mouth stiffens before turning downward, and I can't help but sense where this conversation is heading.

"I wish your mother was still here. She would have made this move easier on all of us. She always knew what to say and do."

"Well, she's not," I snap. "Mom left us."

"Mom didn't leave us, sweetie; she died."

"Well, it's the same thing."

Dad sniffles, and his eyes well up with tears. I didn't mean to upset him, but Mom left us, whether it was by choice or not.

She's gone.

I feel bad for my outburst, but nothing I can say will change the mood in the car. It's best to let this ride itself out now. I close my eyes, pretending to fall asleep. We've barely made it out of the greater Seattle area, and I've already set a precedent for the long drive.

I let my eyelids fall heavy from the weight of my words. As I allow myself to fall into a relaxed, almost meditation-like state, I'm jolted by a familiar and haunting image.

Sondra's horror-struck expression flashes through my mind and imprints itself as a reminder of that day. It doesn't last long before the image shifts, and she falls backward with one arm reaching out toward me.

Her ginger tendrils tangle in the wind, followed by a bloodcurdling scream, "Izzy, no!"

CHAPTER 02
NEW BEGINNINGS

After nearly three thousand miles and three restless nights of sleeping in dirty, old roadside motels in Montana, Wisconsin, and Pennsylvania, we finally arrive in East Gate, Connecticut. Our drive was quiet, with a lot of thoughts and feelings left unexpressed. Our usual father-daughter banter was abandoned and left with a hollow unease. It rested heavy in the car like the thick northwest blanket of fog that's now far behind us. But now, here we are, pulling into our new life.

Dad slows down to read the welcome sign conveniently nestled in an array of maple trees.

Welcome to Historic East Gate

Founded 1788

Population 9,431

Did I read that right? "Dad, less than ten thousand people!"

"Yes, it's on the smaller side, but it will be a nice change from our hustle and bustle city lifestyle. I promise you will grow to love small-town life."

I roll my eyes. "You can't be serious. I knew the town was

small, but I didn't realize just how small. I won't be able to blend in. All eyes will be on me. Do you get how hard that's going to be?"

"You have the entire summer to figure it out and maybe make some friends before the school year starts. I'm sure it will all work out."

I shift my entire body to face the window. "Ugh, whatever. I sure hope you're right."

We continue driving in silence through a hilly, picturesque landscape of dense trees. Dad takes the first right down a narrow street that could hardly lead us to civilization. After five miles or so, I'm pleasantly surprised to see the town finally coming into focus.

Massive church steeples tower in the distance with rolling hills of green behind them. I carefully let myself imagine what it will look like in the fall when all the leaves turn their beautiful, deep autumn colors. But I don't let myself get too invested because, after all, I'm a sulky teenager who just found out she moved to the world's smallest town. I'm being dramatic, but I can't help it. It's how I'm programmed.

"Come on, Izzy. Cheer up. Let's move past what was said earlier in our trip. We've had three days of moping; it's time to move on. This is our fresh start. It's going to be a nice adventure for the two of us. Isn't this town quaint and beautiful?" Dad says while nudging my knee, searching for a joyous reaction.

"Dad! Stop pushing this town on me. It's only been like five minutes. Give me a second to breathe! I'll stop moping when I'm ready."

"OK, I will leave you to your sulking, but I'm excited, so please don't rain on my parade. I'm sorry I didn't tell you about the town's size. I assumed you would have remembered. I forget how young you were and how things appear when you're that age. I'm sorry, sweetie, but please try to be open to our new life. I was hoping to drive through downtown and by the school before we head to our new home."

"Fine," I respond with little enthusiasm.

"You are going to fall in love with downtown when you see it," Dad says with excitement brewing in his voice, obviously ignoring my request to stop pushing. He rolls down all four windows, and a cool spring breeze invades the car. Dad's thick dark hair flaps against the wind, messing up his side part. I can't help but laugh at the sight.

"Ah, there she is. My sweet little Izzy is back."

I quickly cover my mouth and shoot Dad one of my classic annoyed expressions I've mastered over the years.

Dad doesn't skip a beat and continues to blabber on. "I remember coming down here as a kid and taking in a movie at the old theatre. I sure hope it's still there. I'd always stock up on snacks at the candy store. Back then, you could get single pieces of candy for just pennies."

"OK, Dad, now you're dating yourself," I respond playfully, but quickly remember I'm sulking and resume my quietude.

This car ride has my moods all out of whack. I'm better at brooding when I can slam a door and hide in my bedroom. Dad always lets my mood run its course. It works for us. But being stuck in a car for this long is uncharted territory.

"Hey, now. Watch what you're about to say. I'm still hip," Dad jokes, but I don't respond, continuing my teenage mind tricks.

We pull into downtown, and it's breathtaking. Dad was right. I love it, but I don't dare tell him that. I wouldn't hear the end of it. I bite my bottom lip to force it from turning upward into a smile. As I peer out the window, I become excited. The city has the quaintness Dad suggested. The town is older, but they've done a suitable job maintaining its historic charm as the welcome sign boasted. I give him the side-eye, catching a smile forming in the corner of his mouth. He sees right through me; he knows I'm getting excited.

On Main Street, both sides of downtown are lined with blooming cherry blossom trees. The trees are so large they nearly reach out and touch the branches from trees on the opposite side of the street, like a scene from a painting.

Once we pass the first block, I notice a small park to the left of our car. It's a lovely area with more trees, of course. A beautiful tall green weathered clock and a gazebo sit near the middle of the park. A couple of girls are sitting on a blanket near the outdated structure. They appear to be about my age. I bet they'll be in my high school. One girl turns to face my direction as our car passes. Her platinum blonde hair effortlessly blows with the wind, making her beauty even more striking. I instantly feel inadequate and run my fingers through my hair to caress down the flyaways. As our car passes them, I turn my head to get a longer glimpse, but they're out of my eyesight in seconds. The stress of a small school intensifies by the sight of them. How will I fit in here?

More girls like Sondra to. . . *Stop it, Izzy.*

To get my mind off the girls, I attempt to note some of the stores we pass. Rex's Hardware—I doubt I'll need that one. A ladies' clothing boutique that looks like it's more for older women than the stylish teenagers I saw in the park. I wonder where they shop.

Stop thinking about them, Izzy.

Back to my mental notes. A bakery that's uncreatively named East Gate Bakery and an adjoining coffee shop called The Perk.

"Ah, Izzy, look!" Dad shouts, interrupting my thoughts. "It's the old theatre. It's just as I remembered it. Oh, and the candy store is still here, too. I know what we're doing this Friday night," Dad says with a childish giddiness in his voice while pointing at each building as if I can't find them for myself.

"Sure, Dad. It's not like I'll have anything else going on," I sadly respond, remembering the girls in the park again.

Izzy, you're doing it again.

We pass a small grocery store on the left, and I hope it's not the only one in East Gate. I haven't seen a Whole Foods or Trader Joe's anywhere. I can't imagine they have a wide selection like what I'm used to in Seattle.

"We will head back down here later once we get settled. We can grab a bite to eat at the cafe and pick up some groceries. So, start making a list. We will have to see what dishes Gran-gran left us, since the moving truck won't arrive with our stuff for another three days."

Yup, it's the only grocery store.

We soon approach the school. Although this could have been our first stop. I think Dad tried to butter me up with downtown first because we're making a loop.

Sneaky.

He knows I'm dreading my senior year, and he's right. But first I have to survive the summer before I can wrap my head around my final year of high school.

My new school is an ornate brick building with a courtyard in the middle. Everything in this town is old and historic. It resembles a castle more than a school. The only evidence it's a place of education, not a palace for kings and queens, is the football field that's just behind the structure. It's also bigger than I imagined for a town of this size. I bet other kids get bused in from smaller towns. That's the only thing that makes sense.

Dad rolls into the parking spot closest to the front of the castle—I mean school.

"Here it is, Izzy. I know it's not like your last one. No big-time tech donors here to add a new wing each year, but it sure has that historic charm like the rest of the town. Don't worry; you will still get an excellent education. I promise."

"Well, it's not what I imagined."

It's only a year. One school year.

"I'm excited for you to make new friends and move on from things at your old school. If you ever need to talk about what happened with Sondra, I'm all ears. I won't judge. We've removed ourselves from that situation, but always know you can come to me."

I shift sideways in my seat. Anger percolates inside me,

and I can't help but shout, "Dad, for the millionth time, I'm done talking about Sondra! I didn't do it. Everyone lied. So, can this please be the last time you bring it up? New beginnings, remember!"

I immediately regret my explosion, especially after we just tried to patch up our last one, but he needs to stop prying into the situation that's already been put to bed.

We drive the rest of the way to our new home in silence. Dad knows better than to bring up Sondra.

We pull up to Gran-gran's house, and my mouth drops. Even Dad gasps at the sight of our new home.

"It's much worse than I imagined. Oh, this is bad," Dad says with a quiver in his voice.

"I'm not living here! I can't! I won't!"

The decrepit house sits back on a hill with a dark, dense forest towering behind it, casting a shadow over the property. The outside is far from what I remember. It's literally falling apart. The brown siding is faded in spots while other areas are peeled away from the house. The foundation has a crack, and the white paint around the floor-to-ceiling windows has chips of paint flapping in the wind. The roof looks like it's about to cave in, not to mention the tiny, creepy, single round window on the third floor. And the amount of overgrowth and weeds overtaking the property is alarming. You can hardly see the multiple levels of steps climbing the hillside, leading up to the front door. Gran-gran is probably rolling in her grave at the sight of her home.

"We can deal with this. The house has good bones. Sure, it needs a lot of work, but we need to stay positive," Dad says, trying to convince me, but I think he's also trying to convince himself.

"Needs a lot of work. Dad, it needs to be condemned!"

"I bet it looks better on the inside," Dad says with hopefulness in his voice.

"I thought you were paying someone to mow and take care of the yard work and upkeep."

"Well, about that. . . I had to let Hank go when money got tighter. I didn't think it would matter. I never thought we would resort to living here. I figured I would sell the house when I had time and pay someone to get it ready for sale, but then life happened. Don't worry; everything is going to be OK."

"OK?! How is this going to be OK? You keep saying that. We lost our house to the bank. You don't have a job, and I had to leave my friends my senior year and move across the entire country to live in a should-be-condemned house that looks like something straight out of a horror film."

"Come on, Izzy. I know this move is hard on you, but please give it a chance."

"I'm not getting out of the car!" I scream, tears welling in my eyes. The big kind that feels like once one drop falls, the floodgates will open, and it will be hard to control.

"Izzy, the house was built in 1859. It's an Italianate-style home."

His description of the house makes it worse. Like I even know what an Italianate-style home is. One more word, and the tears will fall. I swear.

"This style of home has stood the test of time. It was built to last. It has so much potential, Izzy. I wish we could've seen it in its prime. Yes, the curb appeal needs some work, but I bet the inside is fine. Come on, grab your bags and let's check it out."

"How are we going to pay for all this?" A huge teardrop falls from my eye, followed by a river of tears now streaming and streaking my face.

"Oh, sweetheart, don't cry. That's not something you need to worry about. I have money set aside. I knew the house would need work. I was somewhat prepared for this. Come on, let's go."

Dad hands me a napkin from the center console to wipe my eyes, then he exits the car. He opens the back door and takes his time rummaging through his bags. I suspect he's hoping he won't have to continue coaxing me inside. But I can't bring myself to get out of the car. Once I step foot outside the vehicle, this is my new reality. I feel sick. My life was good, well, good before the incident with Sondra, and good before Dad went broke trying to keep our way of life afloat. And good before Mom left us. OK. Maybe it's been a shitshow for a while now, but I was comfortable. I can't deal with *this*.

I take a deep breath, stare up at the run-down structure, and my stomach churns. But something catches my eye.

Something moved!

Upstairs, in the round window on the top floor.

Did I imagine that? No, I didn't—something passed by the window again.

"Dad, there's someone in the house!" I scream.

CHAPTER 03
REFLECTIONS

Someone is in the house.

"What?" Dad shouts.

"Dad, there's someone in the house. Look."

"Sweetie, it's all in your head. You are putting off going inside."

"No, look up there at the small window on the third floor. Something is moving up there!" I shout, stepping out of the car.

"Honey, I don't see a thing," Dad insists.

"Dad, I saw someone. Please, we need to call the cops."

"I think you're overreacting. I'm sure it's nothing. Come on, grab your bags."

"I'm not going in there unless you have someone come check it out. I saw something. You need to believe me. Dad, please."

"Fine, I will call the police and have them come check things out. If you really saw something, I guess it's better to be safe than sorry." Dad pulls his phone from his pocket. He glances at me again to make sure I'm not lying, then dials the police.

"Um, hi, this is Steven Beswick. I'm the owner of the home on 1803 Jefferson Place." Dad pauses for a moment as he paces next to the car. "Yes, that's the one. We just pulled up, and well, my daughter thought she saw someone inside. Can you send someone to come take a look?" He pauses again. "OK, great. We really appreciate it. Thanks." He presses end on his phone and slides it into his back pocket.

"Police don't think it's anyone, but they're sending someone right away. They think it could be an animal," Dad says.

"How would they know it's nothing? They aren't here. What if we have squatters? The home has been vacant for five years."

"Well, the officer will deal with whatever it is when he gets here," Dad reassures me.

About ten minutes pass when a patrol car pulls up behind our black SUV. The officer steps out of his vehicle and walks toward us. He's squinting and giving my dad a funny look.

"Steven, is that really you?" The officer hollers to us as he continues to move in our direction.

My dad reciprocates the squinting and funny grin.

"The call came in over my radio, and I had to see it for myself. Man, what's it been? Five years?" the officer says to my dad.

"Tim, it is you. I didn't recognize you with the uniform. It threw me for a loop. What, you're a cop now?" Dad excitedly replies, apparently recognizing the man.

They shake hands when they finally approach one another.

"Yep. I'm a man of the law now," Tim says, tapping on

his badge. "The factory shut down, and the station was hiring. It was destiny," he laughs. "I really do enjoy it, and it pays a lot better than the factory."

"The uniform looks good on you, man," Dad responds.

"Sorry to hear about Isobel, but what brings you back here?" the officer says to my dad, raising his right brow in confusion.

"Thanks for that, Tim. Gran left us the house, and, well, we're moving in," Dad responds.

"Wow, I never thought I'd see the day. Well, welcome. We need to catch up, but first, I heard over the radio you think you may have an intruder?"

"My daughter, Izzy—" Dad begins to say, but Officer Tim cuts him off.

"Oh, my gosh. This can't be little Izzy. Oh, my, how you've grown. Where does the time go?" Tim gushes over my inevitable growth spurt and aging. I can't say I recognize the man.

I give a snide grin. I'm annoyed with our unproductive banter and game of catch up, so I continue with our issue at hand. "I saw someone upstairs. Right up there. In the small window on the top floor. I swear there is something up there. You need to go look now," I inform Officer Tim.

"Well, I doubt it's squatters because we don't see much of that in East Gate. It's more likely to be a ghost," Tim snickers. "I'm only joking. It's probably a raccoon or a possum. If it's all right with you, I'll check things out first."

"Yes, of course. Here are the keys," Dad says, producing his keyring.

"I'll be right back. Hang tight." Tim grabs Dad's keys. He pivots and runs up the steps overgrown with weeds.

"Dad, who is that guy?" I ask once he's out of earshot.

"We used to play together when I summered here as a kid. We saw each other a few times when I came back over the years. You met him when you were younger. He has a son—Riley. Do you remember him?"

Oh, my goodness. That's Riley's dad. My crush Riley. Maybe I should have been more pleasant to Officer Tim. I wonder if Riley is still as cute as when we were twelve. Something exciting to look forward to, perhaps.

"I barely remember Riley," I lie.

I'm not ready to talk boys with my dad. I know I'll slip and say something embarrassing. My cheeks flush hot thinking of the potential of running into Riley again. I turn toward the house to avoid making eye contact with my dad. I really hate lying to him, but it's become surprisingly easier the older I get, especially as I have more secrets to keep.

Room by room, the lights turn on in the house. Officer Tim makes his way through the second story. Light after light illuminates the house until we see the final glow peek out from the tiny round window on the third floor—the creepy one.

Several minutes later, he appears in the entryway. "Come on up, Beswicks; it's all clear." Tim motions for us to join him.

"Dad, I swear I saw something," I plead.

"Well, whatever it is, it's gone by now. Come on, Izzy, grab your bag; let's see what Tim has to say."

I pull my bag from the back seat, and by the time I turn around, Dad's already up the stairs, resuming his chat with Officer Tim.

I take my time joining them as I dramatically walk up the three separated levels of stairs through the overgrown weeds that are sprawled across nearly every cement step.

"Must have been the wind blowing the curtain. The house has a pretty gnarly draft," Tim tells us when I finally reach the house.

"Are you sure there's no one there? Did you check everywhere?" I question Tim.

"Yes, I promise you I checked everywhere. You have nothing to worry about, except maybe the layer of dust you're about to inhale. It's pretty rough in there, Steven," Tim says, pointing back inside.

I permit myself a moment before I step into the house. Dad and Tim are already inside, and they don't notice I'm not following them. I shut my eyes and take a deep breath, preparing myself for what's on the other side—my new life. When I'm ready, I step through the doorway.

A coolness flushes through my body as I lift my eyelids. It seems as though I've taken a step through time. Everything in the foyer is exactly as Gran-gran left it. Little scraps of memories swim around my mind, and I swear I smell her perfume. Oh my gosh, it's overwhelming, almost suffocating. The floral notes of her fragrance nearly choke me as I swallow, burning my throat. I take in a few deep breaths through my nose to ensure I'm not imagining it. No, it's real. I smell her.

How is that possible?

Suddenly, my head is bombarded with forgotten memories from this very spot, and I'm dizzy. Visions of Gran-gran teaching me to tie my shoe on her beloved hall tree bench. I remember her talking about her antique furniture and how much she cherished each item in her collection, because each piece had a story—a history. I run my fingers over the elaborate hand-carved mahogany wood of the Victorian hall tree, stopping when I see my reflection in the darkened mirror. Something appears to be wrong. The words on my T-shirt aren't reversed as they should be. I can read them. My mind must be playing tricks on me. I glance at my shirt in confusion and then back at my reflection.

The words *Seattle Sounders* stare me straight in the face.

"Dad!" I shout. "Come here now!"

Dad and Tim appear in seconds.

"The mirror. It's backward. Look."

I position myself in front of the mirror again, and the words on my shirt are reversed as they should be—normal. What? No, that's not what I just saw.

"Sweetie, it's a normal reflection. You must be tired. We had a long trip," Dad says, writing off my moment of insanity.

Tim gives me a sideways grin. Maybe I did imagine it. Suddenly, I don't smell Gran-grans scent anymore, either. I shake my head in confusion. Maybe Dad's right. It must be the long drive messing with me.

"I need some sleep, I guess," I respond.

"Well, I'll let you get settled. But seriously, Steven, this house needs a lot of work if you two are going to make this your home. I could swing by with my tools and give you a hand on Thursday. It's my day off. Maybe I can see if my lazy son can help too."

Riley. My heart flutters.

"That would be wonderful. We'd love the help. It's much worse than I thought it would be." Dad rubs his forehead.

"OK then, I'll let you guys get settled, and I'll come over around nine on Thursday. I'll pick up some doughnuts and coffee for us all."

"That sounds like a plan. See you in a few days. Nice seeing you again, Tim. Tell Riley we say hi," Dad says, leading him to the doorway.

My cheeks flame at the thought of seeing my childhood crush, but the feeling is soon replaced by the dizziness from earlier. My knees wobble, and my legs give out from underneath me.

"Izzy, Izzy. Are you OK?"

CHAPTER 04
GOOD BONES

I'm pretty sure I'm dreaming, except it feels so real. It's as if I'm in a bubbled version of reality—one where I can see myself lying lifeless on the floor. Dad and Tim frantically hover over me. I move freely and effortlessly around the chaos, turning to face the mirror again. Everything is as it was the first time I saw my reflection in the old antique mirror. I stare straight ahead, and the words Seattle Sounders read precisely as they appear on the shirt. The words aren't backward as they should be in a reflection. The side part in my shoulder-length dirty blonde hair is reflected on the opposite side. There must be something wrong with this mirror.

"Izzy!" Dad shouts, bringing my attention back to my body lying on the dirty floor.

Tim checks my pulse.

"Izzy, wake up," Dad says with panic.

I simply observe.

The longer I see myself lying on the floor, the more I'm convinced this is not reality. This is a dream. I'm not in two places at once. Am I?

"Dad, I'm here," I say out loud, but neither Dad nor Tim flinch. "Dad!"

"Izzy, can you hear me?" Tim asks.

They can't hear me.

What's going on? This is the strangest dream I've ever had—so real.

I turn back around to face the mirror. Something is drawing me back to it. The back of my hand begins to burn the longer I stare at my reflection. It's intense. Like fire.

I should call out again. I need my dad and Tim to hear me. My mouth opens in my reflection, but the words release from the me on the floor.

"Dad. I'm fine." The words sputter out of my mouth.

I look past them, searching for a second me in the room, but I'm the only Izzy here. A shiver flushes down my back, and I recoil into myself. I'm shaken by what happened, and I don't know what to say to the adults in the room. They will think I'm insane, and maybe I am.

"She's back," Dad says, hovering over me.

Tim grabs my arm, lifts me up, and gently sets me upright on the bench.

"You gave me quite a scare. What happened?" Dad caresses my hair.

My eyes dart around the room.

Nothing.

I was dreaming.

I swallow hard, and my mouth is dry.

Tim walks away. I hope he's getting some water.

"How long was I out?"

"About a minute or so. Are you sure you're OK?"

"Yes, Dad, I'm fine. I promise."

Tim returns from the kitchen empty-handed.

"Um, Steven, there aren't any clean cups, and there is no soap or anything to wash them with. Everything in your cupboards has an inch or two of dust inside them." Tim struts past us, heading for the door. "I think I have a bottle of water in my car. I'll go check."

Dad's eyes lock on me, observing my every move. I'm afraid to say anything because I'm unsure what to say.

Tim reappears moments later with a Dasani water bottle. He hands it to me. The safety band is already broken around the lid. Usually, that would bother me, but I'm so parched I can't help but chug half of it immediately.

"Well, OK. Izzy seems to be all right, and since we don't have any intruders, I will let you folks be. I should probably get back to patrolling the mean streets of East Gate. Take care, Beswicks. I will be back on Thursday. In the meantime, don't hesitate to reach out if you need anything. Izzy, take care, my dear." Tim nods in my direction.

"Thanks. I appreciate it, Tim. We will see you then," Dad responds, and Tim disappears out the door.

Dad turns back to me as soon as the front door latches shut. Concern lurks across his face.

"What happened?" Dad asks again.

"I'm not sure. I felt dizzy. That's all I remember."

"Maybe we need to get you some food and see how you feel. Let's go to the café. We can work on this mess after getting some calories in us," Dad says.

"No, I'll be OK."

"Sweetie, you just fainted. I feel like I need to take you to a doctor or something. I'm not being a good parent if I let it go. Your mom wouldn't approve of this."

"No, I swear I'm fine. Please stop asking. It's really no big deal. I promise."

"Fine, at least let me order us a pizza then. I will see what this town has to offer as far as delivery goes. But I'm keeping an eye on you all night."

I nod in agreement to the pizza, but *all night*? I need to explore this place on my own. I know I saw something, and Dad and Tim wrote it off as the wind. Then there's my unexplainable incident in the hallway. We've been here all of five minutes, and I have two unanswered questions that need resolving. I can't lie to myself; I'm pretty shaken, but I have no explanation. I need answers now. I reach for my bag, and I'm nearing the spiral staircase when Dad tears his sight away from his phone.

"Hey. Hold your horses, girlie. You want your usual?"

"Of course. Cheese and black olives. Is that even a question?"

He laughs and dials the phone number. "I'd like to place an order for delivery, please. . ." His voice trails off as he disappears into the next room.

I resume my strut toward the staircase. I carefully avoid running my hand up the wooden banister as it looks like it will give me more than one splinter. Another thing in this house desperate for repair. The house is in such disarray that it almost feels like it's grieving and sad. It's only been five years, but it looks like twenty-five. The way grief eats at a person, it's eating at this house.

When I land on the second floor, I'm greeted by a long, grand hallway with five doors. I didn't get to explore much as a kid. Gran-gran kept me on a tight leash here. I always stayed in the first room and didn't venture further than I was told. Plus, there was the fear of getting lost. This place is massive.

I'm surprised at the sudden burst of memories that regain their spot in my mind. It's like every step I take unlocks a new set of memories.

I carefully open the first door, half expecting a squatter to jump out with a knife, but I let out a sigh of relief when that doesn't happen. It's my old room—I think. It's pretty unremarkable and simply decorated. I mosey down the hall and open every door, peeking inside. I'm pleasantly surprised that each room is larger than the last. Gran-gran was holding out, keeping me in the smallest of the rooms. I think the second room was where my parents stayed, but it isn't familiar. Maybe I'm mistaken, and they stayed on the other side of the house.

When I reach the final door, I'm excited to see it's the master bedroom. It's bright and spacious. A king-sized bed occupies the middle of the room with tall bedposts and a sheer white canopy. It's rather pretty but needs to be cleaned.

Three large windows face the street. Since the house sits back upon a hill, it showcases a glorious view of the town. The gold-plated church steeples jump out amidst the green trees. It's beautiful.

No closets. That's strange. I don't recall seeing a closet in any of the rooms.

"Great bones."

A chill rushes down my spine. I spin around.

"Oh my God!" I shriek. "Dad, you scared me half to death. This place gives me the creeps. You can't sneak up on me here!"

"It's just old, nothing to get creeped out about." Dad enters the large room and walks the perimeter, stopping in front of the windows. He places his hand against the wall. "See, I told you the house has great bones. And a huge bonus, we each get a wing. The east wing faces town, and the west wing faces the forest. Which wing do you prefer?"

"First, stop saying great bones. It just adds to the creepiness of this already eerie house. And second, I think I would prefer to stay in this wing if it's OK. You had me at west wing, but lost me at forest. So, I'll take the side that faces civilization."

Dad laughs. "See, you're starting to see the potential. It just needs a new layer of skin."

"Ew, Dad. Not the right choice of words. Can we bulldoze it down and start over?"

"That's not an option right now, so we will work with what we've been given."

I give Dad an over the top dramatic pout, which he ignores.

"All right, the east wing is all yours. Are you going to take this room? It's the best one in the house."

"Dad, are you sure you don't want it? You don't mind me taking the best room in the house? It really should be yours."

"I've always preferred the west wing. I have fond memories there. So, please take this one. I think you'll be happy here."

"All right. I think I will. But where's the closet?"

"Oh, sweetie, this house was built before closets were a necessity. Closets used to be taxed as a room or something silly like that. Plus, people didn't have as many clothing options as you have nowadays, so they added a wardrobe instead of adding a closet."

"Like the C.S. Lewis book? Is it going to take me to Narnia?" I joke.

"No, but you will probably need all the wardrobes in this wing to fit your clothes and maybe some in mine." Dad laughs. "This room is big. I will see what I can do about adding a closet, eventually. It's time this house got some upgrades."

"I really don't remember this place being so big. You'd think as a child I would remember this house being bigger because everything seems huge when you're little."

Dad tussles his fingers through his hair. "You would think, but for some reason, this place didn't faze you as a kid. You were desensitized to it or something."

"Hey, what's on the third floor? I don't think I've ever gone up there, or at least I don't remember."

"You know, come to think of it, I haven't been up there either. Gran always said it was off-limits. I assumed it's where she kept her mess. Every old lady has a room of mess they don't want their guests to see."

"Well, it's our house now, so I guess it's our mess. Can we go check it out?"

"Sure, I don't see why not."

At first, I thought I wanted to explore on my own, but I think I'll feel better if Dad is with me.

The third level is where I saw something earlier. Tim was up here. He didn't lie. I saw the light go on, but I must see it for myself. I won't be able to sleep until I do.

I rush out of the room; Dad follows slowly behind. I leap up the steps, taking them two at a time. I'm eager to explore and less frightened now that Dad is behind me. When I hit the landing, I see one large open area. No mess like Dad suggested. There it is: the tiny window I saw from the street. A simple ivory handmade curtain hangs off to the side. It hardly seems necessary as the window is so small and lets in very little light. The floorboards creak underneath me as I walk to the window.

"Well, this isn't what I expected. There is nothing up here. Almost a letdown," Dad says.

An intrusive rapping comes from the front door. "Ah, must be the pizza. That was speedy. I sure hope it's cooked all the way. I hate when they rush to get your order out, and it's all gooey. Let's go, Izzy. There's nothing to see here."

Dad rushes away to get the door. I'm about to follow, but before leaving the third floor, three narrow wooden steps in the room's corner catch my eye. The steps are virtually unnoticeable in the darkly lit edge of the room, opposite the tiny, creepy window. I cautiously tiptoe across the wooden floorboards to the base of the small hand cut planks serving as stairs. Each step groans from my weight, and I'm hardly 110 pounds soaking wet. At least if they give way, I won't have far to fall. I steady myself on the last step, facing a closed door. I twist the brass knob, but the door doesn't budge. It's locked. Dang it. There must be a key somewhere. I'll search for it later.

"Izzy, pizza's here. Come downstairs," Dad hollers from the first floor. His voice is faint by the time it makes it to my level.

I twist the handle one more time to make sure it won't open. No luck.

"On my way down, Dad," I holler, walking backward down the steps.

A sudden breeze whips past me, stirring up my hair, giving me goosebumps.

"Welcome home," a voice whispers in the wind.

CHAPTER 05
SUMMERTIME BLUES

A month passes in our new home. Despite the first day making me want to run for the hills, nothing odd happens on the ensuing days. So, I'm leaning more toward temporary insanity caused by trauma from our move, plus lack of food. But of course, I have my guard up, and I sleep with a night light, you know, just to be safe. Anything could be lurking in this creepy old house. Every creak, draft, and squeak has me on edge, but I'm slowly adjusting. I try to think of the noises as white noise like my calming Puget Sound back home.

Officer Tim brings doughnuts and coffee every Thursday and Sunday. He spends both of his days off with us, and thanks to Tim's help, the house is slowly coming together, almost livable. I think Dad and Tim are actually enjoying the work, and they've become best buddies in the process—a beautiful bromance. My dad seems genuinely happy here. A light I've never seen has been flipped. It's like all the stress and sadness he had in Seattle is gone. Because of Tim, Dad has an IT job working for the city. He mainly fixes old computers, but he's happy, and the money is OK.

Life hasn't been as fun for me. I haven't met anyone yet. Dad and Tim are my only friends here. Pathetic, I know.

My hopes of reconnecting with Riley have been spoiled. Each time Tim pulls up in his red Ford truck, I anxiously wait for Riley to exit the passenger side, but it's always the same result. Tim exits the vehicle alone with a box of doughnuts and three coffees, along with an excuse for his son.

The many cute outfits and great makeup days prove pointless, as only Tim shows up without Riley, time after time. The man probably suspects I have a crush on him. Ew gross, but for a man in his early forties, he's a hot dad, I guess. From what I remember, both he and Riley have the same light brown hair and the same thin nose. I'm dying to see if he's still as cute as when we were twelve. But I guess Riley doesn't care to reconnect with his childhood friend. I must not have left an impression on him. Ugh, the one thing I had to look forward to has been nothing but a disappointment week after week. Maybe today will be the day he shows up.

I brush my teeth and jump in the shower. Sing a few songs while I scrub. Dab on a layer of makeup, adding bronzer to the sides of my thin nose, making it appear even smaller, and just enough under my cheekbones to highlight them. I brush a thick layer of light pink gloss over my average lips for a little extra pout. I even tempt my patience, using my flat iron, giving myself some S-waves starting halfway down my locks. My hair is desperate for fresh highlights, so the curls make it appear like an intentional ombre style. Maybe I can convince my dad to pay for a cut and highlight before the school year starts. I usually strive for perfect hair; roots this atrocious aren't acceptable. Back in Seattle, students ridicule each other for things like their hair. Teenagers can be so mean. Good thing school doesn't start until next month. I have time to fix it.

Sondra's mean words hum in my ear. "Izzy, you know people can tell you're poor now."

Not today, Sondra. Not today.

My Thursday morning routine is wrapping up when the sound of Tim's truck revving up the hill notifies me he's almost here. I take a final glimpse of myself in the mirror, feeling satisfied with my appearance, even with Sondra's words looming in the back of my mind.

I rush over to my bedroom window just as Tim parks his truck. Like clockwork, Tim opens his door, gets out, reaches back in for his drink carrier, and places it on the truck's roof. Then he pops back into the vehicle for his box of doughnuts.

But wait.

He reappears with no box. He always has a box. What's up with that? I look forward to my delicious bi-weekly pastries. I quickly rush downstairs to greet Tim at the door, hoping maybe Riley is coming after him with the pink box of yummy treats. For fear of disappointment, I'm afraid to let the optimism uncork.

"Hello, Tim. What, no doughnuts?" My voice is unusually high-pitched.

"Dang, Izzy. I didn't even have a chance to knock. It seems I have you spoiled. Sorry, the grocery store was out of doughnuts today. I guess a busload of vacationers beat me to it this morning."

"Oh, bummer. Is Riley coming today?" My voice fluctuates on his name, and my cheeks redden in embarrassment.

"Riley has football camp this week. He's been a busy guy. I hardly see him these days. He won't be with me this Sunday, either. I'm sure you two will eventually reconnect at school."

At school! That's still over a month away. Ugh, this is the most boring summer of my life. I want to run upstairs to my oversized bed and scream into my pillow, but Dad appears in the foyer, foiling my plans.

"I overheard no doughnuts this morning," Dad says with a chuckle.

"OK, now I know I've spoiled this family. I would love to hear a, 'Hello, Tim. It's good to see you. We appreciate your hard work and enjoy your company with or without doughnuts'," Tim jokingly responds.

Dad lets out a deep, boisterous laugh. He reaches into his wallet, pulling out a twenty-dollar bill. "Izzy, why don't you head downtown and check out that bakery on Main Street you've been wanting to go to? Get three of whatever looks good."

Perfect. I need to get out of this house—finally, my first outing alone in East Gate without my dad.

"OK, thanks, Dad. I'm walking, so it might be a while."

"No rush, sweetie."

I take the twenty from him, shove it into my jean shorts pocket, and grab my coffee from Tim. I'm disappointed

Riley isn't here, but maybe he's ugly now and is too self-conscious to see me. I highly doubt that's true, but it makes me feel better.

It's a beautiful morning, and the sun is shining. It's about time I get out and explore. So far, Dad and I have been ordering take-out and spending our days cleaning and unpacking. It's been boring and uneventful, without even a visit to the old theatre.

Gran-gran was a packrat. When the movers brought our items, we condensed her stuff into the unoccupied rooms while we figured out what to do with it all. I suggested a yard sale, but Dad shot down that idea. I think he wants to keep all of her things. So, I didn't press the issue. At least the mess is mostly hidden behind closed doors. We still have a lot of work ahead of us, but it's coming together.

I walk along Main Street under the cherry blossom trees, which have lost their bloom. It's still pretty, but not as picturesque as our first day here. I pass The Perk before entering East Gate Bakery.

I toss my empty coffee cup in the trash outside and step inside the brightly colored establishment. Wafts of sweet vanilla and cardamon aromas pleasantly greet me. It's delightful. My mouth begins to salivate. I join the long line in front of me, and that's when I fear I'm being watched, but I can't confirm it until I hear the snickering and giggles.

It sounds eerily familiar. My heart sinks to the pit of my stomach. *There will always be girls like Sondra.*

I carefully glance over my right shoulder, and there they are. The three girls from the park on my first day in town.

Thoughts of inadequacy and self-consciousness creep into my headspace. I tug at the fabric around the midsection of my shirt and pull at the strands of hair lining my face. The beautiful blonde one is facing me, while the other two girls have their backs to me in the booth.

I accidentally make eye contact with blondie, and the other two girls turn and stare in my direction. Their glare is cold, cutting through me like a knife. The three girls snicker amongst themselves, and I direct my attention back to the moving line.

Just like Sondra—always girls like Sondra. A shiver rushes down my spine at the thought.

When it's my turn to order, I realize I forgot to look at the menu. I quickly choose the first item and prepare to announce my order when the cashier catches me off guard. "I've never seen you in here before. Are you on one of those vacation buses that pulled into town earlier this morning? I thought they'd already left," she says with a husky voice that seems too low for her features.

"Um, no. My Dad and I just moved here from Washington State a month ago. It's my first time in."

I shift uncomfortably, feeling the stare of the girls behind me. I know their eyes are pinned on me, watching my every move, waiting for me to make a mistake.

Always girls like Sondra.

I rock restlessly back and forth on the heels of my feet. My hand starts to burn again as it did in my dream in the foyer. The heat intensifies with each counting second.

"We don't get many new people in town. I didn't know

we had any houses for sale in the area. Where do you live, sweetie?"

What is this, an interrogation? It serves me right for leaving the house. I should have been happy with my coffee and Tim's company today. Instead, I'm in an awkward conversation and regretting going out in public. What was I thinking?

I don't want to answer this nosey woman, but she's staring at me, waiting for my response. I tuck my hair behind my ear, and as my hand passes by my eye, I check to see if it's on fire because it feels like it is, but it appears normal. "We moved into my great-grandma's house. She passed away five years ago and left us her home," I respond.

"Oh, that was nice of her. Who did you say was your great-grandma?"

"Um, I didn't say. Her name was Isobel Beswick. Did you know her?"

"Oh, you're a Beswick?" Her husky voice fluctuates on my last name. She glares at me for a few moments before taking a step back from the counter.

I carefully peek over my shoulder to see if the girls in the booth are still observing me. All three of them are staring wide-eyed. Once they catch their gaze on mine, they turn back to the table.

"Well, anyway, what can I get for you?" Her nosey friendliness shifts to a cold, generic tone.

"Three blueberry scones," I quickly spout out, ready for this encounter to end.

"I'm sorry, we're fresh out of 'em."

"Um." I uncomfortably stare back up at the menu.

"Three croissants."

"Sorry, out of them too."

Oh my God. I just want this to be over. I want to be home with my dad, peeling old wallpaper off the kitchen walls. I scroll down the menu to the next item.

"Fine, what about three bacon breakfast sandos then?"

"Yep, we got those. Do you want to add avocado to them?" Her words come out monotone and flat.

"Sure," I respond.

The girls giggle, but I don't turn around. I know they're making fun of me.

"Okay, that will be twenty-one dollars."

Oh no. You have to be kidding me right now. I want to crawl under the counter and hide. I'm horrified as I pull the single twenty-dollar bill from my pocket.

"All I have is a twenty. I guess just make it two."

The cashier scowls at me. She doesn't change the order. She simply waits for me to produce another dollar. Like I'm going to pull it out of thin air.

The prettiest of the three girls stands up from the booth and confidently marches in my direction. She waves a five-dollar bill in front of me before setting it on the counter. "Don't forget to tip." Her sassy voice is condescending. She pivots to walk out the door, pausing to wait for her minions.

In unison, all three girls turn their heads and stare at me for five whole seconds before exiting the bakery. Their gaze is haunting, and the burning in my hand ceases, leaving it ice cold. Goosebumps quilt my body, and I think I'm going to die from embarrassment. I'm horrified by what just happened. Not only am I the odd new girl, but now I'm the girl who can't afford her own breakfast. Great, this will make the school year so much fun.

The cashier snatches the five-dollar bill from the counter and hands me back four ones. I reluctantly add them to her tip jar now that she's expecting a tip. Plus, I'm not going to crawl back to the girl with her change.

I quickly step aside to wait for my order. But the girls are still lingering on the sidewalk outside of the bakery. The audacious blonde one is the only one I can get a good look at. Her long platinum blonde hair is sleek and lustrous. She has straight bangs across her forehead. Of course, she can pull off bangs. The hair that falls along her face is perfectly framed around her sleek jawline. Her pink summer dress flatters her slender figure perfectly. Her haunting, big blue eyes pierce through me as her eyes catch mine for another awkward moment. I quickly turn back to the counter, just in time for my order to be called out.

Please leave.

Please leave.

I take my time grabbing extra napkins. *Please leave.* I don't dare peek again until I'm ready to exit the building. I reach back for a few more napkins, buying me a couple of extra seconds. I shove them into my bag and take a deep breath.

I push through the door, and I'm relieved to see the three girls are across the street and heading toward the park.

I swear I can still hear them snickering.

Always girls like Sondra.

CHAPTER 06
THE CLIQUE

Disappointment. That word describes my summer perfectly. I still haven't seen Riley. Every visit, Tim has an excuse, so I eventually quit asking. My only friends are my dad and Tim—still. But today is the first day of school. My stomach flutters, wondering if I will finally see my childhood crush. Surely, I must. He's a senior, just like me. The odds are in my favor—I hope.

Dad offers to drive me to school. I tell him I'll walk; of course, he insists on driving, but I leave before he gathers his things. It isn't a far walk to the school. Since we're broke, I don't see a car in my future, so I better get used to it. The walk to school is lonely, but at least the sun is shining.

One year. I can do this. One year and I'm done.

Once inside the ornate building, I glance down at the schedule they printed for me yesterday at orientation. Everything about this town is a step back in time. Who prints things these days? Hello, have you ever heard of an electronic schedule? If I told Dad about this, I know he'd jump into tech mode and brainstorm ways to move this place into the twenty-first century. But I don't think I want my dad hanging around at school, so I'll keep this to myself until I graduate. Then he can assist them.

I have first-period history with Mrs. Jamison. My stomach is a ball of nerves as I walk down the hall, searching for room A103—a few faces glance in my direction. *Yes, I'm the new girl. Quit looking.* Thankfully, Dad paid for me to get a haircut and highlights. That's one less thing to feel self-conscious about.

I wore something basic today because I didn't want it to appear as if I was trying too hard. So, I opted for my go-to frayed denim shorts and a black V-neck pocket T-shirt. I let my hair hang straight today with a side part and went light on the makeup. Before investing in my look, I want to see what everyone else is doing. I wasn't exactly popular at my old school, but I had friends. The school was so big that we had a lot of cliques, and almost every clique accepted me, except the elite popular clique. Sondra's clique. That is, until junior year when they started talking to me. I felt special. Sondra, Evelyn, and Mackenzie asked me to sit with them, and of course, I didn't think twice about it. I abandoned all of my other cliques to join theirs—the worst mistake of my life.

The first-period bell rings, echoing through the hall.

I'm late.

I sprint down the newly abandoned hallway, my backpack sliding off my shoulder. I rush into the room, nearly panting, and everyone is already seated. The entire room stops what they're doing and stares at me. I attempt to catch my breath.

"Oh, you must be our new student, Isobel Beswick. Oh my, saying that name gives me goosebumps. I knew your great-grandma," Mrs. Jamison says. Her expression is hard to read.

"Um, yes. That's me, but it's Izzy," I shyly respond, nervously tucking the hair behind my ears.

"Welcome, Izzy. You can take a seat. It looks like the one in the middle is open."

The middle. I should have planned better and been the first one to class, ensuring I could sit in the back of the room where people can't stare. But now I'm dead center—all eyes on me. I quickly grab my seat. I dig in my backpack for a notebook and pen, and that's when I recognize two of the girls from the bakery. Not the blonde one, but the other two. The duo I didn't get a good look at.

"Since it's the first day, I'll do roll call. This will help Izzy learn everyone's names," Mrs. Jamison says.

Great, everyone knows each other, but me—the new girl.

Mrs. Jamison calls out two names before shouting mine again. "Isobel Beswick."

"It's Izzy, remember?"

Light laughter erupts from different ends of the room. I'm not trying to be sassy, but I already told her my name. Mrs. Jamison gives me a nod, accompanied by a flat smile, and continues calling out the names.

I stop paying attention until I hear, "Riley Hawkins."

"Present."

My pulse races and my heart flutters. I slowly shift in my seat, nonchalantly tossing my chin over my left shoulder. It's

Riley sitting two seats behind me. My Riley. I barely recognize him. He's a full-grown man now, and he's beautiful. I want to give all my attention to soaking up his details, but I can't because it would be too obvious. So instead, I turn back around in my seat.

"Tahlia Latham-Hart."

"Here." The light and airy voice comes from one of the bakery girls.

"Margo Hawley."

The second bakery girl raises her hand.

Both girls are stunning. Instead of paying attention to Mrs. Jamison, I observe them. Before I know it, my pen is pressed hard on my paper, and I'm doodling them in my notebook.

Tahlia's skin is creamy golden brown with earthy yellow undertones. She has strikingly high cheekbones with a rosy, pink blush that accentuates them. Her thick black curly hair is pulled into a loose and wild bun piled on top of her head. Loose curls fall in every direction. Her wild eyes are as green as moss.

The blonde girl from the bakery is pretty, but I think Tahlia is even more beautiful. She is slender and tall like the blonde one, but Tahlia is more toned with the posture of a ballerina. The black sundress she's wearing hangs on her lean body. I'm now slightly obsessed with her style, secretly wanting to imitate it right down to the accessories like the black choker necklace tied tightly around her neck to the black nail polish on her manicured fingernails. So much black in one outfit would normally scream gothic, but it's not—it's radiant.

Margo is different from the other two. She's shorter and curvier, but not fat. Her chest is voluptuous in her tight purple tank top. She's wearing a large antique-looking, purple, and black pendant necklace. Margo has a very round face with even rounder dark chestnut brown eyes. Her brownish-red corkscrew tendrils that hang mid-back bounce every time she moves, stirring up a coconut scent that makes its way to my desk. She has one small braid framing the left side of her face. Her nose and cheeks are sun-kissed and pink with a light dusting of freckles.

Each girl is beautiful and intimidating.

No one else in this room competes with them. Well, except for Riley.

***

Four classes tick by without me talking to anyone. This isn't how I imagined my first day of school. People glance and stare, but no one is curious enough to even say hi.

When lunchtime rolls around, I follow the tide of the hall traffic into the cafeteria.

Following a group of students into the hot food line, I grab a slice of sausage pizza that looks like cardboard and probably tastes like it too. I skip all the other options because they look just as bad.

Once I exit the food line and get my lunch card stamped because, once again, technology is lacking here, I'm suddenly faced with a huge fear. I have nowhere to sit. I scope out the table options and check out the different cliques. Each table clearly has its social place in the cafeteria. As I study everyone, I realize they're studying me too. Everyone is eyeing me, wondering where I will sit on my first day. I'm standing here with my tray—classic first-day new girl scenario. Usually, in the movies, you see the new girl eating alone or sitting on the toilet munching on her sandwich or, in my case, cardboard pizza. I won't be that girl today. Plus, it's insanely unsanitary.

This decision will probably be the most important one I make at this school. It will set a precedent for my entire senior year.

Of course, Riley is on my radar, and I spot him immediately. He's sitting with the jocks; his back away from me. At least he isn't witnessing my embarrassment. I still can't believe he hasn't said hi, or at least a gesture of acknowledgment that he remembers me. Ugh, guys can be so frustrating. Maybe I should just go over there and slam my tray down next to him and remind him who I am. But I know I'm not going to do that, so I better figure out where I'm going to sit now. This is getting more awkward by the second.

I scan the cafeteria once more, trying to land on my next move when I spot the three girls—they're sitting alone near the back of the lunchroom. Margo catches my stare, and her arm jolts up into the air. She vigorously waves her hand, while the other two gaze with scrutinizing eyes in my direction. They should enter a staring contest for as much as they stare at me. I bet they'd win.

Is she waving me over? I glance around in every direction to make sure she's gesturing to me to avoid embarrassing myself, and when I see no one else acknowledging her, I slowly move toward their table.

Margo calls out, "Hey, new girl, come sit with us," as I get closer.

Parts of me are screaming and throwing up warning flags. It's just like last year with Sondra and the elites. *Go sit on the toilet alone and eat your cardboard. Keep your head down until graduation. You don't need friends here. You won't be here long. Make friends in college.* But my feet continue to disobey me and before I know it, I'm setting my tray down next to Margo and across from the other two girls who are sizing me up with their not-so-subtle glares.

I'm nervous and my stomach does a million somersaults as I cautiously lower myself into the seat. I take my time in case they start laughing and this is all an evil joke. But the girls don't laugh at me, and relief floods my veins. All right, I'm here. Now let's see what they want with me.

"Hi, I'm Margo, and this is Tahlia and Jessa." Margo's voice is pleasant and friendly, catching me off guard. It's not what I thought it would sound like. I thought it would be shrill and pitchy for some reason.

I'm grateful I now have a name for the blonde one. It's Jessa. Her name fits her perfectly.

Before I can reciprocate the introduction, Jessa cocks her head so far that her long blonde hair sweeps across the table.

"So, is it true?" Jessa asks in the same sassy voice as when she waved the five-dollar bill in front of me.

"Is what true?" I reluctantly ask, biting at my bottom lip. There is no way they know about what happened in Seattle. I'm three thousand miles away from that problem.

"That you're Isobel Beswick's great-granddaughter?" Jessa says.

I'm relieved. Not the Sondra thing. Thank God.

"Yes, that's true. Why are people acting funny about that?" I respond.

"Well, because she was a witch. A real fucking witch. Don't tell me you didn't know that?" Jessa says.

I let an uncomfortable laugh slip through my glossed lips. "That's insane. My Gran-gran wasn't a witch," I respond. They must be joking. Right? Ha ha, let's mess with the new girl. I should have known better than to sit with them.

"Oh, Gran-gran. How cute," Margo coos.

Jessa glowers at Margo.

"Well, Gran was indeed a witch, and you're living in her house now. Everyone is scared of that place. It's so old and creepy, you know," Jessa continues, adding to this not so funny ruse.

"There is no way—" I respond, but Jessa cuts me off.

"People say your Gran isn't dead. She's simply hiding and waiting for us all to die off so she can come back to her home and start over again. You know she's one of the original Salem witches?"

I let out a loud, uncontrolled cackle. I can't help but snicker at her ludicrous story. "OK, now I know you're insane. That mathematically can't be true. Gran-gran was born in 1924, not the 1600s. I'm sorry to disappoint you," I respond.

Jessa's eyes blink rapidly, like I've just said something in a language she doesn't understand. She leans across the table, inching her way closer to me. "Rumor has it she was born in the 1600s and was one of the Salem witches who was going to stand trial in 1692, but she vanished before her trial date. Never to be seen or heard from again, that is, until the 1900s, when she turned up in East Gate, Connecticut." Jessa recaps her story like she's telling it over a campfire in the middle of the forest with a flashlight held below her chin, trying to scare young campers.

I roll my eyes, giving myself a moment before responding. "How would that be possible? She would have been over 200 years old."

"Duh, she's a witch. Like I've been saying. Can you please keep up? Are you slow or something? She probably put a witchy spell on herself to hide during the trials and didn't come back until the 1900s when the coast was clear. She clearly tried to start over, but somehow someone found out who she was, and she went back into hiding."

"I'm pretty sure there isn't a record of this. If I google her name, there won't be anything related to her and that event in history."

"Duh, Izzy. Are you not getting it? She probably erased all records of herself with a witchy spell," Jessa replies with almost too much certainty.

"Does everyone believe this?" I ask.

"Most people. Everyone in East Gate was terrified of her," Jessa says.

I shift uncomfortably in my seat. If everyone thinks

this, then I'm the freak-show new girl. I pick a piece of sausage off my pizza and shove it into my mouth, avoiding conversation. I want to gag as it slides down my throat. It does taste like cardboard. Note to self: pack my own lunches.

"Can we come over to your house after school?" Jessa rudely poses.

I let out a cough, nearly choking on the remnants of my disgusting lunch.

"Um, I don't think that's a good idea. My dad and Tim Hawkins have been renovating the house. It's a mess. I don't think my dad would like anyone in the construction area."

"Officer Hawkins? Riley's dad?" Margo questions.

"Yes," I respond.

"That can't be. He told us never to go to that house. Why is he spending time there? Now I really want to see this place," Jessa demands.

Why would Tim say that? A pang of disappointment slugs me in the gut.

"Are you going to tell her?" Tahlia butts in. It's the first time she's spoken since I sat down. I nearly forgot she was sitting with us.

"Shut your mouth, T," Jessa snaps.

"Tell me what?" I demand.

"Nothing," Jessa says. She picks a long strand of her stick straight blonde hair to twist around her pointer finger. "So, can we come over? What time does your dad get home?"

"I don't think it's a good idea. He gets home around 4:30," I respond.

"OK, that's perfect. I promise we'll leave before Daddy

gets home. We don't want to get you in trouble. We're your friends now. You can trust us." Jessa flashes me a bright white smile.

I don't believe her, but my gaze falls to Margo. Her big brown eyes stare back at me with kindness, stirring a warmth inside me. I don't dare look at Tahlia. Her stillness is kind of creeping me out, plus her green eyes are fiercely pinned on me. I can feel them.

"Come on. Daddy won't know you've had any company, I promise. I'm not taking no for an answer. After school, I can drive us all. Meet me in the parking lot at 2:45. My car is the white Jeep parked near the exit."

"All right," I respond.

I don't know what else to say to get her to stop asking. I guess what harm is there? There is nothing for her to find anyway. Right?

"So, why'd you move here?" Jessa bats her long, perfectly mascaraed eyelashes.

"Um." I try to stay motionless in my seat, but my foot taps compulsively under the table. I don't want to tell them my dad lost his job and I'm running away from my problems. "Um. We inherited the house and Dad was ready for a change," I respond flatly, leaving little room for questions.

"Do you, like, miss your old home? Where was that anyway?" Jessa presses, her voice slightly valley girl, reminding me of the old movies my mom used to watch.

"Yeah, I guess so. We moved from Seattle. It's hard to switch schools your senior year," I respond.

"Why didn't your dad wait out his 'change' one more year?

That only makes sense," Jessa says, her words cutting deep into my open wounds. I don't want to talk about this with these girls I just met.

I quickly attempt to switch the subject. "So, tell me about yourselves. Have you all lived here your whole lives?"

"Yes. All three of us," Margo says, seemingly proud of never leaving.

"What's there to do for fun around here?" I ask.

Jessa bites her bottom lip, turning her nose up. "Stuff."

Very vague, Jessa. "Like, what kind of stuff? Shopping? Parties?"

Margo chimes in, "Yes, parties, but no good shopping around here. We drive to New Haven for the good stores."

"Oh," I generically respond, accidentally letting my eyes wander to Tahlia, who's been a little too quiet. She's studying me from across the table. Her green eyes glowing, mouth pursed, and arms tightly folded below her tiny chest, appearing too serious for a senior in high school.

My eyes bounce around the cafeteria, searching for a new place to sit tomorrow. My gaze lands on Riley, but I'm quickly drawn back to the girls as Margo pulls me back into our conversation.

"What class do you have next?"

"I have chemistry with Mr. Fuller," I respond, glancing back toward Riley, but he's already exited the cafeteria.

"Me too. Great, we can walk together," Jessa responds in a vibrant, upbeat tone.

***

In Chemistry, Mr. Fuller doesn't assign seats, and Jessa insists we sit together in the back of the classroom. No one else seems to pay any attention to me like Margo, Jessa, and Tahlia, especially with what the entire town thinks of Gran-gran. You'd think the spotlight would be on me—the new girl. Mostly people ignore me with a few occasional stares, but other than that, they keep to their cliques without giving me another thought. Even Riley. Cue my heart breaking into a million tiny unmendable pieces. Especially now that he's even hotter. F my luck.

But back to my *new friends*. I can't wrap my head around their accusations of Gran-gran. I mean, her house is creepy, but I don't remember it being that way when she was alive. It's grown that way over time. Gran-gran didn't have any creepy witchy vibes that I can recall. But does that explain the strange occurrence in the foyer with the mirror? Does it explain the voice I thought I heard in the attic or the burning sensation?

No, Izzy, that's absurd.

All those things happened when I was exhausted, stressed, and hungry. There is no such thing as witches, and my Gran-gran was like ninety-eight when she died. She died from old age, and she's not coming back.

These are stories kids make up to scare each other. Every old town has someone they've made into a spooky figure. Like old man Rickets, back in Seattle. People said he was an axe murderer, but he was just a creepy old man with a lazy eye who sat on his porch swing all day and night. He didn't really murder people with an axe; we just made that up to get a rise out of the younger kids in the neighborhood. Gran-gran is the old man Rickets of East Gate. Poor Gran-gran. I wonder if she knew what people thought of her.

Jessa pokes me with her pencil, rudely interrupting my mental breakdown. Her blue eyes are animated, while a smile tugs from ear to ear. "I still can't believe you're really here and that we get to see *her* house. I'm so stoked. Everyone is going to be so jealous we met you first." Her voice is hushed as the class begins, but I highly suspect no one else cares I'm here.

***

Unfortunately for me, Jessa, Tahlia, and Margo all show up in my last class. Trigonometry—my least favorite subject. What are the odds—least favorite class mixed with some girls I'm not sure about and possibly want to ditch, but now I can't.

Luckily, we have assigned seats, so I get a mini break from my new crew. We sit alphabetically, and Megan Calhoun, a pretty girl with blondish-brown hair sits behind me, following Jessa Dewitt. It's only one person, but I welcome the space, and Jessa can't poke me with a pencil in this class. Margo and Tahlia are a row away, but out of my line of sight, and I'm grateful for that.

As much as I hate trigonometry, it's the first time I pay attention all day. I even take notes instead of doodling. The mind-numbing math is a nice break from the madness that has been my day.

The bell will eventually ring, and I'm in the lion's den with nowhere to go. So, it looks like I'm taking my new friends home with me.

CHAPTER 07
DEAD GUYS

Reality quickly sets in as the four of us pile into Jessa's pristine white Jeep. It still has that new car smell. I should feel lucky they chose me. No one else has. Not even Riley. So, I'm in no place to turn down potential friends, even if that means taking them to my house. Once they see nothing witchy, they will forget about it, and we can move on to normal teenage things like parties, shopping, and boys.

I'm dying to ask them about Riley. These girls seem like they would have the scoop on everyone in our class. But now isn't the time. I still can't believe he didn't acknowledge me all day. It's like I was invisible. I'll have a pity party for myself later, but I can only deal with one thing at a time.

Jessa rolls down all the windows and cranks the volume on her stereo, making it hard for us to chat. I suspect it's an intentional move. That way I can't beg them to back out of this crazy idea. She doesn't ask me for directions because she already knows where to go.

Head straight out of the parking lot and directly to the witch lady's house on the hill. The one where every small child is apparently afraid

*to walk past. Yep, that's the one. The place I call home. See, no
directions needed.*

Jessa pulls up in front of my decrepit house. She shifts her
car into park, and I catch a glimpse of her smile growing
in the rearview mirror. I quickly yank on the door handle,
eager to get this little fieldtrip over, but suddenly I'm slapped
with a new feeling—humiliation. The real reason we're here
suddenly fades into the background. I'm embarrassed that I
live here. I don't want the girls to see how I've been living all
summer. Sure, we've made improvements and I'm getting
used to my new life, but it's nowhere near the lifestyle I used
to have. In fact, it's a million miles away from that. If these
girls could have seen my large house on the Puget Sound
with the wrap-around porch, swimming pool, and private
sandy beach, they would think differently of me.

But this is what they see.

This is the me I'm putting forward.

I've been burned, and that little voice of insecurity
rears its cruel head. They don't want to be my real friends.
They're using me for this little mission.

But maybe it's not like that.

A strange tingle swirls in my belly, directing me to a new
image, one where we're friends. I sense a powerful pull to
them, especially Margo. She seems kind. All three of them
are beautiful too. Jessa with her straight blonde hair, Tahlia
with her tight black curls, to Margo and her full reddish-
brown thick bouncy hair. This type of clique was everything
I desired back home. But I also thought I wanted to be
Sondra, Mackenzie, and Evelyn's friend, and look where

that got me. They were nice, until they weren't. It was like a switch flipped. Suddenly, Sondra hated me and the other two followed suit. I need to play it safe with my potential friends, even if my gut is telling me otherwise.

I take a deep breath and meet the girls on the sidewalk. I hope they ignore the yard, even though it's more presentable than before. Dad and Tim have been working on it. Yes, we still have weeds, but they're no longer past the stairs, and the lawn is freshly mowed. But it would still make a landscaper cry.

No one speaks, taking in the image of the witch's home and all its eerie wonder. I hope this will satisfy them, and they will change their mind and we can go shopping or something else—anything else.

"OK, Jessa. We saw it. Now can we go?" Tahlia begs, while tapping on Jessa's shoulder.

Wonderful. This is perfect.

"Oh, hell no. We're here. We're finally going to see inside the infamous Isobel Beswick's house." Jessa prances around the girls in a full circle, waving her fingers delicately at them in a magically calling way.

Her excitement deflates any hope I had of them abandoning this idea.

"OK, let's do this," Margo quickly agrees with Jessa, who is clearly the leader of this group.

"T, don't be a baby," Jessa snaps. She wraps her hand around Tahlia's tiny wrist, pulling her up the steps behind her.

Margo and I dutifully follow.

"Thanks, Izzy," Margo says softly to me.

I flash her a small smile. Margo is kind, but I can't let my guard down.

"Come on, slowpokes. Let's get this show on the road. Daddy will be home soon if you don't hurry this up," Jessa shouts from the front doorstep.

Once Margo and I rejoin Tahlia and Jessa, I set the rules.

"OK, you must respect our home and put everything back as you found it. No snooping in drawers or rooms without me. I'll tell you what was hers and what's mine. I'm warning you, it's a disaster, and most of Gran-gran's things have been moved, so I'm not sure what you're looking to find."

"Oh, we'll know when we see it," Jessa responds.

I reluctantly unlock the door. Margo and Jessa excitedly rush inside, scattering out of my view. Tahlia lingers on the doorstep, causing me to pause. I haven't spoken one on one with her yet. She's standoffish, making her intimidating. She's too quiet for someone so pretty.

"Are you coming in?" I ask.

She's frozen like a statue, and suddenly, I realize I shouldn't be afraid of her. I think she's frightened of me and this situation. I have the upper hand.

"It's OK. I've lived here all summer, and I haven't seen anything to be afraid of." I gesture for her to come inside. Of course, that's a lie. I think. I'm still uncertain about the weird occurrences on my first day here. But there's strength in numbers. Right?

"Come on in. It's OK," I continue to reassure her, lending my hand out.

Tahlia ignores my hand, so I quickly drop it to my side.

Her face is tight as she pulls in a deep breath, taking the first step inside. She doesn't release her breath until she's halfway into the foyer.

"You did it," I respond in a silly congratulatory tone, attempting to lighten the mood. "Now, let's go see where the others went off to."

Tahlia brushes past me, ignoring my kindness, not even offering a simple smile.

OK, maybe she's just a bitch. I'll keep my eye on that one.

Don't let your guard down, Izzy.

I take a moment to regroup my emotions.

I can do this.

I locate the three girls in my dining room. Clearly, they aren't listening to my warning. This is one room still full of Gran-gran's things, and they gravitate toward it like a magnet.

Jessa has the curio cabinet open, staring at the items inside. "Hey Izzy, who are all these men?"

Jessa grabs a framed photo from the cabinet and shows it to us. Is this your Gramp-gramp?" She laughs, finding humor in her lame attempt to make fun of me.

"Um, I'm not sure," I respond.

"How do you not know who your great-grandpa is?" Jessa asks.

"Jessa, not everyone has a perfect family life that fits into a normal box," Margo says, standing up for me.

Jessa snootily sticks her tongue out at Margo.

"Well, I think he died before I was born. I really don't know what happened to him. It was never brought up," I respond.

"And you never asked?" Jessa presses.

"No, it didn't seem important. Remember, I moved here from Seattle, over three thousand miles away? I wasn't here with Gran-gran all the time. The time we spent together was quick and is mostly erased from my memory since I was so young."

Jessa hastily reaches into the cabinet, pulls several frames out, and lays them across the table.

"Look, it's a different guy in each photograph. Who the hell are all these men?" Jessa asks.

"Does it matter? I'm sure they're just a bunch of dead guys now. Dead and gone, like Gran-gran," I respond.

"Yes, it matters, Izzy. This is a clue to who Isobel was. If we're going to unravel her mystery, we need to know more about her life."

"Maybe they're her brothers or something. Can we let it go?"

Ignoring me, Jessa flips a photo over and removes it from the frame. A name in Gran-gran's handwriting is on the backside of the photograph in pencil.

Markus Thompson 1942

She does the same thing to each photograph, and before we know it, the three of us are staring at seven names and dates.

Henry Hancock 1946

Robert Tucker 1958

Frank Hermiston 1960

Hank Becker 1962

Timothy Palmer 1976

"What was Isobel into? This is messed up. Did she date or marry all these men?" Jessa asks.

"OK, that's strange," I curiously admit.

"Yes! Our first clue." Jessa takes out her phone and snaps a photograph of the names. "Something to investigate," she says with delight in her voice.

"Don't you find it strange she never took any of their names if she married all these men? Did she ever have a husband with the Beswick name? Or is that her maiden name?" Margo asks.

"I honestly don't know."

"Another thing, why is your name Beswick? Shouldn't it be something else?" Jessa boorishly asks.

"So, my grandma—I just call her Anna—we're not close. . ."

"The plot thickens." Jessa jabs, cutting me off.

"Anyway, Anna got pregnant at eighteen with my dad, and she never told the father. Or at least, that's what I've been told."

"Or perhaps she didn't know who the father was?" Tahlia says, insinuating Anna was a slut. This could also be true. I don't really know or care.

"Can I please finish?" I shoot Tahlia and Jessa a spiteful glare before continuing. "So, since Anna was a Beswick, my dad was named Beswick, and then obviously I was too."

"Did Anna ever marry?" Margo asks.

"No, I've never even known her to have a boyfriend, but we aren't close," I respond.

"That's some messed up stuff there, Beswick." Jessa rests her hands on her tiny hips.

"You can't choose your family, but you can choose your friends." I stare icily at Jessa.

Maybe my feelings about them are wrong, and we won't be friends. I'm sure I can find someone else to sit with at lunch for the next year.

"OK, point taken," Jessa says, getting my not-so-subtle hint for her to cool it. She dramatically flips her hair over her shoulder before turning and exiting the room.

Tahlia follows behind like a little puppy dog, leaving their mess on the table.

Rude!

"I'm sorry if we're being intrusive," Margo says, helping me put the frames back together. "Jessa has always been fascinated with this house, and I suppose we've been curious too. There's something about this place. I hope you're not mad at us."

"It's fine. Hey, let's go find Jessa before she turns my house upside down," I suggest, while putting the frames back into the cabinet.

"Good idea," Margo agrees.

"Jessa, Tahlia," I holler from the foyer, uncertain which direction they took. My words echo through the house.

"This place is huge," Margo says. "I bet you could get lost if you didn't know where you were going. My house is very tiny; a mouse couldn't get lost in it."

"Yeah, it's pretty big. Especially for two people."

"Why did Isobel need such a big house?" Margo questions.

"Up here. Come quick!" Jessa shouts.

Margo and I race up the stairs, putting an end to our

conversation, which I was glad to do because I really didn't have an answer.

We locate Jessa and Tahlia on the third floor, trying to pick the lock that leads to the attic with a bobby pin that must have come from Tahlia's hair. A long strand of black curls dangles in front of Tahlia's left eye.

"Give me the key," Jessa demands with her hand reaching toward me, palm out.

"I don't have it," I respond.

"I bet your dad has the key somewhere," Jessa insists.

"No, he can't find it either," I lie.

I need to ask him about the key still. I don't want to face what happened to me on my first day in the house.

"Don't you think that's strange he can't *find* it?" Jessa asks, testing my patience.

"Maybe," I respond.

"There is something behind this door, and we need to see what it is," Jessa presses.

"You guys, I'll try to find it, but my dad will be here soon. You said you'd leave before he gets home from work."

"Yeah, Jessa, let's go. We don't want to get our *new* friend in trouble," Tahlia says with a snark in her voice.

I don't know what I've done for Tahlia to be so cold to me. Margo seems like the kind one, always giving me empathetic eyes when Tahlia and Jessa do something rude. Jessa is the leader, the Sondra of the group. The one who you don't cross.

And Tahlia. . .

"What was that?" Margo shouts, interrupting my thoughts.

"What was what?" Jessa asks, giving Margo a curious expression.

"That," Margo whispers.

Tahlia, Jessa, and I respond with questioning eyes. I shrug my shoulders.

"That," Margo repeats. "It's like a knocking noise. You guys really don't hear that? It's so loud. Make it stop. Stop!" Margo shouts, covering her ears with her hands. "Make it stop!"

The three of us rush over to Margo to calm her down.

"We honestly don't hear it, Margo," I gently tell her, trying to caress her hair, but my fingers get lost in her tendrils.

Margo backs away from us. "Make it stop. It's so loud. It hurts!" Margo screams, running toward the stairs.

She's out of our sight before we can process what's happening.

Tahlia, Jessa, and I try to catch up, but Margo's fast. She's out the front door, down the long entryway of steps and out on the sidewalk by Jessa's Jeep by the time we finally catch up to her.

"It stopped," she says, hurled over and panting.

"What the hell was that?" Jessa demands, out of breath.

"You seriously didn't hear that loud knocking?" Margo softly asks.

"No," the three of us respond in unison.

"It was so loud that it pounded through my chest. It felt like my ears would explode if I didn't get away from it."

"Now, are you going to believe me, Izzy? That's some witchy fucking shit right there," Jessa says.

"You guys are messing with me," I accuse them. "That's

not cool. That's so mean. I let you into my house, and you screw with me like that!" I shout, feeling defensive.

"No, I swear, Izzy. That was so real to me. I felt that if I didn't get out of the house—" Margo's big brown eyes lock on mine and bore straight into my soul, and I can't help but think she's telling the truth.

After all, Margo is the only one who's been nice, so I need to give her the benefit of the doubt. They don't know about the mirror, my dream, or the voice. Which now I'm beginning to think was real. But how could it be?

Was Gran-gran really a witch?

No, there is no such thing. Izzy, you're letting them get into your head.

"Is that your dad?" Jessa nods her head to the SUV pulling up behind her Jeep.

"Crap. Yes. It's him."

"Izzy, your dad is hot," Jessa responds, elongating the word hot.

"Ew, please never say that to me again."

"Hello, Mr. Beswick." Jessa waves my dad over to us.

"Hey, Dad. These are my new friends from school. They drove me home today. This is Jessa, Tahlia, and Margo."

"Hello girls, it's nice to meet you. Thanks for giving Izzy a ride home. That was very kind of you," Dad says with a beaming smile. I'm sure he's happy to see I'm finally making friends.

"Mr. Beswick, Izzy and I were talking about how fun it would be if she could have a slumber party this Friday for her new friends," Jessa says, completely going over my head.

We didn't discuss such a thing. What is she doing?

"Oh, I think that is a great idea," my dad responds without glancing in my direction to see if I even wanted this. If he did, he would have seen the warning flags in my eyes before responding.

"Oh, wonderful. Thank you, Mr. Beswick. We're going to have so much fun."

"You girls can call me Steven."

"Thanks, Steven," Jessa says in a flirty voice.

I want to vomit.

"See you inside, Izzy. Take your time with your friends. It was nice meeting you girls. See you in a couple of days."

"Bye, Mr. Beswick," Margo and Tahlia say as my dad leaps up the stairs.

Thank God they didn't call him Steven too.

"What was that? Why did you ask my dad? You could have asked me."

"Well, I want to see more of your house, and after Margo's experience, we must spend the night. I doubt you would have really asked him. He didn't seem to mind we were here, as you suggested," Jessa responds.

"Next time, go through me. Not my dad."

"I don't think I can go back in that house, Jessa," Margo shakily responds.

"Well, if it happens again, you can leave, but come on, you must try. You were fine until we got upstairs. There's some freaky stuff happening up there, and we need you, Margo," Jessa responds with little sympathy for her friend.

"Whatever. But if it happens again. I'm out for good," Margo says, tossing her hands in the air.

"OK, we all have our homework before Friday. Izzy, you

find that key. If your dad has any insight into Isobel's love life, pry it out of him. Tahlia and Margo, stock up on snacks, and I'll do some digging into Isobel's mystery men. This is going to be so much fun. We're going to get to the bottom of this," Jessa says with too much excitement in her voice.

Poor Margo is traumatized, and Tahlia's expression is hard to read. Go figure.

"Ah, do you have a Ouija Board? Or maybe we can play light as a feather," Jessa laughs, like this is all some kind of a joke. "I'll bring the tarot cards."

Everyone ignores her.

"All right, T and Margo, let's go. See you at school tomorrow, Izzy." She blows a kiss in my direction before disappearing into her Jeep. Her music blares as she and the other two girls drive away from my house.

What just happened? Jessa is a bulldozer. Just like Sondra.

CHAPTER 08
OFF-LIMITS

After the girls leave, something in the house doesn't feel right. A disturbance lingers in the air. The entire night, I feel like I'm suffocating. It could also be the humidity and the fact that my window air unit is working on overdrive to cool down my room. But I swear the house is creaking more than usual. I stretch to hear the knocking sound that sent Margo screaming out of my house, but nothing of that sort comes to my attention.

In the morning, I quickly shower and get ready for school, putting a little more effort into my appearance to match my new friends: a denim skirt, a tight, white V-neck T-shirt, and a simple silver chain necklace. My hair is wavy today; it's my best look. To finish my second day of school appearance, I add a little more makeup than yesterday. I don't want to go full-blown since I was pretty basic on day one—a little color on my cheekbones and a light shimmer on my lips. Maybe today Riley will notice me. How can he not remember me? Plus, his dad is working on my house. This makes very little sense. I might have to grow a pair for the two of us and make the first move.

I meet Dad in the dining room for breakfast. Usually, we eat cereal or peanut butter toast. We save the calories for Tim's visit, which is now only Sundays because of my dad's work schedule.

"Morning, Dad."

"Hiya, kiddo. Did you sleep well? It was a doozie of a heatwave last night. I'm still not used to this kind of humidity. Seattle was cool and humid. This is just hot and sticky."

"No, not really. I think this was the worst night since we moved here. Hopefully, the heatwave is almost over. The house was extra creaky last night too."

"Oh, is that right? I didn't notice. I must have the quiet wing." Dad laughs.

"Hey, Dad, changing subjects. When will we finish moving Gran-gran's things out of this room? It's our house now, and these old photos creep me out."

"As you know, with the new job, I haven't had much time to work on these little projects. Tim and I only get Sundays together now, and we need to focus on the structural things before winter falls. I kind of like this room as is."

"Dad, this room is creepy. It's like a shrine to dead people."

Dad releases a soft chuckle.

"Do you even know which photo in this cabinet is your grandpa? Anna's dad?" I ask, pointing to the curio cabinet.

Dad walks over to the cabinet. His hand raises up to rub the back of his neck as he gazes at each photograph. "Well, sweetie, I'm not sure which one he is. I just know his name was Bob."

The one named Robert Tucker, I bet.

Dad crosses past the dining room table and into the kitchen. He continues talking while pouring me a bowl of Froot Loops. "He passed away when my mom was younger. I don't even think she was crawling yet. We never discussed it, and I didn't press either of them for answers. It just didn't seem important. I had my family, and I was happy with the people who surrounded me."

He pokes around the corner. "Do you want a glass of OJ?"

I get the sense he doesn't want to talk about it.

"No, I'm fine with just the cereal. So, you don't know who the other guys are then?"

Dad appears with my breakfast and sets it down in front of me. I could have done this for myself, as I do every day, but I think he needed an excuse to leave the room, so he didn't have to look me in the eye.

"Sweetie, I honestly don't know, and I don't recall Gran-gran ever being with a man. I always assumed she preferred to be alone."

"In this huge house?"

"Why all the questions?"

"I'm just curious. The more things I see, the more questions I have about Gran-gran."

Dad doesn't say anything, so I pry further.

"Sorry, one more question. Do you have the key to the attic? I thought I could start cleaning it out."

"No, I don't, sweetie. I'm sorry. I highly doubt Gran-gran had much stuffed into that tiny room. You saw the third floor; it was pretty barren. I don't think it's a room we need to worry about. At least not anytime soon," Dad responds.

"Oh," I say, disappointed.

"OK, enough questions. Finish your cereal, or you're going to be late. Do you want me to drive you?"

"I'm going to walk," I respond, returning to my bowl of sugary goodness.

Dad gives me a hopeless frown.

A heavy pounding erupts from the entryway, catching me off guard. The spoonful of Froot Loops that's nearly in my mouth falls from my hand, splattering down into the bowl, leaving tiny drops of milk all over the table.

"Who could that be at this hour?" Dad walks away from me, ending our conversation.

I grab a towel from the kitchen to clean up my mess, and a familiar voice floats down the hallway.

"Hey, Mr. Beswick. Does Izzy need a ride to school?"

What is Margo doing here?

I hurriedly clean up my mess and toss my bowl into the sink. It clinks against the porcelain before settling.

I sling my bag over my shoulder, meeting my dad and the whole gang in my entryway. Margo looks unnerved to be back in the house. She's biting at her lip, leaving remnants of her cherry red lipstick on her two front teeth.

"Morning Izzy." Margo waves at me. "We were going to text you, but we all forgot to exchange numbers. Want a ride?"

I can't say no now. That would be rude. "Sure."

Jessa's casually leaning her thin, lengthy body against the doorframe, twirling her blonde locks around her pointer finger, giving my dad googly eyes.

Gross.

"Bye, Dad," I say, pushing past him, shooing the three girls down the stairs.

"Bye, Steven," Jessa says, waving back at my dad.

"Have a good day at school, girls. Behave yourselves," Dad yells as we're halfway to the car.

Once inside Jessa's Jeep, she asks, "Did you get any information from Steven?" Casually throwing my dad's name around like he's one of her friends.

"No, my dad didn't even know which guy was his grandpa, but he did say he thought his name was Bob. I bet it's Robert Tucker."

"Don't you find that odd?" Jessa presses.

"Well, it's not odd because—" Tahlia chimes in.

"T, not now," Jessa snaps, cutting her off.

"What is Tahlia saying?" I ask.

"Nothing," Jessa says sharply. "Anyway, do you girls want to know what I was doing last night?"

"Looking up dead guys' info?" Margo responds.

"Well, no. I got sidetracked by a text message from Sam Hornsby. And guess what we're doing tonight? We're going out to his farm for a senior year kick-off bash," Jessa exclaims.

"On a Wednesday?" I gasp.

"Yeah, his dad is out of town and will be back on Friday. So, a school night it is," Jessa says, thrilled.

"Oh, I'll have to ask my dad if I can go out tonight," I respond.

"Just text him at lunch. Tell him we have a group

assignment in history, and we're working on it at my place. He should believe you, right?" Margo says.

I give Margo a smile. The truth is, I'm not sure I'm ready for a party. I'm just getting used to these three, and now having to chat it up with what sounds like the entire senior class in a social setting seems overwhelming, especially when everyone thinks Gran-gran was a witch. Although, I can't help but wonder if Riley will be there.

"Hey, what do you guys know about Riley Hawkins?" I shyly ask. It's the perfect time to bring him up.

"You can't have him!" Tahlia barks, practically biting off my head. She shifts her body to face me in the back seat. Her mossy green eyes look like they might pop out of her skull, and my hand begins to burn again.

I look away from Tahlia's scowl and down toward my burning hand, but everything appears normal. It must be in my head. This is how my body deals with stress now, I guess. I bring my eyes back up to meet Tahlia's, but she's redirected her attention to staring out the window.

I softly respond, "Oh. I'm sorry. Is he your boyfriend?"

I never meant to step on Tahlia's feet if that's the case.

"No, he's not my boyfriend. He's just off-limits right now," Tahlia hisses.

"How do you know the Hawkins family, anyway? You're not from here," Jessa asks.

"I used to hang out with Riley when I was younger and vacationed here. My dad and Tim Hawkins are friends. Remember? I told you Tim is helping my dad fix up the house."

"That's so strange," Tahlia says, while keeping her eyes focused on the passenger side window.

I shift awkwardly in my seat. "What's strange, T?"

"It's Tahlia. Use my name," she snaps.

"I'm the only one who can call her that," Jessa pipes in.

"Sorry, Tahlia. I didn't mean to offend you. But what did you mean by 'it's strange?'"

"It's nothing. T's in one of her moods today. Aren't you, T?" Jessa responds.

Tahlia gives Jessa a harsh side-eyed glare and turns up her nose but doesn't respond. Her perfect posture makes the quiet interaction appear bitchier than Tahlia probably intends. Tahlia never seems to want to displease Jessa.

They're keeping something from me. What the hell does off-limits mean? I can't help but feel a little rage inside. Tahlia has been nothing but mean to me. I can't help myself. I'm not putting up with this again. The last time almost ruined my life.

"Tahlia, I'm sorry if I did something to make you hate me, but your snide comments are getting old."

"I don't hate you," Tahlia says under her breath.

"OK. Enough, ladies. I promise T will shut her yap and be nicer," Jessa says.

"We're all going to be great friends. The four of us. It has to be that way. I feel it," Margo adds, reaching over to me, squeezing my arm and giving me a full smile.

"So, the party tonight. We're all going—no ifs-ands-or-buts about it. We must make an appearance and introduce our new friend to East Gate High's social scene. Oh, it's going to be so much fun. I can't wait," Jessa shrieks with excitement.

CHAPTER 09
TIPSY SECRETS

"I poured you a cup of whatever concoction they're making in the kitchen," Margo says as she pushes a plastic cup into my hand, blue liquid sloshing out and up onto my arm. "Bottoms up." She clinks my cup and chugs the entire contents in two full gulps. She runs the back of her hand across her mouth, cleaning away the blue evidence.

I bring the cup to my lips, and the smell alone is enough to make me only pretend to take a sip.

"Do you want a refill?" Margo asks, her eyes already glossing over.

Is she serious? She just handed me the drink. "Um. No, I'm fine. I still have some. Maybe you should take it easy. This stuff seems strong."

I'm thrown off by Margo drinking like a booze hound, but then again, I've only known her a few days.

"Oh, it's fine," she says, shrugging it off. Margo saunters over to a nearby table, grabs another mystery beverage, and takes a long swig before returning to me.

"Hey, where did Jessa and Tahlia go?" Margo asks,

already slurring her words.

"They went to find a bathroom."

Margo's eyes glaze over as she stares through me toward the field, forgetting to acknowledge my response.

"Hello, earth to Margo." I snap my fingers, but she's already moving on.

"Hey, Sam. Get over here!" Margo shouts toward a tall guy with jet black hair moving in our direction.

"Sam Hornsby, I want you to meet Izzy Beswick," Margo shouts, even though it's unnecessary.

"Oh, so you're the new girl I've been hearing about," Sam says.

Margo's feet seem unsteady, and she sways between Sam and me. I place my hand on her arm to steady her.

"Oh, no. What have you heard about me?"

"Well, that you're—"

"Now I have to pee!" Margo abruptly shouts, giving us too much information, cutting Sam off in the process. "Be right back. Izzy, are you good?" Margo says, loosely grabbing my hand and quickly letting it slip free.

I can't help but wonder if Margo had a few extra sips before rejoining me outside, because she appears to be tanked already. How is that possible? Did she pre-game without me noticing?

"Yes, Margo, I'll be fine. Go find a bathroom."

Margo turns toward the barn behind us. Sam places his hands on Margo's shoulders, repositioning her to walk in the other direction toward his house.

"You know, she's been here hundreds of times. She should know where the bathroom is. Margo is a good girl, but she gets tipsy at my parties. Sometimes she passes out, and Jessa and Tahlia have to let her sleep here because they can't coax her into the car."

"So, anyway, back to what you've heard about me," I narcissistically ask, when really I should be more concerned for Margo, but I can't help it. I need to know what people are saying about me. I'm the new kid. It matters.

"Oh, yes. My boy Riley has talked nonstop about you being here all summer."

My heart leaps.

"Wait. Riley Hawkins mentioned me to you?" I excitedly ask.

"Oh, shit. I probably shouldn't have let that slip. Maybe I've had too much of the Wave Rider." Sam shakes his cup at me.

"Is that what you call the blue drink?"

"Yes, this concoction was a total accident. We randomly mixed a bunch of booze together. Pretty much everything we could find got dumped into a cooler, and we road tripped to the coast. We were all so drunk and tried surfing and failed miserably, but everyone loved the drink, so we've been mixing it up for parties ever since. It's crazy strong. I probably shouldn't have sold my boy out like that. I think I started too early on these." Sam tips his drink at me.

Sam stumbles backward into the lighting from the barn floodlight. With his face now lit up, I can see him better. He's good-looking, but his complexion is tainted with acne scars—such a shame.

"Where's Riley tonight? I haven't seen him yet," I eagerly ask, needing to know more.

"He should be here soon. He had to close-up the ice cream shop, Scoops, where he works."

"Is that downtown?"

"Yep. A block or so from the park," Sam responds.

Funny that Tim never mentioned that about his son.

"He should be here soon."

"You already said that," I remind him.

Sam holds up his cup again to jog my memory that he's had one too many Wave Riders. "Well, I have to go play host and make sure my dad's shit isn't getting messed with. Nice to meet you, Witch Girl."

"What did you say?" I ask, stunned.

"I said it was nice to meet you, Izzy. What did you think I said?"

"Um, nothing. Nice to meet you, Sam."

Now I know I'm going crazy. I could have sworn he said Witch Girl. Did I imagine that? Where the hell are the girls? I can't believe they've left me all alone here. This is not how this was supposed to go tonight.

And that new revelation about Riley. He talked about me all summer but never made a point to seek me out. What's up with that? Does it have something to do with what Tahlia said in the car, that he's off-limits or whatever?

I need answers.

Now.

I navigate my way to the farmhouse, where I find Margo asleep on the porch swing. She's mostly upright but slouching awkwardly with a plastic cup tipping over in her hand, spilling out onto her leg. This can't be comfortable.

I remove the cup from her hand and place it on the porch ledge. She needs to lie on her side in case she vomits, so I ease her down. I pull her hair away from her face and grab the elastic band from around my wrist to tie her thick hair into a ponytail.

I don't think people should drink these Wave Riders anymore. Poor Margo. Shouldn't Jessa and Tahlia care to look after her if this is her normal behavior? Friends should look out for one another. Some friends they are.

Margo makes a soft murmuring sound, and her eyes flutter. She reaches out her left hand and grazes it over my cheek. "I like you. You're nice." Her words are faint and sleepy.

"I like you too, Margo," I softly respond.

"I hope it's not true," she drunkenly whispers.

"What are you talking about?"

Margo's eyes fight to stay open, but ultimately enclose, and she passes out again. I softly pat Margo's head before leaving her. I need to find Tahlia and Jessa so we can get Margo home. We haven't been here long, and I would love to stick around and wait for Riley, but Margo needs a bed. She's going to feel awful tomorrow. I've never seen someone get so drunk so fast.

I step into the kitchen where Megan Calhoun and a few guys I recognize from my trigonometry class are playing beer pong, but they've substituted Wave Rider in place of beer. Everyone will be so hungover for school tomorrow, and it's only the third day. My Seattle friends are crazy, but this is a whole new level I've never witnessed. I guess kids can get away with more out here in the sticks.

I round the corner to a long hallway, and I spot Jessa and Tahlia in the room at the end. A group of at least ten people are surrounding them. Jessa's movements are animated, like she's telling a story. I wonder what has her so excited. I take a few steps closer, so I can listen. Then I'll tell them about Margo.

"I totally went inside her house. It's fucking creepy. Isobel was into some weird shit," Jessa tells the group of eager listeners.

My heart plummets to my feet. I might be sick. This can't be happening again. I keep trusting the wrong people.

"The rumors are probably true about Izzy," Tahlia says in a haughty voice.

I clear my throat loud enough for them to take notice. Tahlia and Jessa whip their heads around, their faces shocked.

"I thought you guys wanted to really be my friend," I yelp.

They're just like Sondra. I shouldn't have let them into my home. I'm so weak.

Everyone lies.

Everyone sucks.

I won't let them see me cry. Tears fill my eyes—the big ones. They're about to fall.

I rush back through the kitchen and past Margo sleeping on the swing.

I don't know where to go.

They're my ride home.

But I know I can't be here right now.

Dashing down the porch steps, I turn toward the parked cars in the field, passing the barn.

I don't stop.

I keep running, only slowing my speed to toss a quick glance over my shoulder to see if they're following me.

Before I can twist my head forward again, my body slams into something—someone.

"Whoa, watch where you're going," a low, masculine voice says.

"Oh, I'm so sorry," I respond, keeping my head down in embarrassment. I putter past the person, hoping to avoid further conversation.

"Izzy?" the voice calls out, stopping me in my tracks.

"Yes." I slowly turn around, shocked to see the voice belongs to Riley Hawkins—my Riley. He's standing right in front of me, saying my name. He looks so different, but hearing him call out my name reminds me so much of the playful young boy he used to be.

"Are you leaving already?" Riley kicks at the rocks below him.

"Huh?" is all I can spit out.

"It's me, Riley. Tim's son. Don't you remember me?" He pushes his sandy brown hair away from his eyes. He practically towers over me. He must be at least six feet tall now.

"Yes, of course. I remember you," I respond with my heart skipping a few beats. This is the moment I've been waiting for since I moved here.

"Are you OK?" he asks. "You seem a little disheveled."

"No, I'm not OK. I'm leaving."

"Leaving already? The party just started."

"Well, I've had enough."

"Did you drive yourself?" Riley asks, his deep blue eyes sparkling in the moonlight.

I feel almost intoxicated in his presence, like my feet might give way, leaving me to fall into his perfectly sculpted arms. I desperately want to stay now, but I've committed to my dramatics.

"No, I'm going to walk."

Riley gives me a concerned expression. "It's at least an hour's walk from here to your house. It's not safe this late at night on these back roads. You'd get lost."

"It's fine. I'll be OK. Don't worry about me. It's not like you worried about me all summer or even bothered to say hi at school. We have history class together, for God's sake. And now you're talking to me."

"It's not what you think. I haven't had anything to drink yet. Let me drive you home, so I can explain."

"I'd prefer it if you'd just answer me now," I demand, stomping my foot into the ground like the dramatic little girl he used to know. "Why did you pretend like I didn't exist all summer? Your Dad was at my house every week. You had your chance to talk to me. Riley, we used to be friends. Do you know how that made me feel?"

I can't believe I'm letting myself be so open with my feelings. All my pent-up emotions are flying out of me, and I have no way of reeling them back in.

"I'm so sorry I hurt you. I didn't, um, I had no choice." He shifts uncomfortably on his feet and runs his fingers through his hair.

"What the hell does that mean?" I demand. My five-foot-four stature barely graces his chin. I wish I could make eye contact with him in this moment as he searches for his excuse.

I rock restlessly back and forth on my heels, imprinting in the dirt below. Riley's brows furrow, and his face contorts into a discombobulated mess.

"Um. My dad—"

"Ah, there you are!" Jessa shouts, popping out from the darkness. "Izzy, I've been looking everywhere for you."

"Not now, Jessa. I'm in the middle of something else," I crudely respond, shooting daggers into her eyes.

Jessa stumbles backward. "I'm so sorry," she says, regaining her balance and ignoring my warning to leave me alone. "I've had a little too much to drink. I didn't mean to talk about you. I'm truly sorry. These Wave Riders always get to me. You'd think I'd learn my lesson. Everyone was asking me questions about you, and I'm sorry I shouldn't have said those things. T is sorry too. She's out looking for you as well."

"Hey, Izzy. Since your friends are here, I'll let you guys do your thing. I'll catch you later." Riley keeps his head down, avoiding looking me in the eye.

He shuffles his feet quickly, leaving Jessa and me alone in the darkness. I keep a watchful eye on him. As he approaches the barn, Tahlia appears. She wraps one arm around Riley's neck, pulling him close to her body. She whispers something into his ear before letting him go. He turns back toward Jessa and me and shakes his head before disappearing further into the party.

I turn my attention back to Jessa, who gives me sad puppy

dog eyes. She seems remorseful, but I don't know if I can trust her. This might be one of those keep your enemy's closer kind of things.

"Friends don't talk about each other behind their back, Jessa."

"I'm sorry. We're sorry," Jessa says, nodding to Tahlia as she approaches us.

"Yes, I'm sorry," Tahlia mirrors Jessa's words with lesser sincerity.

"What's going on? Everyone is acting strange around me, and no one will give me a straight answer. Everyone is being so cryptic. Is it because of that silly story about Isobel? If so, that's ridiculous."

"I promise I'll tell you, but not here. It's best if we're alone," Jessa says.

"What the heck does that mean? See, you're being cryptic!" I shout, flailing my hands around.

"Not here," Jessa whispers.

"None of you can drive. Give me your keys," I demand.

"I'm fine now. I'll be fine," Jessa insists.

"Whatever. Let's grab Margo and get the hell out of here!" I shout.

We find Margo in the exact place I left her. Tahlia and I hoist her arms over our shoulders, dragging her. Margo's deadweight is exhausting to pull, but we finally make it to Jessa's Jeep. We stuff Margo in the back seat. Her body flops over into the middle of the row.

"Seriously, let me drive. You've been drinking," I request again.

"No, I swear I'm fine now. I know these roads like the back of my hand. Get in the back seat and take care of Margo."

I reluctantly do as Jessa asks, sliding into the seat behind her. I move Margo's body upright and fasten her seatbelt. Her head bobs as Jessa takes the first right onto the country road, leaving the farmhouse illuminated in the back window. To say you could cut the tension with a knife would be an understatement, but I can't bite my tongue any longer. I must know.

"Now, can you tell me what the hell is going on?"

Jessa shifts her entire head, taking her eyes off the quiet, dark road ahead of us, her face hard to read and dimly lit up by the blue dashboard lights. Her pink lips purse, and her blue eyes soften. "There isn't an easy way to say this—"

"Jessa, look out!" Tahlia screams.

Jessa jerks her head back to her center and tugs on the steering wheel. Tahlia reaches over and grabs the wheel from Jessa, pulling the Jeep in the other direction.

Tahlia lets out a loud sigh. "Oh, thank God we avoided the deer. Keep your eyes on the fucking road," she says, exasperated.

The sudden movement of the Jeep sends Margo's heavy head onto my lap. Her erratic open mouth breathing releases boozy scents into the car, nauseating me.

Everyone goes quiet, letting Jessa focus on driving when an intense thud sound reverberates throughout the car. My head wobbles from side to side

"What the hell was that?" Tahlia screams.

A second thud echoes near the back of the car.

"We must have hit the deer. We drove over something," Jessa exclaims, slamming on the brakes. She steers the car off to the side of the road.

"No. I saw it. We missed it," Tahlia says, puffing at her words.

"Well, we hit something," I clamor from the back seat.

"Run," a voice whispers.

Every hair on my head stands up straight. "Margo," I say, nudging her. She doesn't move. The words aren't coming from her.

"Run," the voice whispers again.

A gust of wind flutters my hair. I jerk my head around, but none of the windows are open. I'm losing my mind. This isn't real.

"Stop!" I shout.

"I am stopped, Izzy," Jessa cries. Her voice is frazzled.

It's not Jessa I'm talking to. *OK Izzy, get a grip on yourself. Focus on our situation, not your insanity.*

"It was probably a different deer. They always travel in packs," Jessa says with unsureness coating her voice.

"Do we get out and see?" Tahlia questions, her voice shaky.

"I've been drinking, and we've got Drunkie in the back seat. We can't stay to check it out. I'll get in so much trouble, and so will Margo. It was just a deer. Yes, just a deer." Jessa pulls the car back into our lane. She doesn't wait for us to say no.

I glance over my shoulder, and something moves on the dark ground behind us. I can't find the words to tell Jessa to stop. All I can think of is the voice—run. And that's what we're doing. We're running away.

CHAPTER 10
SLEEPWALKING

"If my Jeep is wrecked, I'm screwed. We're all screwed," Jessa says, anxiously shifting the Jeep into park outside of my house.

Jessa gets out first, with Tahlia following behind. I'm frozen in my seat, as I have been since we pulled back onto the road. I can't help but think things would have been easier if we stayed in Seattle. I could have dealt with the snickering and rumors about what happened with Sondra. But this is a whole new level of uncertainty. We hit something, and I'm Witch Girl—granddaughter of Witch Lady. Everyone is talking about me, and something is going on that no one will tell me. Plus, I'm insane now and hearing voices. So, there's that.

Tahlia paces in front of the car as Jessa frantically rummages through her purse, finally pulling out her phone. She shines the phone's flashlight at the front end. The sight of their faces drastically shifting from frightened to confused cause me to stir in my seat.

I need to move.

I can do this.

I can face whatever this is. Pulling in a deep breath, I place my fingers on the handle and push the door open. The muggy air slaps me in the face, making me ill.

"How is that possible?" Tahlia asks, as I approach them.

"I swear we hit something. If it were the deer, my front end would have evidence of it. There isn't damage. No blood. Nothing. We're in the clear," Jessa says, elation erupting from her voice.

"It was probably just a small animal like a raccoon," Tahlia says, reassuring herself.

"Either way, you guys, I don't want to be alone tonight. I'm too shaken up by all this. Plus, we can't take Margo home; we need to keep an eye on her. Can we sleep here?" Jessa asks.

"No, my dad will freak. You've all been drinking; he'll know."

"Well, *you* haven't been drinking, so you do all the talking if he catches us. Your house is so huge he probably won't even hear us. I promise we'll be quiet, and we can sneak out before he knows we were here. Please, Izzy," Jessa begs.

"Won't your parents care? And what do we do about Margo?" I ask.

"T, call your parents. Tell them I got too tired to drive you home and you're staying at my place. Izzy, grab Margo's phone and text her mom that she's staying at my house for the same reason. I'll tell my parents I'm staying at T's place."

I frown but do as Jessa requests. I don't want Margo to get in trouble, and I'll feel safer if I can monitor her tonight.

"We do this all the time. Our parents trust us for some crazy reason," Jessa says with a laugh. "OK, now the tricky part... getting Margo in the house quietly."

Tahlia looks at me, and I nod. Both of us know darn well Jessa won't help. Once we get Margo out of the car, she surprisingly assists us in walking up the steps. Jessa opens the door and serves as our lookout. We successfully make it to my bedroom without alerting my dad.

Tahlia and I lay Margo down on my bed, and the three of us join her.

Silence veils over the room as each of us process the night's events. I get lost in my thoughts and before I know it, my eyes are heavy. I want answers, but I also need sleep.

***

"Find her."

I'm startled awake.

"Find her," the voice calls out again. It's airy and drawn out, almost unreal. It's the same voice from the car and my first night in this house.

"Find her."

Goosebumps prickle up and down my arms.

I jolt upright in bed and glance to my left, where Tahlia and Jessa are fast asleep. Then to my right.

Oh no, where did Margo go?

Shit.

"Margo is gone," I whisper, shaking Jessa awake.

Jessa groggily stares at me in confusion, rubbing her tired eyes.

The ceiling groans above us as pitter-patters of movement coincide with creaking floorboards. The activity ceases and is replaced by a scratching or dragging sound, causing every hair on my body to stand erect.

Something isn't right.

A wide-eyed stare immediately replaces Jessa's grogginess. Her pupils seem to double in size as she nervously tugs at her hair. "What should we do?" she whispers.

"We need to find Margo," I respond in the same hushed voice.

Jessa nudges Tahlia awake. "Margo's gone." Jessa nods to the ceiling groaning above us, catching Tahlia up to speed with very little explanation.

The three of us quickly but quietly exit the bed and file into the hallway. We cautiously climb the steps to the third floor—a place I never thought Margo would go alone.

We come to a halt on the last step before entering the third floor.

"Is she sleepwalking?" Tahlia asks.

"What is she looking at?" Jessa questions.

Margo is crouched in the center of the room below the small window, hovering over the floor. There is an unnatural curve to the way she's hunched over.

"Margo, sweetie, are you all right?" I cautiously take the first step toward her.

She doesn't respond, so I slowly tiptoe up behind her.

"I think I read somewhere that you're not supposed to wake a sleepwalker," Jessa says, but I ignore her. I don't think she's sleepwalking.

"Margo," I repeat her name.

She still doesn't move.

I continue to inch closer to Margo until I'm directly behind her. I gently place my hand on her back, and a familiar burning sensation runs through my fingertips to my wrist. I push past the feeling, ignoring it for the moment. "Margo, can you hear me?" My voice is low and calm, careful not to startle her.

I lean in further, peeking over the top of her head. The burning intensifies. I ball my hand into a fist, trying to calm down the sensation, but it doesn't help.

A bloodcurdling shriek releases from my belly, not from the burning pain I'm in, but at the sight of Margo's actions below me. Blood is dripping down Margo's hands and running down the length of her arm. The nail on her pointer finger is peeled back from the skin and gushing blood.

Tahlia and Jessa seem to be frozen in terror, as they are still on the top step.

I stretch to listen for any sounds indicating we've woken my dad. Luckily, I don't hear any movement. He must be too far away. In this moment, I'm grateful for this large house.

"What's going on? I'm scared," one of them whispers, but I can't tell which one.

"Margo, what are you doing?" My words shake as they leave my mouth.

Margo slowly turns her head, her eyes glossier than

before. Her mouth meets my ear, her breath hot on my skin. "They need me to find it," she whispers.

"Find what?" I cautiously ask, afraid of the answer.

I direct my attention back down to Margo's bloody hands. She's digging her fingers into the wooden floorboard below her. Scratch marks and blood coat the three boards beneath her.

"Margo, stop!" I shout, pulling her hands away from the board, only stunning her momentarily.

"They need me to find it," she repeats.

"Come help me!" I scream.

The three of us pull Margo backward, away from the boards, but she fights us to resume. Her arms thrash wildly as she tries to get back to her task.

"They need me to find it."

Jessa straddles Margo and slaps her straight across the face, knocking her from her trance. I manage to pull both of her hands back as blood flies in every direction, leaving rust-colored speckles on my white shirt. Tahlia drags Margo to the middle of the room, and Margo falls flat on her back, sobbing.

"What the heck was that, Margo?" Jessa demands, offering little sympathy.

Margo sucks in the air and puffs out choppy breaths, trying to respond. She can't quite catch her words. "I... I—"

I don't wait for an answer. I jolt out of the room without a word, sprinting downstairs and into the kitchen, searching for Dad's tools.

I pull a hammer from his toolbox and grab the first-aid kit from the drawer before dashing back upstairs. I toss the kit at the girls, assuming they will know how to clean up Margo's wounds.

Using the claw side of the hammer, I yank the blood-soaked boards up one at a time.

"Um, you guys. Get over here now!" I scream.

CHAPTER 11
TOLD YOU SO

The four of us gaze dumbfounded into a dusty, cobweb-infested hole. Margo's blood dots the floor like constellations in the night sky. A sick reminder of the twisted events that led to this moment.

"Do I touch it?" I ask.

"What the heck is it?" Jessa questions.

"I think it's a book," Tahlia responds.

"Margo, how did you know there was something in the floor? Do you remember waking up and coming up here? You kept repeating, 'they need me to find it.' Do you know what any of this means?" I press.

Margo gulps and swallows hard before answering, "Remember when I ran out of here screaming? The noise was the same, but somehow different. If that makes any sense. It woke me, but this time it didn't drive me mad. It called to me—asking for help. You guys will think I'm banana bonkers, but I heard a voice. I know that sounds insane."

"No, Margo, that's not insane," I respond, giving pause to my next words, afraid to say them out loud. "I've heard voices too. Like a faint whisper." I reach over to Margo and squeeze her arm, careful to avoid her poorly bandaged hand.

Jessa crosses her arms tightly under her chest and huffs a couple of times. Instead of appearing frightened by my revelation, Jessa seems almost jealous. Could she really be envious that I hear voices, or that Margo and I have the same freaky connection? Or could it be the sudden attention Margo is getting? Maybe I'm imagining things.

Jessa shifts her weight on the ball of her heels. "Did you know you were hurting yourself?" she asks, once again with little sympathy.

"No, I didn't feel the pain until you pulled me away." Margo directs her focus to her wrapped hand with blood soaking to the end of each fingertip.

"OK, so what do we do? I'm afraid to touch whatever *that* is," Tahlia says. "Maybe we should leave it, cover it back up, and forget we ever saw it."

"Whatever it is, it called to Margo, and something's been calling me. I feel like we need to see what it is to move on," I respond.

I'm unsure about revealing the truth about my experiences in this house. The messages in the voices, the burning in my hand, the mirror, or the sudden burst of memories. It all led us to this thing in the ground.

A withered, almost wrinkly looking item taunts us from the hole. Do we or don't we touch it? Both scenarios bounce rapidly through my mind.

"Grab it," the familiar airy voice calls out.

I glance at the three girls. Their gazes are unchanged.

They can't hear it. Not even Margo. This message is for me. Just like Margo had her own message earlier, bringing her to this very spot. We're being directed, but for what reason?

"Grab it." The elongated, airy words float down into my eardrum.

"What are you doing?" Tahlia shouts.

Giving little thought to my actions, I bend down, lock my fingers under the heavy item, and tug it out of the hole. I carefully set it on the ground, and a cloud of dust puffs up from the movement, making us all cough.

A massive purple leather-bound book stares back at us, dusty and strung full of cobwebs.

"No fucking way! So, it is true? I told you so," Tahlia says in a smart-aleck tone.

"What are you talking about? What's true?" I demand, clueless about their secrets once again.

"Don't you understand? Everything we said about Isobel is true. This must be her spellbook," Jessa says. "She's a witch, Izzy!"

A smug grin spreads across Tahlia's face. "Well, Jessa, then that means the other thing is probably true. Izzy deserves to know the truth."

"Tell me the truth! Now!" I shout.

I can tell Jessa's enjoying having a hold over me. She knows things I don't. She takes her time gathering her thoughts and tugs at her straight blonde hair before answering. "Isobel was cursed." She smacks her lips as if she recently applied lip gloss and then brings them together in slow motion, pausing for dramatic effect and puckering them into a duck face.

"Spit it out!" I demand, tiring of her antics.

"I don't know how to say it… If the rumors are true, which they look like they are"—she nods toward the dusty old book on the floor—"then you're cursed too." Her top lip turns upward, and a satisfied smirk tugs at each end.

"Cursed? Like how?" My eyes flash to Tahlia and Jessa, searching their faces for answers that are slowly seeping out. Why must they drag everything on?

"And where the heck is Margo?" I shriek with annoyance.

My eyes dart to each dark corner of the room, with Margo nowhere to be found.

"The book is gone," Tahlia says in a low, hushed voice.

I'm finally uncovering the truth, and Margo has gone and messed it up.

Dang it, Margo.

"Um, you guys. The attic door is open." Tahlia shakes her hand toward the small steps leading to the attic.

A faint light glows from the crack in the doorway.

"What the heck!" I exclaim. "How?" I approach the ajar door, slowly pushing it open. "Margo?" I cautiously take a step inside, and my jaw drops.

At least a dozen candles illuminate the room.

Margo is directly in the middle of a faint white circle drawn on the floor. The dusty old book is sitting in front of her, wide open.

"The key was inside the book," Margo says gleefully, unfazed by her odd actions.

Her crazed eyes are nearly translucent.

"You shouldn't have opened it without us," I say.

"I had to. It wanted me to," she responds.

"Did you light these candles?" I question.

"No, it was like this when I opened the door. Isn't it beautiful?"

"Margo, why are you so calm? I'm freaking out. This isn't normal." My skin feels like it's going to crawl off my bones.

Margo starts humming to herself. A tune that I can't place.

"What are you singing?"

"I don't know. It's something in my head," Margo responds, smiling.

"Sweetie, you're freaking me out," I admit.

"Come, have a look. They want you to see it, Izzy." Margo extends her hand for me to join her in the circle.

"Who wants me to see it?" I warily respond.

Margo ignores my question. Instead, she keeps her hand extended outward, inviting me inside the circle.

I carefully step into the chalk outline, half afraid I'll burn up upon entry—like something out of a horror film.

But nothing happens.

Tahlia and Jessa daintily follow behind me, cautiously avoiding stepping on the white line. The four of us sit in a circle around the old book. I reach out to turn the item to face me. After all, this is my house, so I should be the one with the best view. I caress the withered-looking page in front of me. My hand tingles, and a burning sensation rapidly rushes from my fingertips to my elbow. The more I touch the book, the more the burn intensifies. But I can't help it. I can't physically pull myself away from it.

The ink is nearly unreadable on the browned and tattered

page. The burning sensation flushes the entire length of my arm, and the ink darkens on the pages.

"Holy cow. That's impossible," Jessa screeches.

The words come to life in front of our very eyes as the burning escalates, creeping across my shoulder and down the length of my other arm. My mind says to run, but my body doesn't budge.

I rub my eyes to ensure that what I see is real. None of this feels real, like a dream. But here we are in an old house, in a secret attic with a relic book of spells laid out on the floor in front of my three new friends.

The words are there. The proof is there. Isobel was a witch. It's in writing. I can't deny the truth. The first page says it all.

Thy Book of Shadows belongs to:
High Priestess Isobel Beswick
Property of: The Wives of Salem Coven

Practitioner's Warning:
Only a Bloodline Witch may invoke the spirits
and cast a circle.
Only the coven bloodline may call upon the
quarters.
If ye shall not abide by the rules set forth,
ye shall suffer.

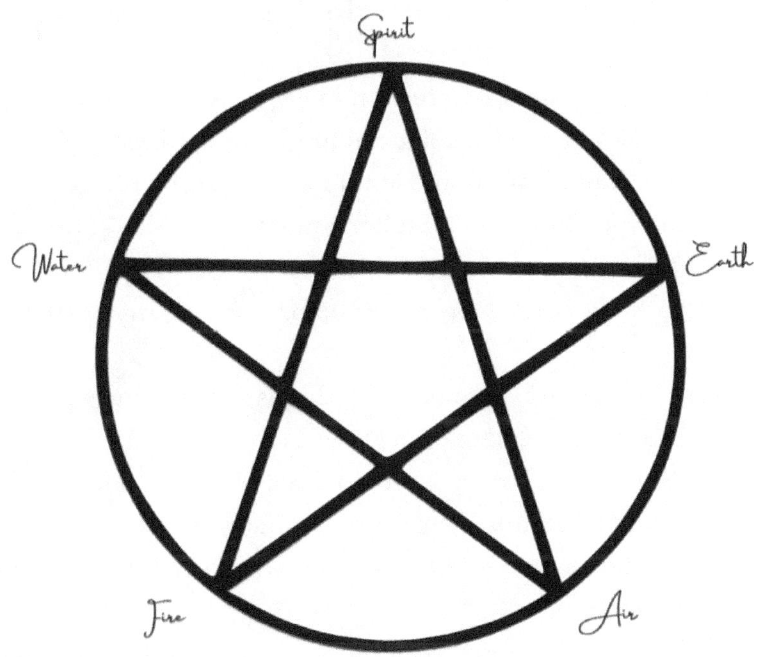

"OK, so now do you believe us?" Jessa asks, her voice low and shaky.

"Whatever *this* is, it involves Margo too. She was the one who found the book and let us into the attic," I remind them.

"It has to be four of us. Four elements to complete the circle, see?" Margo points to the diagram. "Earth, air, fire, and water. There are four of us."

"Well, who is the spirit then?" Jessa asks.

"They said we don't need to worry about that. Izzy will know what to do."

"I don't know what to do," I respond. "Are they talking to you now?"

"Kinda. It's like I can feel an energy," Margo says.

"This is some dark magic juju going on here," Tahlia suggests. "I don't think we should keep turning the pages."

"I think it's time you all tell me more about this supposed curse before continuing. If this book is a real spellbook, I need to know what you know before we go any further," I say.

Jessa clears her throat. "So, this is the tale we heard. Remember, Isobel fled Salem, Massachusetts, before her trial? She started over here in East Gate, Connecticut, many years later. But she carried a curse with her. One that forever toiled her love life. Anyone who loved an escaped witch would die."

"Who cursed them? Wouldn't they have to be a witch too?" I ask.

"I'm not sure. This is just the tale passed down. Maybe the answers are in this book," Jessa says.

Tahlia takes a long deep breath, and her sorrowful big green eyes meet mine. "But the worse part of this curse is that it follows her bloodline. It's passed down forever, cursing anyone in the coven bloodline. That means you, Izzy."

I nervously gnaw at the inside of my cheek, recalling my conversation with Tahlia in the car this morning. "Is that why you said Riley is off-limits and why he's avoided me all summer? Everyone really believes this, huh?"

"The curse seems to be true. We were keeping Riley safe from you. We've known each other our entire lives. He's like a brother to me." Tahlia's eyes fill with tears. "I don't hate you, Izzy. I just can't let you get close to someone I care about. I have to protect Riley."

"No, that can't be true. That's ridiculous," I respond.

"Look at what we're doing right now. We're sitting in a room with freaky candles that Margo said she didn't light. You two are hearing voices, and we can't argue that sitting in a circle with an old book isn't real. This is real, Izzy. The rumors are true," Tahlia says.

"So, if Officer Tim knows about this curse and warns kids to stay away from this house, then why is he here all the time?" I ask.

"Maybe to keep an eye on things and to make sure you stay away from his son," Tahlia replies.

"There's more," Jessa says. "I wanted to tell you at the slumber party on Friday, but it seems now is a better time. I spent my entire time in chem class on my iPad, googling Isobel's men. The dates on the back of the photographs weren't the year she married them, but their death dates. Every man she got close to died. All six of them. So, there's a reason for the rumors, Izzy. They aren't just stories people made up. They saw it firsthand. Her lovers all died. Sure, the stories could have been fabricated as a way of understanding all that death, but this book is reason enough for us to believe."

"Why didn't you say something sooner?" I demand.

"I wanted to surprise you all on Friday. I thought we could do a seance or something cool, but that was before things got real," Jessa says sheepishly. "I honestly never expected things to turn out like this. I was hoping for something interesting to happen, but never in my wildest thoughts could I have imagined all this."

The room is spinning. I'm dizzy. I bring my knees up to my chin, so I can rest my head. Everything is unraveling, and I can't put the pieces together fast enough. I feel a hand on my back, but I don't turn around to see whose hand it is.

"I really hate to bring this up, but where is your mom?" Tahlia gently asks.

My heart drops at the mention of my mother. How dare they? "Mom got sick. It wasn't some stupid curse, if that's what you're implying."

"What kind of sickness, cancer?" Tahlia asks.

"I'd rather not talk about that." I lower my head further into my legs. I want to disappear right now.

"Izzy, this is important. Please, you can share this with us," Margo says softly. "You can talk to us."

I raise my head, making eye contact with Margo. I speak like she's the only one I'm talking to. "No, it wasn't cancer. The doctors didn't know what it was. It was some unexplainable disease. They didn't have answers, and it took her fast, so there wasn't much time for them to research it." I choke back tears. "Plus, my parents were together fourteen years. If it were a curse, don't you think it would have taken her sooner?"

"I don't know, but it's still a coincidence. Don't you think? Maybe the curse doesn't follow timelines. Maybe it takes a person when it will hurt someone the most," Tahlia says. "Do you think your dad knows about any of this?"

I leap to my feet, ready to defend my family. "I don't want to believe that. My mom got sick. There was nothing anyone could do. It wasn't a stupid curse. And my dad hasn't let on to anything witchy or curse related. He lost his wife to a disease, and he's trying to move on."

"I hate to bring this up when you're so emotional, but we need to figure out if it's true, so we can help you. Didn't Anna say she didn't tell the father about her baby—your dad? Well, maybe she knew about the curse, and she was protecting the father. This all makes a lot of sense. The dead guys, your grandpa being MIA, and your mom passing from an unknown disease. This is all connected," Tahlia says.

"I can't be cursed."

"Maybe there are some answers in this book?" Jessa suggests with her finger on the page, ready to flip. "Ouch."

"What happened?" Tahlia asks.

"The book zapped me," Jessa says, shaking her hand.

"Zapped?" I question. "Like you felt hot?"

"No, it like shocked me," Jessa responds. "T, you touch it."

Tahlia turns the page. "My hand felt warm, but it didn't zap me. It tingled, but it didn't hurt."

"Margo, did it hurt you when you carried it in here?" I ask.

"No, it was warm, but that's it," Margo responds.

Jessa tries to touch the page again. "Ouch."

"That's so strange. Maybe you're not supposed to touch it," I suggest.

Jessa rolls her eyes. "Whatever. What's on the second page?"

Wives of Salem Coven must abide by the law set forth.
Failure to abide will cause great harm.

Thy Rule of Three
In loving harmony and loving trust abide ye must
What ye send out, ye will receive times three
In loving harmony and loving trust
With open eyes and open heart, ye must abide
In loving harmony, we meet and in loving trust, we part
So shall it be.

"What the heck does that mean? It's all like ancient wording and stuff," Jessa huffs.

"I think it's like Karma. What you put out, you'll get back, good or bad, so practice wisely," I respond. "We can't mess around with magic." I shut the book.

"No, keep flipping. There must be something in here about the curse," Tahlia suggests.

"You guys, I think I've had enough for one night. Plus, the sun is coming up, and my dad will be awake soon. I'm surprised we haven't woken him yet. Blow out these candles. I'll put the book and key back in the hole for now. No one breathes a word of this to anyone. You got it? They will think we've lost our minds. I mean it. I'm already a freak to everyone, but this will confirm it."

"We pinky promise," Margo says, lending her pinky to the group.

"Fine, we pinky promise too," Jessa and Tahlia respond in unison, locking their pinkies together.

CHAPTER 12
MR. BARISTA

I told the girls I would meet them at school. Margo seemed OK this morning for someone who was drinking like a fish, then spent the night digging holes, breaking fingernails, and hearing voices. I helped her clean her wounds and disguise them better so no one would ask questions. They left my house around five a.m., thankfully avoiding detection.

I quickly get ready and walk down to The Perk for an iced mocha latte, skipping breakfast with my dad. I splurge for the large size since I got zero sleep, and I'm cursed. It's a lot to take in before 8 a.m. I can't wrap my head around it all. My mind is swirling with all my newfound information.

"I have an order for Izzy. Iced mocha latte," a handsome guy about my age with wildly dark eyes calls out, knocking me from my dazed thoughts.

I lean in, extending my arm across the counter, reaching for my drink in his hand. My fingers accidentally rub across his, giving me a little zip of fire. I tug the large drink toward me, ready for this awkward interaction to be over. But he doesn't let the beverage slip from his grip.

"Hey now, eager one. I get a little quickhanded too when it comes to my morning coffee, but you didn't say if you wanted whipped cream on top," the barista says, catching me off guard and pulling the cup back.

"Oh, um, sure," I stutter. "I guess I can use all the sugar I can get today," I respond with an uncomfortable grin.

"You look like you could use some chocolate sprinkles too." The man with golden brown skin and velvety colored eyes says with a wink that makes my stomach flutter.

Is this guy flirting with me? I guess I can flirt back. Riley was MIA all summer and ditched me last night once my friends showed their faces. Plus, I don't know if Riley even likes me. So, there isn't any harm in getting a little attention, right?

"Thanks, sprinkles sound good." My smile widens.

I search for a name tag, but come up with nothing. Not even a lanyard. Dang it. I suck at this flirting thing. If you can even call what I'm doing flirting.

"Here you go. Now you're all set for the day ahead. Fully caffeinated and with as much sugar as one can legally fit into a large cup." He tilts the beverage back toward me.

I reach for the iced coffee, letting our hands graze during the pass off. His touch causes my hand to burn hotter this time, and a shiver runs up my spine. My breath catches as we exchange an awkward smile.

"Have a good day, Izzy," the gorgeous barista says, tilting his head. His lip curls upward, leaving me dizzy with emotions I can't explain.

"Thanks, you too, Mr. Barista."

Mr. Barista! Oh my gosh. Who says that? I'm so embarrassed. Yep, I suck at flirting.

I quickly turn for the door, but unable to control myself, I flip my head over my shoulder to see if he's still looking.

I'm nearly knocked off my feet by the strangely curious glare he's giving my backside. I shudder at his possible thoughts and quickly strut out of the building. It's a good thing I suck at flirting, I guess.

With my overly caffeinated, overly sugared beverage in hand, I mull over last night's events. I need answers, and I need them now.

Are we really hearing voices or slowly going insane? Maybe we have a gas leak causing us to hallucinate.

Did a voice really direct Margo to those specific floorboards?

Were the book and the attic an elaborate prank to scare the bejesus out of me? If so, it worked.

Is Tim Hawkins aware of the rumors and, if so, could he really believe them? That explains why he's keeping Riley from me. But Tim's an adult and a cop. Would he let silly stories get in his head? Then again, a lot of the adults in town act strange around me—the lady in the bakery, Mrs. Jamison, and I'm sure there are more.

Am I really cursed?

Sweat beads its way down my back, soaking through my shirt to my backpack, making me uncomfortable.

Another humid day. Great.

This morning on the news, the weatherman said this heat is unusual for this time of year. Go figure, the summer we move is the hottest on record.

My latte is sweating and nearly slipping through my hand. I take a long gulp, trying to cool myself down, when a burst of mocha slides down my throat. A young boy flies by me on a skateboard, knocking me off balance and causing me to choke.

"Everyone knows what you did to her, Izzy," the boy hisses.

"What did you say?" I shout, wheezing and swallowing hard to avoid choking a second time.

The skateboarder abruptly stops his board, pressing his foot hard on the tail end and popping the nose up to his hand. A solid mix of confusion and annoyance spreads across his face.

"Huh? I didn't say anything to you."

"Are you sure?"

"You should probably lay off the drugs. Ain't no one talking to you, lady." His board hits the ground and he skates away.

I shake my head to dislodge my insanity. Maybe I should check myself into a mental institution. I need help. Witches aren't real, and neither are the voices in my head. I'm going crazy—but the book. It's hard to argue against. I held it in my hand. It's real.

My thoughts of delirium come to an instant halt when I near the school. Flashing blue lights reflect off the car windows in the parking lot, directing my attention to the police cars lining the front of the building.

What on earth is going on?

CHAPTER 13
MISSING PERSON

The closer I get, the more patrol cars come into my view. I spot the girls pulling into Jessa's usual parking space. Maybe they know what's going on. I sprint the rest of the block to meet them before they're swallowed up by the crowd of students waiting outside.

"Do you guys know why there are like ten patrol cars here?" I ask, nearly out of breath and sweating like a hog, with my hair sticking to the side of my face.

"No clue. We just got here." Jessa pulls her backpack from the back seat. For someone who got zero sleep last night, she appears well rested. Her sky-blue eyes even have a twinkle in them. How does she do it?

I feel dull and tired. My hair even looks tired, hanging lifeless without any volume. Come to think of it, I'm surprised the barista paid any attention to me. I had no energy left to attempt anything cute today. Last night took everything from me.

Margo's appearance is the same as always. Her hair bounces with each movement.

Tahlia, on the other hand, is wrecked. The bags under her eyes don't help either. It's odd seeing her so unkept. I know last night got to her in more than one way. I think it's time I ease up on her and give her a second chance. After all, her crudeness was just a front to protect Riley.

The four of us saunter toward the school entrance shoulder to shoulder.

"I need everyone to get into two single-file lines. One for each doorway, please," Mrs. Jamison loudly instructs.

"What's going on?" Jessa demands.

"Miss Dewitt, you will all be asked a series of questions once you get inside the building."

"About what?" Jessa questions.

"I'm sorry, I'm not at liberty to say," Mrs. Jamison responds, letting her head hang as she backs away from our group.

Loud chatter erupts from the two lines forming.

"Hush, no talking in line. I need everyone to be quiet. We need to let the police do their job," Mrs. Jamison says with a heaviness in her voice.

We do as we're told.

When we approach the entryway, an officer comes up to me, as I'm the first in my group. "Name?"

"Izzy Beswick."

"Izzy, I'm going to have you come with me." The officer escorts me into a classroom alone.

I catch a glimpse of Riley being accompanied into the room across the hallway. He catches my eyes and offers a slight smile before the officer closes the door behind me.

"Izzy, my name is Officer Massey. You can take a seat if

you'd like." He points to the row of desks behind us.

I slide into the first chair, but he remains standing, making me feel small.

"Can you tell me if you attended a party last night?"

I fidget in my seat, unsure if I should answer truthfully. I don't want to get in trouble my first week of school, but I didn't drink, so I should be OK answering.

"Um, yes. I went to a party with some new friends. I didn't drink, if that's what you want to know."

"No, that's not what we are here about today," he responds.

A flush of relief rushes over me but is quickly replaced by a layer of unease. If he's not here to bust us for the party, then why is he here?

Officer Massey studies me and I can't help but tense up, like I did something wrong. "A student was reported missing last night by her parents, and we're trying to locate her. She was last seen at the Hornsby farm."

"Oh my gosh," I gasp. "Who?"

"Megan Calhoun. Do you remember seeing her at the party?"

"Yes, she was playing a game with some guys, but I don't recall their names. I'm new here. Sorry, I'm not much help in that department." I bite my lower lip with my two front teeth, but quickly stop myself. I shouldn't fidget, even though I have nothing to hide. It makes me look like I do. I know this routine all too well. *Sondra.*

"Do you know what time that was?"

"I honestly don't recall. I left the party shortly after I saw her."

"Who did you leave with, and who was driving?"

"I left with Jessa Dewitt, Margo Hawley, and Tahlia Latham-Hart. Jessa drove."

As soon as the words leave my mouth, I regret it. I don't want to get Jessa in trouble, but who could prove she was drinking at this point?

A second officer enters the room. He doesn't speak, but nods to Officer Massey.

"Excuse me for a moment." He joins the second officer near the doorway.

I carefully observe the interaction between the two men. The second officer whispers something in his ear. Officer Massey shakes his head, letting it drop low before nodding again. I can't help but fear something bad has happened to Megan. The second officer frowns and then exits the classroom.

Officer Massey takes slow, thoughtful steps back to me. He pulls in a deep breath, letting his pointer finger rest in the dimple of his chin. After opening his mouth to speak, he quickly closes it. Perhaps he's rethinking his next question. He twists his body toward the door, breaking eye contact with me.

"You didn't happen to take Highway 30 home last night, did you?" he questions.

My heart drops to the pit of my tummy as bile lunges up my throat. The familiar burning sensation returns to my hand.

Lie, Izzy. Lie.

"I'm sorry, I don't know. Remember, I just moved here."

"How old are you, Izzy?"

"I'm seventeen."

"OK. That's all the questions I have for you at this moment. If anything else comes up, I know where to find you," Officer Massey says. "Please head to your first period classroom, unless it's occupied, then you should head to the gymnasium."

Confusion lurks across my face as I stand up. "Good luck with your search for Megan. I hope someone finds her safe soon."

His expression drops as he nods his head toward me. Tears well in his eyes before he shifts his head away from my gaze. He knows more than he's letting on. Something bad happened to Megan. I know it. I fear this investigation has gone from a missing person case to something worse.

I enter the hallway with my stomach churning. Why did he ask about Highway 30? We hit something last night. What if we did something to Megan?

I want to vomit, but I hold it back. I anxiously search the hallway for the girls. We need to get our stories straight if we didn't already throw ourselves under the bus—poor choice of words right now.

Principal Miller nearly collides into me as he pushes his way through a crowded hallway of students and teachers. "Please go wait in your first-period class for further instructions!" he shouts. His voice is high and agitated as he shoos the lingering students away from the interview rooms.

I take my seat in Mrs. Jamison's history class with two empty desks next to me. Where are Margo and Tahlia?

Mrs. Jamison slinks into the classroom; her eyes are pink and puffy like she's been crying. She takes her seat behind her desk without addressing the room. The entire class sits in silence, waiting for further information. The only noise in the classroom is the sound of rustling tissues. Uncertainty hangs heavier in the air than the humidity.

Margo and Tahlia sullenly enter the room, weaving through the rows of desks.

"Finally," I whisper as Margo and Tahlia move past me. "Can you believe the news?" Static erupts from the loudspeaker, cutting us off.

"This is Principal Miller speaking. I'm sorry for the disruption in your schedules this morning, but as most of you know by now, one of our brightest students, Megan Calhoun, was reported missing last night. Our small, tight-knit community and police officers have been searching for Megan since last night." Principal Miller pauses to sniffle.

I swear the entire classroom stops breathing in anticipation of his announcement.

"It truly breaks my heart to deliver this news. The search team discovered Megan's body this morning on Highway 30. I'm sure this information is coming as a shock to everyone. So, due to this awful tragedy, I feel it's best if I dismiss class for the day. If you want to talk to a counselor or a teacher, please stick around, and we will assign someone to talk with you. If you don't want to go home and would rather stay here to grieve with your classmates, you are welcome to do so. We have notified your parents and guardians.

"I have to ask that if anyone has information that could be useful in piecing together Megan's last hours, please contact the East Gate Police Department.

"Please keep Megan's family in your thoughts and prayers. Class dismissed," Principal Miller concludes. His voice is ragged and choppy, assumingly fighting back tears, trying to stay brave for his students.

"Do you guys think—" I ask, but before I can get the horrid words out, I notice Margo's crying.

Margo's eyes are bloodshot, and her face is red and splotchy. How insensitive of me. I forgot these girls have gone to school with each other for twelve years. I'm slightly detached because I'm new. Instantly, I feel heartless for my lack of reaction.

I reach out and rub Margo's arm. "I'm so sorry for your loss. Was she a friend of yours?"

"I don't want to talk about it," Margo sniffles, folding her hands across the desk before laying her head down. Her curly hair falls all around her, creating a shield of distance between her and the rest of the room.

I want to leave, but I'm not sure what to do. I glance to Tahlia for direction, but she's too busy caressing Margo's hair. I check the back row, searching for Riley, but he's not there. He didn't come to class.

Uncontrollable sobbing and chatter explode throughout the room. I catch bits and pieces, trying not to be rude by eavesdropping, but I have nothing else to do.

"I just can't believe it," one student says, breaking into tears.

A second student attempts to console her, but busts into a full-blown panic herself.

"She was so young and had so much going for her. She was applying to Ivy League schools. Why would she have been out there alone on the highway at night?" another student asks the crying duo.

"It was probably the Wave Riders. She was playing pong with them. I bet she got so drunk she wandered off and got lost," one girl says between sobs.

"Do you think she was hit by a car?" a curly haired guy asks.

"Probably, how else would she have died?" another student responds.

I let out a long puff of air. Thank God Jessa's car isn't damaged. Maybe I'm overreacting. We hit an animal, not Megan Calhoun. Right? But this is a crazy coincidence. We hit something and our classmate is dead on the same highway.

Tahlia moves to the empty desk in front of me and twists her body to face mine. In a hushed voice, she says, "Margo was passed out in the car; she doesn't remember anything. Do you think we hit Megan?"

My stomach drops as she says the words out loud. "I honestly don't know, but the Jeep would have been damaged if we did. It couldn't have been us. A possum or maybe even a squirrel, but we didn't hit a human. Right?" I whisper. "I wish we knew more about how she died."

Tahlia's green eyes gloss over with tears. "I'm scared, Izzy."

"Me too," I respond, nodding toward Margo. "Is she going to be OK?"

"It's Jessa we should be worried about right now. We need to find her. She's probably freaking out."

"Let's get out of here and find Jessa. She has Econ first period in the B wing." Tahlia swings her backpack onto her shoulder. "Margo, come on."

"I think I'm going to stay and talk to someone," Margo says.

"No, I don't think that's a good idea. We need to go. Margo, grab your bag and hurry up," Tahlia commands, but Margo doesn't budge. "OK, fine, call us later. Please, we need to talk."

My phone vibrates in my pocket. I pull it out and see a text from Dad.

Hey sweetie, I hope you're doing OK. I heard about your classmate. I can't sneak away from work, but I know you will be all right. Please call me if you need me or need to talk. There is some cash in the emergency fund if you need to order some food today. Love you.

I quickly type out a generic response so he doesn't worry about me, even though I know he will.

Thanks, Dad. I'll be OK.

Tahlia grabs me by the arm and drags me out of class. We meet Jessa outside her classroom. The three of us walk in silence to Jessa's Jeep. Once inside the car and a block from school, we finally begin to speak.

"Do you think we killed Megan?" Tahlia asks, her voice quivering.

"No, there's no way. We'd have damage to my car," Jessa responds.

"But we hit something, and it's a messed-up coincidence that her body was found around the same spot. Don't cha think?" I ask.

I'm afraid to admit I saw something moving in the street behind the Jeep last night. If it were Megan, maybe she was still alive, and we could have saved her if only we checked. Guilt twists through all my organs, hugging them tight until I feel a numbness.

"No, we're fine. We have nothing to worry about," Jessa insists. "I'm sure they will release more information soon, and you'll see we're in the clear."

Tahlia anxiously tugs on her ear. It's turning a bright red color. I want to yank her hand away from her face and tell her to stop, but I don't. I remain tucked into my seat in the back of Jessa's Jeep with the weight of my conscience pinning me in place.

"Margo was really worked up about Megan," Tahlia says.

"Funny, I didn't think she and Megan were friends," Jessa responds.

"She was distraught. Even if they weren't close, grief and sudden death cause people to react differently. We should let Margo grieve how she feels necessary," I say, defending Margo.

"Does she know we hit something last night?" Jessa asks.

"She doesn't remember anything, and I didn't tell her," Tahlia says. "She will hate us when she finds out what we did."

"We didn't do shit, T," Jessa snarls. "Drop it. We're fine."

"I need to get home. My mom just texted me. She wants me to talk about my feelings," Tahlia says, annoyed.

Silence settles over the Jeep until we pull up to Tahlia's house. It's a beautiful historic estate with many modern upgrades, unlike my house. I suspect she comes from a family of wealth.

"I'll see you guys at school tomorrow," Tahlia says.

"Bye, T," Jessa responds. "Are you going to get up front, or do you plan to have me chauffeur you around?"

"Oh, yeah," I respond.

I hurry out of the back seat and into Tahlia's spot. I've never been in the front before. It seems everyone has their place in Jessa's Jeep and mine is in the back with Margo.

"Are you the only one with a car?" I ask, since I've yet to see Margo or Tahlia drive.

"Yep. My parents bought me this for my sixteenth birthday. Pretty cool, huh? Tahlia's parents said she could have a new car if she got a job. Something about teaching her responsibility, blah, blah, blah. Tahlia said no thanks. She didn't want a job. Plus, I pretty much drive her ass everywhere so—" Jessa laughs, lingering on her thoughts. "So, you want to hang out now?" She shifts the conversation.

"I think I'd rather be alone. I have a lot to process with the whole curse thing, remember?"

"Boo, you suck." Jessa sticks her bottom lip out.

My phone vibrates. Ugh, my dad needs to stop checking in on me. I'm fine.

I pull my phone from my back pocket. It's a number I don't have saved, but the first line of text pops out at me, and all I can focus on is one word. *Riley*. I immediately shove my phone back into my pocket, hoping Jessa doesn't notice.

"Who's texting you?" Jessa asks, irritated.

"Oh, no one. Just my dad. He likes to hover during tragedies," I lie.

This is a text I can't share with Jessa.

"You make it sound like this isn't your first tragedy," Jessa says, her lips curling for juicy gossip.

She's out of luck because I won't tell her about the worst day of my life.

No matter what everyone else says, it's not my fault Sondra is dead. I didn't kill Sondra.

CHAPTER 14
DEAD GIRLS CAN'T TALK

My hand is on the door handle, and I'm ready to leap out of Jessa's Jeep. The unread text message is burning a hole in my pocket. Not literally, but these days, anything's possible. My stomach is anxiously waning. I'm dying to see who messaged me.

Is it Riley or someone else messaging me about him? Either way, I'm eager to see, but not with prying eyes around me. I've been warned. This is something I can't share with my new friends.

"See you tomorrow." I shut the door to the Jeep.

The squeal of the passenger side window rolling down causes me to pause.

"Don't forget we're sleeping over tomorrow," she hollers.

I turn back around. "Oh, you still want to do that? I don't know if Margo will feel up to it."

"Well, duh, we can't stop now. We just found the good stuff. I'm curious, aren't you? Maybe we can find something to undo the curse." She smiles, wiggling her fingers toward me.

"Whatever," I respond, knowing it's useless to argue with Jessa.

"I'll pick you up for school tomorrow," she shouts, driving away and giving me no time to refute her.

I rush up the steps and dash into the house. The humidity inside hits me like a brick wall. It's worse inside than outside. Our little window air units aren't cooling this old house down whatsoever. Beads of sweat run down my spine, soaking through my top. I hastily dig into my pocket for my phone. I take a deep breath and open the message.

Unknown: Hey it's Riley. I got your phone number from my dad's phone. I hope it's OK I message you. Would like to talk. I want to explain. Can I come over? Please. . .

My heart feels like it might burst from my chest. Alone with Riley. It's everything I've been dreaming of all summer long. It's finally happening.

Izzy: Sure, I'm home. Swing by.

I send the text before I have time to overthink things. If Riley and I are just friends, the curse can't hurt him, right?

Unknown: Be there in an hour. My dad wants me to stop by and check on Mrs. Calhoun.

I have an hour to spare. Good, just enough time to freshen up for Riley. He can't see me like this.

I shower quickly and slip into a tight, low-cut black tank top and a denim miniskirt. I slide my mirror over so I can sit in front of the air conditioner unit; I don't want to sweat off my makeup. I add enough lipstick to make my lips appear poutier and kissable, just in case.

"Eh, this stupid curse," I shout to an empty room, but somehow, I feel someone or something is always listening.

I shouldn't lead Riley on if this curse is real, but if it's not, he needs to see me at my best. I'm not a monster, just a teenage girl. I can't help myself.

Maybe Jessa is right; I need to search the spellbook for something to undo this curse. If, of course, it's real.

Seriously, how is this my life now?

I take my time adding some waves to my hair and give myself a final once-over in the mirror. I look pretty darn good, if I do say so myself.

I check my phone; it's been nearly an hour. I should wait for Riley downstairs. I don't want to accidentally miss him. If he knocks, I might not hear it up here with all the A/C units humming through the house.

The moment I open my bedroom door, the heat washes over me. My luscious waves begin to fall limp and sweat beads above my upper lip. I wipe it away with my finger while rushing down the long hallway, practically flying down the stairs and into the living room. I crank the A/C to full blast and take a seat on the couch, allowing myself to cool down. I weave my fingers through my hair, attempting to bring it back to full volume cuteness.

The seconds tick by on Gran-gran's old grandfather

clock. The seconds turn into minutes as I wait for Riley. Where is he? I'm sure he's still with Megan's mom. I can't be selfish right now. He'll get here when he gets here.

Where was Tim this morning? I wonder if he was one of the officers searching for Megan. I don't recall seeing him at school, so he must have been part of the search team.

The gravity of last night and this morning begin to weigh heavy on my mind. I'm exhausted mentally and physically, and this heat isn't helping.

Sondra, Megan, the curse. . .

It's all too much.

My eyes fall heavy and visions of Sondra weave through my memories like tiny fibers trying to find their home in my thoughts. They feel misplaced and can never quite get where they belong. Something is missing. A piece—a chunk of memory—gone.

The day in the forest replays like a vivid nightmare.

Flashes of vibrant blueish-green Douglas Fir trees line the dirt trail, popping in and out of focus like scenes from a damaged movie reel.

Sondra is here with me, but ahead of me—her long curly locks bounce off her purple hiking pack with each step. I turn to glance behind me, but the other girls aren't there. The forest is secluding us with no one else in sight, just nature and the wind blowing effortlessly around us.

Then blackness cloaks my vision, but only for a moment, as a shrill scream invades the dark space. "Izzy, no!"

A mess of wild red curls flickers across the back of my eyelids, followed by images of a contorted body that cut in and out like cigarette burns on my damaged movie reel.

I know time is missing when I hear the voices calling from behind, "Izzy, what did you do?"

A knock from the front door startles me, pulling me from my nightmare and back into my safe space. I'm sweating profusely. I quickly stand alert. Riley. It must be him.

A second knock bangs at the door.

"I'm coming," I holler, airing myself in front of the A/C. A lot of good that shower did me.

OK, Izzy, you got this. Be confident.

I rush into the foyer, giving myself a quick once-over in the darkened mirror before answering. I'm grateful nothing strange happens.

"Hi," I eagerly say, swinging the door wide open.

"Hello." Riley rocks on his heels as he runs his fingers through his sandy brown hair.

"How is Mrs. Calhoun? I can't even imagine how she must be doing."

"Not good. During the search this morning, she was the one who spotted the body. Shattered would be the word I'd use to describe her."

"Oh my. That's so horrible. That poor woman, that poor family." My stomach churns. I can't help but feel responsible, even though we don't know for sure what we hit, and I wasn't driving. I could have pushed harder for Jessa to go back.

No, it was just a small animal. Izzy, get out of your head.

"How are you doing? Were you close to Megan?"

"No, we weren't close, but we've known each other since

we were five. So, yeah, it's still hard. Hey, I know right now isn't the best timing with everything going on with Megan, but since I saw you last night, I haven't been able to stop thinking about you. I needed to come see you. I was planning on talking to you at school, but well. . ."

He trails off, and I know he doesn't want to mention Megan again. I take that as my opportunity to switch gears.

"Is that right?" I flirtatiously ask. "You couldn't stop thinking about me?"

"Are you going to invite me in, or are we going to stand outside all day?" He laughs, his cheeks turning red. I can't tell if it's from the heat or if I've embarrassed him by my comment.

"Oh, yes. Please come in. We can go to the living room. It's cooler in there."

Riley's eyes widen as he steps into my house. His eyes immediately react to every square inch of the entryway to the living room. "Wow, this house has changed a lot from what I remember. It looks—"

"Old and decrepit," I finish his sentence.

"Yes," he says with a frown.

"Didn't your dad tell you how bad it was?"

"Nah, he just said he was helping your dad with repairs. But now I see why he spends all his free time here. Dang, Izzy, it's so different than I remember."

"I know, right? I wasn't happy about moving here to begin with, then I found out this was my new home. You can only imagine the fit I threw." I let out a soft chuckle.

"I can imagine. You used to throw such a tantrum when

you were younger if things didn't go like you wanted. I see things haven't changed," he says. "It's good to see you, Izzy. It really is."

"It's good to see you too, Riley," I respond, knowing my face is turning bright pink. "So, in your text, you said you wanted to explain. So—"

"Right." He paces the room. His demeanor drastically shifts, turning uneasy, and his face pales like he might throw up.

What could he possibly have to say that's causing this reaction? My tummy flips a few times as I impatiently wait for him to spit it out.

He rubs his temples and sighs. "My dad told me to be careful around you. He said it was best to keep my distance."

Oh my God, here it is. He knows about the curse. He believes it. Tim believes it. You've got to be kidding me.

"Are you serious?"

Riley stops pacing and stands directly in front of me. His blue eyes are large and cautious. "I don't know how to say this, so I'm just going to come out with it. My dad says you shoved a girl off a cliff, and she died. Is that true, Izzy? Please tell me it's not."

"No, that most certainly isn't true," I respond, heated.

My body convulses in anger. I fall back onto the couch behind me. My head hangs heavy in my hands as I search for the words to explain what happened. Sondra's still ruining my life.

"I, um. I didn't push her. She fell." I slowly let the words leave my lips, wishing I didn't have to say them at all. I never wanted anyone here to know about Sondra.

"My dad said two other girls saw you do it—witnesses, Izzy." Riley continues to press me like I'm on trial.

"How does your dad know this?"

I question whether my dad said something, or if Tim never trusted me and investigated my past when we moved here. My trust in Tim is wavering; I thought he liked me.

The curse suddenly seems easier to sort through than this. A dark shadow looms over the room, suffocating me, pulling me into its darkness.

"He's a cop, remember? Plus, you were the new girl from the big bad city." He laughs uncomfortably. "Dad was just making sure you weren't a juvenile delinquent or something. Turns out he had good instincts." He rubs the back of his neck, turning his head to the ground.

Tears race down my face, clouding my vision. Does Riley really believe I'm capable of something so horrible?

"I swear on Gran-gran's grave I didn't push her. Mackenzie and Evelyn couldn't have seen what happened. They were a good half a mile behind us on the trail. They lied about what they saw. Those girls never really liked me. The truth is, Sondra had her back to the cliff and lost her footing. She fell. That's God's honest truth. I was a minor, and they couldn't prove I pushed her. I was cleared," I respond.

Thank God dead girls can't talk because I don't know what she'd say.

"But did you—do it? You can trust me. I won't tell a soul."

"No. I didn't. I already told you. And can you please keep this to yourself? I can't have this getting out. It's over and I'm trying to move on. It was a horrible accident with a terrible rumor attached to it. Why do you think we moved here? It was easier to start over than to deal with that hanging over my head for the next year."

"OK, I just had to ask. I believe you. The Izzy I knew would never have been capable of hurting another person."

"I'm still the same Izzy, just older," I respond, trying to redirect the conversation. "Can I ask you something? It's silly."

"Anything."

"Have you heard rumors about me and my family being—"

"Witches." Riley laughs.

"Yes," I respond sheepishly, hanging my head in embarrassment.

"They're silly stories, Izzy. Just made up by the townsfolk to scare children. Don't tell me you buy into that nonsense?"

"Well, no," I respond, only feeling like I'm telling half of the truth. "Jessa, Tahlia, and Margo seem to believe it."

"Yeah, about those girls," Riley pauses. "They're trouble. I suggest you find new friends. Margo is a hot mess. Jessa is a snob and a half, and Tahlia, well, she's the worst. Don't trust them."

That's strange. Tahlia says she and Riley are close, like siblings close. Their stories don't match up.

An intrusive knocking rattles from above us. "What's that noise?" Riley asks.

"I'm sure it's nothing. This house is so old. It creaks and groans all the time."

"Should you go check on that?"

"Nah, I'm sure it's nothing," I respond, not wanting to leave Riley's sight.

The noise sounds like it's coming from the third floor, but I'm not dealing with *that* right now. There's no way I'm chancing Riley finding out about my secrets lying beneath the floorboards upstairs either.

"OK, whatever you say, but it sounds like a water pipe might burst or something. You should probably tell your dad," Riley suggests.

"I will." I twirl a wild piece of my hair around my pointer finger.

Silence cloaks the room, creating a new vibe, but not in a bad way. The energy in the room has shifted. My eyes catch his, and the corners of his mouth tug upward into a charming grin.

"So, I wanted to tell you how pretty you looked last night, and well, how beautiful you look right now. Gosh, I hope that didn't come out weird or too corny." He chuckles, turning his head downward. "It's just that it's been so long since I've seen you—then to see you all grown up. I was shocked—but like in a good way."

My heart flutters at his words, and an approving smile gleams across my face. I know I'm blushing, but I don't care. "Thank you. You don't look too bad yourself," I playfully respond, letting my heart take over, leaving my conscience and the curse at the door.

Riley slowly drops onto the sofa, taking the seat next to me. His body turns toward mine, letting our legs touch. "I'm sorry I let something my dad said stop me from seeing you this summer. I realize now that it was silly of me. I should have asked you sooner. I'm so sorry."

"It's OK. You're here now."

Riley reaches out and places his hand over mine, catching me by surprise. I try to remain calm, but my inner excitement begins to show on the outside. A gigantic, joyful smile beams across my face. The warmth from his hand instantly heats mine, and I feel like my insides might melt.

With each movement, his cologne stirs up around him—a rich musk with a hint of spice. I take a deep breath to inhale his scent, hoping to lock it into my memory. I want to cling to this moment and never forget it.

Riley reaches out and cups my chin with his free hand, pulling me into his gaze. His blue eyes glisten with excitement. He slowly leans in and his lips begin to part. As he twists his head ever so slightly, the warmth from his body heat radiates up my arm.

No, wait. It's not from Riley's overheated body.

It's the same feeling as last night.

Crap! Not now.

The heat spreads across my shoulders.

No. This can't be happening.

Logic isn't on my side right now.

If this curse is real, I can't put Riley in danger. I can't help but think of Isobel's men—all dead. Photographs of their existence and dates of their demise are sitting in a cabinet on the other side of this wall. I'm being irresponsible with Riley's life.

I can't. . .

But he's so cute. . .

I shouldn't. . .

In one heartbreaking move, I turn my head away and then softly tug my hand from under his. I scoot my body to the far side of the sofa, creating a cushion of space between us.

I'm afraid to let Riley's eyes greet mine. After a few uncomfortable seconds, I meet his gaze. His eyes are struggling to comprehend what just happened.

"I'm sorry if I did something wrong," he says. His voice is pained with confusion. "I thought you—"

"No, you did nothing wrong." I try to assure him, cutting him off. But I understand how this must look.

"Well, it appears I did," he says sullenly.

The knocking rattles again from above us, adding to the tension in the already tension-filled room.

"You really should check on that. I think I should go." Riley stands. "It was nice seeing you, Izzy."

"You don't have to leave," I plead, wanting him to stay.

I want to tell him everything, but I'll sound insane if I do. He doesn't believe the rumors, and if I tell him I'm cursed, well, then I may as well kiss this relationship goodbye before it even begins. He'll think I'm nuts.

"I should check in with my friends. It's been a hard day for everyone," Riley says, rejection emanating off his body as he beelines for the door.

"OK. I'm glad you stopped over. Don't be a stranger," I quickly add, trying to lighten the mood, but he's already out the door.

I feel awful, wretched, and torn apart. I want him to kiss me more than anything in the world. I want a connection with someone—with Riley.

I slink down the length of the wall, sulking in my sadness, knowing Riley is probably running down the stairs as fast as his legs will allow. After my rejection, he'll never be able to look me in the eye again. He put himself out there and I through a red card in his face.

Plus, I'm not sure I told Riley the whole truth about Sondra—the missing chunks. But it's better that way. To have distance from that situation. No one here needs to know the details of that horrible day—my nightmare.

My head hangs heavy as my heart shatters. I now understand the dramatics of all the crushing love scenes in my favorite movies. The way my heart would ache for my favorite characters is relatable to this moment. I might have given up my first chance of love for some stupid rumor, but what if it's real? How can this story have a happy ending with a three-century old curse damming me to a life as an old spinster?

More knocking rattles the ceiling above me, louder and more intrusive this time.

"What the hell do you want?" I shout to an empty house. "You're messing with my life!" I scream so loud that my words scratch my throat.

I pick myself up from the floor. I pass by the darkened mirror in the hall tree. The movement freezes in the reflection as I glide past.

I stop. I wave, but my reflection doesn't mirror my image. Gran-gran's perfume lingers through the air again.

"I guess I'm a fucking witch!" I shout to my reflection that remains unchanged. "I'm losing my mind. Is that what you want from me?" My voice echoes through the house as the knocking intensifies above me.

CHAPTER 15
HUNTERS

On the third floor, the three bloodstained boards responsible for mangling Margo's fingertips mere hours ago, rattle viciously. The floorboards vibrate like tiny earthquakes insignificant to the rest of the world, while wreaking havoc on my minuscule life.

Over the past twenty-four hours and witnessing what appears to be magic, I'm coming to the realization that reality has wrinkles. I picture it as tightly woven strands through time and space. I'm one of the few who sees through the rumpled mess.

As much as I want to resist, it's not possible. I'm aware of things most people can't imagine—let alone see—because for some unknown reason, I'm special. I can't fight against my wrinkled reality as it keeps taunting me and forcing me to see through the cracks. I don't know how else to explain it. I should be afraid, but fear isn't the emotion rushing through my fibers; it's curiosity with a hint of annoyance.

In my newly realized moment of twisted clarity, I yank the boards up, one by one, placing them on the dusty floor next to me. The hot and damp air hangs heavy like a veil across the open space. Sweat trickles down my back from my burst of movement.

The large leather-bound book stares up at me—calling to me—wanting me to pull it out. If you asked me to explain the feeling, I wouldn't be able to, but it overwhelms my being. It's as if I lack self-control, like an alcoholic who can't say no to the beer in front of them. I do as the book wants. I heed no warning from the hairs on my arms standing on end or from the intense fire coursing through my limbs. Instead, I heave the book from its hiding place and lay it out wide open, this time for my eyes only.

The silver key glistens in the perfectly hollowed-out hole as I flip the page, staying steady in its home like it's obeying orders—like magic. The pages with the familiar practitioner's warning and the karma rule of three peer back at me, stirring up a new feeling I can't quite understand. A pull of desire tugs at my gut, coaxing me to continue.

I flip the pages, careful not to tear them since they're delicate. Each page is crammed with spells and notes in Gran-gran's handwriting. I can't help but feel close to her, as if she's sitting right here next to me, writing in this very book.

Each page is detailed with diagrams—most a circle with a star in the middle—and organized by elements, colors, and a list of things required for each spell. Most spells require four coven witches and candles of colored variations, depending on the spell. Other pages are lists of herbs and their magical properties.

But one thing that strikes me as more curious than the crafty spells is the dates on the bottom of each page. Some pages date back to 1691, before the Salem Witch Trials even began. If these dates are accurate, somehow through the wrinkled reality, Gran-gran was there documenting in this book with four other unnamed witches, solely known as the Wives of Salem Coven.

Who else holds the witch's curse?

What other bloodline is faulted like mine?

Who is responsible for placing such a curse damning their spawn for generations to come?

A sadness creeps over me as I realize the curse must be as real as this book. As real as the voices that call to me. As real as the images in my memories, the out-of-body experience I had on my first day, and the events that led me here.

The thought that my mom could have been taken by this curse hangs the heaviest on my shoulders. My dad nor I will ever be able to happily love. We're forever tarnished by this curse, looming over us for a lifetime unless I find a way to stop it from rippling its way through our lives. Not to mention Isobel's many men. But why would she lead her lovers down a tainted road that would end in death if she was aware of such an outcome?

Hours seem to pass by as I study the book, searching for something that can undo this stupid curse. But if Isobel didn't have it figured out after her sixth lover, then how can I? Why did she put so many men in harm's way? I can't do that to someone I love. My heart yanks at the thought.

In the book, there's a spell for everything from curing

a cold to hexing your neighbor, but so far, there isn't any mention of the curse or how to undo it. I flip several more pages, feeling discouraged when the final entry catches my attention. The handwriting is clearer, the ink is darker. It's an addition to the original spells. My stomach churns as I caress the page, feeling closer to Gran-gran than ever before. So many items in this house, but this is the one where I feel her presence the most, even more than the antique hall tree. The page is calling to me, taunting me, directing me to its words. My eyes viciously scan the page below.

This is it.

I found it.

Undoing the Witch's Bloodline Curse

It's real. The bloodline curse is real. It isn't a story or a rumor.

My family is cursed. But if there's a spell to undo the curse, then why isn't it broken? Why did Isobel fail so many times? I feel a strong pull back to the book—to keep reading—to understand—to fix this for my dad and selfishly for myself.

This spell comes with heavy warning and shan't be taken lightly. It's of utter importance that every rule is followed as laid before thee.

Those who tried have failed to undo the witch's curse. So, I caution thee.

First a hunter must fall.
Then a circle must be cast with coven bloodline witches stationed
to call the corners and guardians for thy protection.
Only a high priestess may lead the ritual with a hunter's blood as
offering.
Only then may the coven call and invoke Hera.

Beloved Goddess Hera, please hear our voices.
We ask for your guidance and wisdom for our choices.
May your love fulfill our need.
Protect and cloak our coven in our time of greed.

Hide us from harm and undo the curse
Protect us and immerse us in your heart and leave no hearse.
Sadness and destruction have cometh to our life.
Protect us now and leave us rife.

One final question for thee.
Let this spell bring no curse or harm by spree.
By our coven, this spell is cast.
By the will of Hera, it will be fast.

So shall it be.

I stare at the words on the page before me, feeling more lost than before. This isn't a curse I can break alone. It requires a real coven of witches, and what the heck is a hunter?

The sun that earlier shone through the tiny round window is fading as darkness sets across the sky. I realize I've been up here for hours. I feel faint and hungry. Something else feels off that I can't seem to place, but who am I kidding, everything has been off since moving here. I can't help but think of Riley again, watching him rush out of my house. My pain causing him pain.

Big heavy tears rush down my face, catching on my chin. I blot my skin with the back of my hand, but miss a single tear that plummets to the tattered book below.

"Oh, no. I can't ruin the page," I shout to thin air, but when I look down to see the damage that's been done, I'm shocked to see more words appear on the bottom of the page.

Further notes: Spells may take a new form if not done properly with virtuous intentions

Beware of the hunter, for ye will always be on the hunt. No bloodline Witch will ever be safe until the hunter is laid to rest and his bloodline is put to an end.
A hunter will disguise himself. Don't be fooled.
You must find the hunters, Izzy
and destroy them. . .all.

My body quivers. Isobel was always Isobel, never Izzy. She told me that once. This note is for me. Gran-gran knew I would find her book. She led me to it. I don't know how, but she did.

What am I supposed to do with this information?
And where can I find a hunter?

CHAPTER 16
OUT OF THE BROOM CLOSET

I toss and turn all night as visions of spells dance through my head. After a second night in a row of poor sleep, I'm agitated but also wildly intrigued.

I attempt to fill in the holes for what I don't know about Isobel. If I can believe everything I've uncovered and all the stories about my Gran-gran, then Isobel died a witch older than the state in which she was nearly tried and executed by hanging. But she somehow managed to escape, perhaps by one of the cloaking spells in her ancient book. Gran-gran was a Salem witch with a magic book of spells, but she's also my Gran-gran, dad's grandma, and Anna's mom. So, how did she exist for so long? And why did she finally die at an old age? Was she cloaked in hiding or cloaked in a realm in between, passing through time for centuries? I wish she were here to answer my questions—to help me understand.

If this is all true, then I'm a direct descendant of a witch. That's a lot to process. Isobel, Anna, my dad, and me.

Are there others—escaped witches? Or is Isobel the only one? Were her parents both witches? So many dang questions with no one to answer them.

I also wonder about the hunter's blood. Isobel's words bounce through my mind, trying to gain traction to its meaning. Did a hunter curse the coven? Is the hunter a person? Could the hunters be the men responsible for sentencing the witches to death by hanging? Are there still hunters now?

I can't simply ignore my findings because I fear they'll continue calling to me. Margo heard things in this house. I can't ignore that fact. She must have a connection too. Why would the book choose her and show her things? I can't let my eyes off her tonight. She's special, and I need to figure out why. This is my mystery to unravel. Isobel trusted me to figure it out. I'm out of the broom closet now, I guess.

***

While I wait for Jessa to pick me up as she so sneakily suggested yesterday, I endure an uncomfortable breakfast with Dad. He's quiet this morning. He's carefully watching me, waiting for me to bring up Megan's death. His eyes are heavy with questions. But I have questions of my own that I can't bring myself to ask. It's not Megan I want to talk about—it's Gran-gran. But if I divulge what I know, it will wreck him. That is, if he believes me. If he doesn't, he'll for sure send me to a psychologist to have my head examined. I can't just come out and tell him I think Mom died because of a three-century-old curse and his favorite person in the world was a witch.

Oh, and all those creepy old men staring at us while we slurp our milky cereal are dead because of Gran-gran's failure to break a curse. Plus, Dad, you're a witch. Or is it a warlock? Ugh, I don't know.

But one thing is certain—Dad has no idea. I would know if he did. He's normal. The same as he's always been. Gran-gran isn't calling to him, or he'd be the one with the secret hiding place on the third floor above my room.

Nothing that's ping-ponging through my mind sounds sane.

Dad stares at me, shifting in his seat. I can't help but tense up because I know what he's about to ask.

"Do you want to talk about that girl that died yesterday?" His voice is low and soft. "What was her name? Megan?"

"No, I really didn't know Megan," I respond, keeping my answer short.

"I figured you probably didn't know her well, but you know. . ." He lets his words trail off because he doesn't want to say it.

I scowl at Dad. I know where he's trying to direct this conversation. He's sneakily attempting to ask without asking if Megan's death is stirring up emotions about Sondra. I most certainly don't want to talk about it. It will break his heart if he finds out me and my friends might be responsible for what happened to Megan. A second death I'm mixed up in.

"Just know, I'm here if you want to talk," he says, getting up to remove his plate.

My phone vibrates against the table. It rattles several

times, indicating I have a slew of messages coming in. One
right after another.

*Tahlia: Did you see school is canceled another day? More time for
students to grieve.*
*Jessa: Sweet, let's start our sleepover early. Izzy, can we come over
sooner?*
*Tahlia: That sounds fun. I'm dying to get out of my house. My
mom is driving me nuts.*
Jessa: Great! Izzy? Girl, where are you? Respond!
Tahlia: Come pick me up.

I'm barely done with breakfast, and they already want
to invade my house. I don't see the point in trying to push
back. They will do what they want anyway.

Izzy: I suppose. Margo, how ya doing sweetie?
Tahlia: Margo. Are you awake??????
Jessa: OK, I'll swing by and get you both in 10 minutes. Margo?
Margo: OK. I'm here. I'll be ready.

I shout to my dad in the kitchen, "School's canceled
today. My friends are coming over now. I hope that's OK?"

"I just got the automated message about the cancellation
on my phone. Yes, it's OK. It's probably good to be around
friends today." Dad pops his head around the corner. "You
know I love you, and I worry about you, sweetie."

"Yes, Dad. I know. I love you too."

***

Twenty minutes later, Jessa, Tahlia, and Margo barge through the front door. Their loud chatter alerts me to their presence. I hustle into the foyer, so they aren't left unattended in my home. They have a streak of being intentionally unattended and poking around where they shouldn't.

Luckily, Dad is already at work since they so rudely let themselves in without so much as a courtesy knock. Maybe it's OK for the three of them to do it in each other's homes because they've known each other forever, but I've only known them four days, and a long four days it's been. I secretly miss them when they're away as they're growing on me, but I slightly despise them when they're nearby—a similar feeling from a year ago.

Plus, Riley's words annoyingly tug at the back of my mind. He said they're trouble, but didn't elaborate much. I didn't press him, which I regret. How did I let that slip past me? I should have asked for details.

But I need friends. Well, what I desperately need is three coven bloodline witches, but maybe three high school friends will do the trick.

Earth. Air. Fire. Water.

The spell requests for all four elements to be called, and since I'm currently short three other witches, I can't help but selfishly wonder if I can ask this of them. The thought slithers recklessly from one side of my brain to the other, but quickly evaporates as I gaze at my new friends. I can't ask that of them. It's careless to even consider it.

My eyes fall on Margo. Poor Margo. Her distress is written all over her face, from her sunken eyes, which are a new kind of red—one yet to be named—to the puffy pink skin under her eyes. Megan's death has shaken her. How will she react when we tell her about the car crash mere nights ago? How can we keep such a secret from her—a friendship already toiled in secrets? No good can come from that.

Jessa and Tahlia seem wildly unsympathetic to Margo's condition. They aren't offering her support. For someone who possibly pulled a hit and run, Jessa looks normal. Everything about her appears to be unshaken. Even Tahlia seems fine. As for me, I worry we're responsible for Megan's death. I'm sad for Margo, but I'm also detached. It's a strange place to be.

"So, are we just going to stand here all day, or can we go upstairs and drop our bags in your room?" Jessa says, startling me.

I wonder how long I was zoning out into my thoughts.

I quickly gather my words, "Oh, yes. Of course you can," I respond, following them up the steps. Jessa and Tahlia lead the way, with Margo and I trailing last.

Margo slings her backpack over her shoulder, and a tiny piece of folded-up paper falls to the floor. I reach down to grab it. I'm about to call out to Margo as her foot hits the first step, but instead I unfold the tiny scrap. I hear the girls hit the landing on the second floor, and I skim the note before they notice I'm not behind them.

I had fun on our date at the pond last weekend. I'll tell my parents soon. I promise.

Xoxo Megan Xoxo

My heart plummets to the ground, and I'm instantly sick to my stomach.

This can't be happening. No, no, no!

The floor spins below me, and I want to scream, but I bite my tongue to keep from doing so. This revelation makes things so much worse for everyone.

Margo and Megan were together.

I should have seen it sooner.

My poor friend. She's not just grieving over a classmate; she's grieving over someone she cared for deeply. Someone she could have had a future with.

I quickly fold the note back up and run up the steps and down the long hallway to meet the girls in my room. They're already nosing around. Margo's gazing out the window, so I hastily shove the note back into her bag. I'm not sure what to do with my newfound information. Do I let Margo know I read her note or wait and let her open up to me on her own? It doesn't appear Tahlia and Jessa know about Margo's secret relationship, because if they do, they're doing a terrible job of being sympathetic toward her.

"I thought we could check out the attic some more. See what other secrets Gran-gran is hiding," Jessa suggests, interrupting my thoughts.

I glance to the other girls to see if they agree with Jessa, but their faces are unreadable. I suddenly feel protective of my new magical space and even more so over the book. It's mine. I should call the shots, not Jessa, but I nod, allowing her to bulldoze me once again.

We creep up the wooden steps to the third floor. My eyes are on Margo as my gut twists and turns, hoping Megan's death isn't our fault, but also feeling deeply sorry for my friend's loss, no matter who is at fault. I want to reach out and pull Margo in for a tight hug and tell her I'm sorry we messed up, but I don't.

"Grab the book," Jessa commands.

I quietly huff to myself, but I dutifully remove the book—my book—without arguing. I lead the group into the attic as Jessa suggests.

"Now what?" Jessa asks.

"I don't know what else you hope to find," I respond.

"I was hoping it would happen again, like last time. We didn't have to search. Things just happened, like magic," Jessa says.

"Maybe there's something else to find in this room," Tahlia suggests.

I gently place the book inside the circle. The four of us move through the attic, pressing on walls and stepping hard on the floorboards, hoping for a sign of something hidden within, but after an exhaustive search, nothing appears to be out of place.

"Bummer," Jessa says, defeated.

The four of us enter the circle and quizzically stare down at the book.

"What do you want from us?" Margo asks softly.

With her question barely off her lips, a powerful gust of wind whips through the attic, although there isn't an open window.

I gasp as strands of my hair hastily whip against my face.

The wind dramatically comes to a pause, and one by one, the candles outlining the perimeter of the chalk circle begin to light themselves. Each one makes a poof sound, then a popping noise, as black smoke puffs into the air. The flames grow tall around us, rendering each of us speechless.

The four of us stay silent, stunned by the magic surrounding us. Our instincts suddenly all react at the same time as we each take a step in. We're in a tight huddle and so close I can smell the mint gum Jessa is nervously chewing.

We let the silence invade the attic until finally Tahlia parts her lips, ready to speak, but Jessa beats her to it. "Like this, this is what I'm talking about. We made this happen. Like magic," Jessa whispers, as if something or someone is listening to us. Her blue eyes are wild and bewildered with amusement.

I want to respond, but the magic has other plans. A fluttering sound draws our attention to the ground as the book viciously whips the pages back and forth, as if someone is angrily trying to find a specific page, but no one is there, and the wind is nonexistent now. My breath catches with each inhale, unsure how to react and process what I'm seeing.

"Holy shit," Tahlia cries. "Is this for real?"

The pages come to a brief halt, mid flip, leaving a single page straight up in the air.

Jessa falls backward, tripping over her own feet and landing on her butt. Tahlia steps away to help Jessa back to her feet. I can't pull my eyes from the single page that's now slowly wavering.

Margo reaches out and grabs my right hand, squeezing it hard. A tingle rushes from my fingertips to my palm with her touch. Can she feel it too?

The wavering page falls to the left, leaving the book wide open to a spell I already know—the one from last night— the one that can undo the bloodline curse. My mouth drops open and a tiny sound escapes.

"Wh—what's on the page," Tahlia stutters.

My stomach coils and my free hand burns like it's on fire, hotter than seems possible. I ball my hand into a fist, but it doesn't calm the sensation.

I stare down at the book. I suppose it's time to tell the girls about my day spent reading spells, searching for this very spell to undo the curse. My feelings for Riley and my longing for a normal relationship cause me to slowly reveal what they're questioning.

"It's—It's um—the spell to undo the curse," the words putter out of me as I keep my chin tucked into my neck, afraid to make eye contact with the girls.

"How do you know?" Tahlia asks.

"I searched through the book last night," I respond sheepishly.

"Without us?" Jessa asks, annoyed.

For some reason, I defend my actions. "This is my house, my book, and my curse. I can do whatever I want and when I want," I retort, feeling overly sensitive and suddenly childish for my outburst. But it's all true.

Jessa's eyes widen. "I'm sorry. I thought this was our thing."

"Our thing? Are you the one with a three-century-old curse lingering over your love life?" I dramatically toss my hands in the air, releasing Margo's grip as images of Riley sitting on my couch creep into my memory.

Jessa's mouth drops open, but she quickly closes her lips, letting the conversation drop. She and Tahlia bend down to get a closer look at the tattered page.

Margo suddenly gasps like she's choking for air.

"What's wrong? Are you all right?" I panic and pull her body into mine.

Margo tenses up, freezing in place. I pull away to look her straight on. Tears swirl around her eyes as terror cloaks her stare like a veil. Her fingers wrap around my arm tightly. It's as if a switch flips inside both of us, sending an electric current from her body to mine. Margo's emotions inhabit my body like they're my own.

The feeling is like what she described last night, except I know it's her, not a ghost or spirit or witch. It's simply my new friend Margo connecting with me in an unexplainable way—and she's afraid. I know—I feel—it's the curse that frightens her, but why?

We're connected.

I feel it.

I feel her.

Margo heard noises and voices.

The book called to her too.

Someone she loved who loved her back died.

We don't speak.

Could Margo be—

No, she couldn't.

But all of this is too hard to deny.

Goosebumps quilt my entire body.

Margo is a witch too—and she's cursed—like me—maybe.

Margo nods, as if she's acknowledging my thoughts.

The attic seems lighter by this revelation, almost as if the humid air leaves the house and now there's clarity.

Margo slowly releases her grip on my arm, taking three steps backward, out of the circle. She gives her body a shake as if she's shaking off any bad juju and announces, "We need to be outside. In nature. We need chalk, sage, salt, these candles, and Izzy, the biggest fucking knife you can find."

CHAPTER 17
EARTH, AIR, FIRE AND WATER

We immediately gather the supplies with little chatter or questioning. First, we find a piece of chalk on the ledge of the window in the attic. After Tahlia blows the candles out, she gathers them, brings them downstairs, and sets them on the back steps. Then I grab some salt from the kitchen pantry and a knife with a long blade. The only thing we can't find lying around the house is the sage.

"Is it necessary to have it?" Jessa questions.

"Yes, it's essential. We need to cleanse the area and get rid of anything negative in our space," Margo says, seemingly annoyed that Jessa doesn't know how to use sage.

I don't want to admit it, but I don't understand its purpose either.

"Tahlia and Jessa, can you go into town and see if you can find a bundle or two of white sage? Try that oddities shop on 4th street. I bet they would have some," Margo suggests, shooing them out the door with a handful of cash she produces from her jean shorts pocket. "I doubt they take cards; it's that kind of shop."

It's nice to see Margo taking charge. I like this side of her, plus it feels good to see Jessa take orders for once.

Margo shoves the door closed behind them, and before turning around, she says quietly, "Did you feel what I felt in the attic?"

I walk over to Margo and place my hand on her arm. She shivers and wraps her arms across her chest as she turns to face me. Sweat beads down my back, and Margo shivers. So strange.

"Yes, it's hard to describe, but we were connected. I could feel your emotions. It was intense."

Her upper lip quivers. "I felt the air leaving my body, getting sucked out of me, and then suddenly I became overwhelmed with your emotions; they mixed with mine. I know that sounds crazy, but all of this is crazy, right?"

"Yes, it sounds crazy, but it's real." I pause to let out a deep breath. "I'm starting to accept that I'm a witch, and I have a responsibility to end this curse. But Margo, how are you connected to this? Could it be possible that you're a bloodline witch too? That seems like a far stretch, doesn't it?"

The blood drains from Margo's face, turning pale as a ghost. "I don't know, but I can't help but feel like I am. I sense things in this house. And when I'm around you, I'm different. I heard the voices." She raises her hands in front of her face. "I mean, look at my hands. I hurt myself, and I don't know why. I was drawn to the book and the attic for some reason. I was drawn to you." She pauses, and her right eye wells up with one fat tear. She blinks and it rolls down her freckled cheek. "Megan," she whispers, with more tears flooding down her face.

I kindly coax Margo over to the bench, where I take a seat next to her. I let my hand rest on her thigh, attempting to ease her sorrows because she might not forgive me for what I have to say next.

"I accidentally saw your note from Megan. I'm so sorry. I didn't mean to intrude on your privacy, but it fell out of your bag."

A partial lie, but Margo doesn't question it. Instead, her lips tremble, and more tears flush down her already pink and splotchy face.

"It's all my fault," Margo says through her loud sobs. "I loved her, and now she's dead. I did this to her."

"So, you believe you're cursed, too?" I softly question. "Like me?"

"I have to be. The book called to me. If I'm cursed like you and Megan loved me back—which I believe she did—I killed her. It's all my fault, Izzy."

"There is no way you could have known that. You had no idea you were involved in this. You can't beat yourself up over it. Does anyone know you two were together?"

"No, why? Will someone connect the dots? Do you think they will find me out? I can't go to jail."

"Oh, no, there is no way anyone will think you're responsible for what happened to Megan. Especially if her parents didn't even know you two were together. Everyone is scared of Isobel and her offspring, but no one has any reason to believe you're cursed, plus could they really charge you for being magical? That would be insane. It's not 1692."

Margo leans over, and her reddish-brown corkscrew tendrils dangle toward her feet. Her back heaves as she releases loud sobs that echo through the foyer.

I get up to grab a box of tissues from the other room. I place the box next to her and rub her back in an attempt to soothe her, but I know it's useless. It's best to let her cry it out. She needs to. It's what I did when my mom died. I just wanted to cry.

After a good ten minutes of tears and a pile of tissues forming around our feet, I ask, "Do Jessa and Tahlia know about Megan?"

"No, I couldn't tell anyone. I promised Megan I wouldn't say anything until she told her parents." Margo pauses to blot her wet cheeks. "We started dating at the end of last school year. We only saw each other once a week in our secret place—the pond. I didn't care who knew, but she was afraid of what her parents would say. They had her on a tight path, and dating girls or boys or aliens, for that matter, was out of the question until she graduated. Even then, they wanted her to apply to Ivy League schools where they said she needed to keep her eye on the prize. They didn't want her to get distracted and thrown off their plan.

"Plus, my mom isn't well liked around here. She's kind of a black sheep. I doubt Megan's parents would have approved of me anyway, so it was best we kept it a secret. I didn't push her. Poor sweet Megan was under so much pressure. I'm sure that's why she drank so much that night.

When I went inside for our drinks at Sam's party, she was already plastered and wouldn't talk to me. She said it wasn't safe to talk there. So, I gulped down an entire drink before I met back up with you. I was sad."

That explains Margo's sudden intoxication that night. Knots twist their way through my belly, forming a ball right in the pit of my stomach. If Margo is cursed like me, then the curse is why Megan died, but that still doesn't make us innocent. I can't let Margo take all the blame. She feels awful, and she doesn't know the entire story. I swallow down the lump that's made its way up my throat.

"There's something else I need to tell you, Margo. The night of the party, you passed out and—"

A rush of warm air invades the foyer as the girls bust through the door. "We're back. That shop was so crazy. They had so many weird things. How have we never gone in there before? O.M.G you guys should have come with us. T flirted with the shop owner, and he gave us the sage for free. It was awesome," Jessa shouts.

Tahlia laughs and takes a bow at her craftiness.

Margo stands up suddenly alert and quickly dabs her eyes again with the tissue. "We need to work on this spell. Let's take this outside. We need to connect with nature to do this right."

And just like that, Margo sucks in all her sadness and confusion to put on a brave face for the other girls. She's back to taking charge, and my secret is still buried in the pit of lies that are quickly piling up.

I grab a plastic bag from the kitchen, placing the book and

the items inside—except the knife, which Margo carries. I also snag a lighter, but I'm unsure if we'll need it as the candles always seem to light themselves.

We hike toward the tree line just beyond my house. The trees tower in the distance, creating an ominous entryway into the deep forest. I don't have a good feeling, but I don't dare speak up. I fear this forest is full of secrets. I'm sick to my stomach, but it could just be the dark secrets I'm holding on to.

"Hey, doesn't a stream run through this forest?" Margo asks.

"Yes, I believe so," Tahlia responds.

"OK. We can't stop until we meet the stream. We need to connect with all the elements, and being close to a water source will be helpful," Margo says, sure of her words.

"Margo, how do you know all of this?" Jessa asks.

"I'm not sure. I just feel it. I can't explain it."

I know how Margo feels it because I feel it too.

We walk for another twenty-five minutes or so until the sound of rushing water invades the air.

"We're getting close," Margo says.

Once we come to the stream, I open the bag, taking out all the supplies. I light the sage and pass it to Margo. She makes a counterclockwise circle around the group, waving the sage through the air. She cleanses herself with it, starting at her feet and ending with her head. I mirror her actions when she passes it to me. We don't speak until we all do the same.

"We need to draw a circle," Margo says.

I begin with the chalk, but it proves to be useless on the

ground. Not knowing what else to do, I grab the container of salt and create my circle with it. This will work.

Tahlia sets up the candles around the perimeter just as they were set in the attic. They don't light this time. I'm slightly disappointed. Maybe our magic only works inside. Tahlia takes a lighter to each candle until all are lit.

"The air is the air we're breathing. Water is the creek next to us. Earth is the ground below us, and the fire is from the candles. I think we have the elements covered," Margo states.

I open the book to one of the diagrams.

"We need to position ourselves like the elements in the pentagram," Margo says.

"Who stands where?" Tahlia asks.

"Well, Izzy is the bloodline witch, so what do you think, Izzy? Remember, Margo said you'd know what to do," Jessa says.

The burning sensation returns to my hand like I'm on fire. Margo talks of the air being sucked from her lungs, so Margo is air. The others are just feelings. I'm not sure if I'm correct or how much this matters, but I give each girl their post.

"Tahlia, you stand with Earth. Margo, air. Me, fire and Jessa, water."

I flip to the last page in the book. I read the words out loud.

"This spell comes with heavy warning and shan't be taken lightly. It's of utter importance that every rule is followed as laid before thee. Those who tried have failed to undo the witch's curse.

First a hunter must fall.

Then a circle must be cast with coven bloodline stationed to call thy corners and guardians for thy protection.

Only a high priestess may lead the ritual with thy hunter's blood as offering.

Only then may the coven call and invoke Hera."

I pause after reading the first part. I'm ninety-eight percent sure I'm a bloodline witch, but does that make me a high priestess? I'm the best we have, so I guess so. I'm fifty percent sure Margo is bloodline or something close to it, but what about Tahlia and Jessa?

"You guys don't have to do this. You're not bloodline, and something bad could happen if we try this spell. We also don't have a fallen hunter, whatever that means. We're grasping at straws and have no clue what we're dealing with. There isn't a guarantee this will work."

"No way. This is so fucking cool. I want to try it. I want to help," Jessa says, with Tahlia nodding in agreement.

Margo doesn't offer a word, but I know she wants to try. She feels responsible for Megan's death and believes she might be bloodline too, even if we don't understand how that's possible. She needs this to work as much as I do. She needs some hope right now.

"You can back out, and I won't be mad," I state, giving them one last chance to get out of the circle, but no one moves.

"What about the hunter's blood?" Jessa asks. "We don't have that."

Margo picks up the knife and diagonally slices her hand

just above her palm. "Blood is blood," she says, surprisingly without wincing from the pain. "I can feel your eyes on me. What? This is how they do it in the movies." Her eyes shoot around the circle, landing on the plastic bag floating through the air. "This will do." She snatches the bag in mid-air.

Margo lets a few drops of blood drip into the bag and passes the knife to me. I do the same, but I wince, and so do Tahlia and Jessa when it's their turn.

"I hope regular people blood will work." I swirl the blood with the tip of the blade. "We need to call the corners—the elements. Visualize yours as you say the word out loud." I nod to Tahlia to begin.

Tahlia calls out, "Earth."

Margo calls, "Air."

I follow with, "Fire."

Then Jessa chimes in with, "Water."

Soon, the four of us are all chanting together, "Earth, air, fire, water. Earth, air, fire, water. Earth, air, fire, water."

I dip the knife back into the blood, raise it above my head, and then dive the blade into the ground below. I can't help but feel a little dramatic as I do so, but it feels right.

The group's eyes widen with exhilaration. The hairs on my arm stand erect. The familiar warming sensation heats my entire body, and I'm electrified as it courses through my being.

I extend both of my hands outward. Jessa grabs my left one and Margo my right. Tahlia joins with Margo and Jessa until we're forming a smaller circle within the circle.

Jessa's hand is cool to the touch, and it feels strange mixed with my warmth. Margo's hand burns inside of mine; a drastic change from her shivering earlier. With the meeting of our hands, the air within the circle drops drastically, and every noise inside the forest intensifies. The birds chirp louder. The frogs croak deeper, and the wind rustles faster. I swear I can smell the moss growing on the surrounding trees. The moss matches the color of Tahlia's eyes, which also has intensified in color. I see the particles of air that float all around me. They shimmer and dance in the sunlight.

Margo's reddish curls are more vibrant, and everything seems more alive and vivid. My pulse beats within me, escalating in sound and vibration. I can feel Margo next to me experiencing the same thing. Her aura glows around her. I switch my focus to Jessa, but she seems darker. The light that usually surrounds her is gone. Her hair is without luster, her face paler, and her eyes ghostly. I give pause to caution, but I can't stop now. Sensing my mood shifting, I slide the book over with my foot, so I can read it below me.

"Beloved Goddess Hera, please hear our voices.
We ask for your guidance and wisdom for our choices.
May your love fulfill our need.
Protect and cloak our coven in our time of greed."

The sky darkens above, and a thick heavy cloud replaces the bright sky from mere moments ago. A shadow is cast on the circle as the cloud grows in size.

I take a deep breath, and Margo squeezes my hand, urging me to continue with her energy coursing into my arm.

"Hide us from harm and undo the curse.
Protect us and immerse us in your heart and leave no hearse.
Sadness and destruction have cometh to our life.
Protect us now and leave us rife."

The wind begins to viciously whip around the circle. Fallen leaves dance around the ring but do not enter. The flames from the candles burn tall and flickers with the wind but don't burn out. The water in the stream stops mid-movement, reverses, and flows upstream.

Margo's hand tightens around mine as lightning breaks through the sky.

"One final question for thee.
Let this spell bring no curse or harm by spree.
By our coven, this spell is cast.
By the will of Hera, it will be fast.
So shall it be."

A rolling rumble of thunder cracks through the sky, sending a wave of energy through the circle, ripping our hands from each other's grip and knocking us off our feet.

Darkness casts over my eyes as I succumb to a heavy weight of slumber that I can't fight.

CHAPTER 18
DARK MAGIC

A sharp pain behind my eyes blinds me. Every muscle in my body aches and cries for attention. I desire comfort, but nothing about this moment is comforting. I toss my arm out, letting my hand search for my blanket, but my fingers aren't greeted with a cozy touch. Instead, my fingers slice through something long, narrow, sharp, and wet.

Blades of grass. Morning dew.

I'm in the forest. I nearly forgot.

How long have I been here?

All night?

My heavy body searches for energy to propel me into motion, yet I lie still.

Last night.

The spell.

Did it work?

A wet kiss of dewy humid air tickles my cheeks, and with it a familiar airy voice, "Thank you." The words are long and strung out.

A smile tugs across my facc, along with a sense of

accomplishment. We must have done it. We lifted the curse. I wrap myself in my embrace, feeling satisfied with my successful deed.

"Isobel, what have you done?" A shrill, pitchy voice shouts.

My eyes shift open. I wince in pain from the sunlight as it burns, quickly closing my eyes. I cover my eyes with my hand, peeking through the cracks as I separate my fingers.

"I was hoping I wasn't too late, but it appears I am. What have you done?" the voice cries.

I search through the cracks for the person the voice belongs to, and an outline of a pale, tall, slender woman slowly comes into focus. The sunlight bounces off her long, wiry, gray hair like tinsel on a Christmas tree.

My voice is hoarse when I try to speak. "Anna?"

But how?

"Isobel, get up," she demands.

"Anna?" I question a second time.

"Get up! All of you."

I rub my tired eyes, searching for clarity.

I can't believe what I'm seeing. It's my grandma—Anna.

"Wh—what are you doing here?" I stutter, trying to prop myself up. My body flinches with each movement.

"You used up all your energy on the magic. You will feel like that for a good while," Anna says unsympathetically. "Wake them up." She points at my friends who are sprawled out, lifeless inside our circle.

"You know about the magic?"

"Of course, I know. I'm a Beswick. I was *her* daughter, but I didn't want anything to do with it, and neither should you.

It's bad, Isobel."

"It's Izzy," I correct her.

"Isobel, you've made more of a mess than you can even imagine." Anna claps her hands together. The loud smacking of her old skin reverberates off the trees.

Margo slithers through the grass, her body moving like a snake, trying to gain traction.

"Get up, now!" she shouts at my friends without stepping foot in our circle.

Margo, slowly coming to with a curtain of fear plastering her eyes, crawls on all fours until she's right on my hip.

Anna swipes her finger between us. "You two shouldn't be friends; no good can come from this friendship. You must stay away from each other," Anna scolds us, her eyes cold and distant.

Margo gives me a curious look. "Who is this lady?" she asks with a groggy voice.

"Anna, Isobel's daughter," I respond softly.

"Oh." Margo turns her head down.

Tahlia shifts on the ground a few feet from us. She attempts to prop herself up with her elbow, but slides back down on the dewy grass. She must be feeling like me, useless and exhausted, as I can't muster the energy to stand yet.

Anna points her finger toward Tahlia. "And this one, this half-breed. Isobel, you must not be friends with her."

"Whoa." Tahlia summons what little energy she has, pushing herself up, and standing. "What? Is that because I'm half black?" she says defensively, leaving her mouth hanging wide open in disbelief.

I gasp. I don't think of Anna as a racist. A bitch, but not a racist.

"Oh, race doesn't have anything to do with this, sweetheart, but I suspect you already know that. Don't you?" Anna says with spite in her voice.

"Tahlia, what's she talking about?" Margo asks.

Tahlia gives us a confused frown and shrugs her shoulders. She takes a few steps back, nearing the border of our homemade salt circle.

"Blondie." Anna points to Jessa lying lifeless on the ground. Her hair sprawled out around her head. "You shouldn't have brought her into this."

"I, eh—" I try to explain.

"You're just like her—my mother. I knew it the day you were born. I knew you were weak, and she'd get to you. But not my Steven. Sure, she tried, but he wasn't weak. He couldn't be called like you."

"Wouldn't you say that makes me special? I'm helping the family. I'm helping break the curse—I think we broke the curse," I shyly respond, assuming she knows what I'm talking about.

"No, Isobel, you're not, and you didn't. You're messing with my mother's dark magic. Yes, the curse is real, but it's not the curse she wants you to undo. Don't you see that child? She's using you. She needs you."

"No, Gran-gran wouldn't do that to me."

"She would, and she did. Look at you four. You're doing her dirty magic."

"Whatever. You can believe what you want, and we'll

believe what we want," I respond, my voice coming out more smoothly and confidently. "I was tasked with this, and I'm doing what's needed to help—to help my family."

Anna lets out a loud cackle. "Silly, silly girl. It doesn't work that way."

"If you don't practice magic and stuff, then how did you know to come here?" I question.

"Just because I don't practice doesn't mean I don't feel things. I'm a powerful witch if I want to be. I have great strengths, but I choose not to use them. I knew you girls were up to no good. I felt it in my bones. I drove all night from North Carolina nonstop, but it turns out my timing was off."

I frown at my loss for words. I don't want to believe Anna. I trust Gran-gran. She would never put me in harm's way. Anna's been absent and Gran-gran was there—for me and my dad.

"Does my son know any of this nonsense you girls have been up to?"

I turn my head down. "No, I've kept it from him."

"Good! Let's keep it that way. I've shielded him his whole life from this awful world. We moved away when he was young, but my mother wanted a relationship with him. She promised no magic, but there was always magic. Thankfully, Steven didn't notice. He was obtuse to the ongoings inside this house. We'd leave, but he always found his way back to her. More so as an adult. But she never got to him as she wanted. I would know. I would feel it just as I felt she got to you." Anna walks the edge of our circle. "You must never tell my son what you and your misfit friends have done. No good can come from messing with the dark magic."

"Why do you keep calling it dark?"

"Are you not listening, child? It's not good. It's used for evil. Clean up this mess. Wake *that* one up and disperse." She nods to Jessa on the ground. "You will never do this again. Do you understand?"

I nod, but I don't mean it. I trust Gran-gran, not Anna. Anna abandoned us, not Isobel. Tahlia and Margo pick up the items we brought with us, and I nudge Jessa with my foot.

"Isobel, I mean it, no more magic. And don't tell my son I was here. He can't know any of this. I'll clean up the mess you've created, and then you won't see me again," Anna shouts, her voice powerful.

Tahlia and I gently hoist Jessa from the ground. Her eyes are glazed and her body is limp. I toss her left arm over my shoulder, dragging her alongside me. Tahlia and Margo sprint toward the house. The second my feet step outside the circle, Anna lunges toward Jessa and I, gripping my bicep tight, pulling me close. Her breath smells of sweet peppermint.

"Isobel, I mean it." Anna shoves me in the direction of the house.

I move as fast as I'm capable, with Jessa dangling next to me, never looking back toward Anna or our magical circle.

CHAPTER 19
MAGIC HANGOVER

"Holy cow. That was intense," Margo shouts as Jessa and I enter the bedroom.

I grin at Margo, who's practically glowing. Tahlia meets me at the door and assists Jessa to the bed. Jessa's body flops lifelessly onto my blue floral print comforter. She reminds me of Margo just nights ago, but Jessa isn't drunk. The spell took a lot out of her—more than us.

Margo pulls me into her embrace. My body is tight against hers.

"That was magical," she whispers into my messy hair that's nested around my ear. An electric sensation rolls through me.

"It was, wasn't it?" I agree. The sluggishness I felt outside is replaced with rejuvenation.

"How are you two feeling?" I ask the girls.

"At first, I felt like I was hungover or got hit by a truck, but now I feel amazing. It's like the world's more beautiful, and I'm more alive. Like the colors in the room are brighter than before," Tahlia says, her voice light and carefree.

"Same." Margo's smile widens. "But why isn't Jessa waking up?"

"I felt awful when Anna first woke us; maybe she has a magic hangover and will feel better in a few minutes—like us," I respond, hopeful. "But seriously, you guys, that was amazing. Everything was so vivid, and I felt colors, if that's even possible. The energy from nature swarmed through me."

"It was beautiful," Margo adds. "Do you think we really undid the curse?"

I think of the airy message from Gran-gran, before Anna rudely appeared. "I think so."

"But what about Anna? She was intense. Is there any validity to what she said? Could we be doing dark magic?" Margo asks.

"I don't know. Something didn't feel right with Anna. Our relationship has never been a good one. She never comes around, so I have a hard time believing her intentions are trustworthy. Once she realizes we did a great thing by lifting the curse, she'll understand. She's had her guard up for a long time. She said she's leaving, so we won't have to worry about her sticking her nose into our business again."

Margo turns her head to face only me, blocking Tahlia's view. She lowers her voice to nearly a whisper. "I get why she said we shouldn't associate. Because I might be a witch, too. But why not Tahlia? And then her warning about bringing Jessa into it? What do you think Anna meant by that?"

"Hey, you know I can hear you," Tahlia pipes up. "I think my senses are heightened, and I'm missing out on something here. Explain!"

Jessa lets out a whimper. I rush over to her.

"Margo, it's your story to tell." I nod to Margo as I crawl into my bed next to Jessa and push the hair away from her face; she's warm.

I listen as Margo fills Tahlia in on her secret relationship.

"I wish you would have told us about Megan. I understand why you kept it from us—to protect Megan. But I love you no matter what, and I hope you weren't afraid to tell me. I could care less who you date as long as you're happy. Always know you can talk to me, Margo."

"I knew you wouldn't care about who I loved. It wasn't that at all. It was to protect Megan until she was ready," Margo says, tears spilling down her face. "And there is more—the book called to me, and I felt things in this house that I can't explain. And after Megan died, I think I'm cursed too. I'm not sure how that's possible, but I can't explain my connection to this house and that book. My dad's dead, and I have like zero family, so I fit the story. I just don't know my heritage. If this is true, I'm surprised no one found out. I mean, somehow, the townspeople knew about Isobel."

Tahlia's eyes fill with dread as her gaze lingers on mine. I know exactly what she's thinking; we're keeping a horrible secret from our friend.

"You can't feel guilty about what happened to Megan. All that happened before you knew your possible connection to this shit," Tahlia says.

"What do you think Anna meant by you being a half-breed?" Margo asks, boldly shifting the conversation away from herself.

"Anna's just a racist. That's all," Tahlia says, biting at each word.

I don't know if I buy what Tahlia's selling. I can't help but feel Anna was trying to tell us something. Anna said it wasn't about race, so what else can it mean? I might not trust Anna, but I also don't fully trust Tahlia either. Plus, Riley said not to trust her. Tahlia and I never clicked as I clicked with Margo or even bossy pants next to me. I want to like Tahlia, but there's always a reason to have my guard up around her. She doesn't make it easy, that's for sure.

Jessa heaves next to me; her entire body convulses. I touch her head with the back of my hand, just like my mom used to when I was sick.

"You guys, she's burning up. Quick, that trash can under my desk. Grab it." I slide Jessa to the edge of the bed, cradling her head over the can that Margo slips under her chin.

Jessa's body heaves harder as she vomits into the receptacle. Black chunks float in a dark liquid.

"What did she eat?" Tahlia questions, squeezing her nose shut to avoid the rancid scent in the air.

"That doesn't look good. Maybe we should take her to a doctor," Margo says.

"I'm fine," Jessa garbles, wiping her mouth with her fingers.

I toss her a tissue, but before she has a chance to clean herself up, she turns her head and tosses more black chunks into the can. She wipes her face, then rolls back over and shuts her eyes.

"Ew. This is disgusting. What's wrong with her?" Margo questions as she sets the can outside my bedroom door. "We need to keep an eye on her. You don't think it's because of the magic, do you?"

"I sure hope not," I respond.

"But what if it's the dark magic? The spell said there would be consequences if we failed. We used our blood, not the blood of a hunter. What if we made a huge mistake?" Margo asks.

CHAPTER 20
SLICES AND STICKS

"Wake up, bitches!" Jessa shouts.

I rub the grit from my eyes, and I realize we must have fallen asleep. "What time is it?" I ask.

"It's seven o'clock at night. You bitches slept all day," Jessa rudely replies. "Don't worry, I checked in with Steven. I told him we stayed up all night playing games, and that's why you're all so tired. Izzy, your dad is so cool—and dreamy."

"Gross! Can you please stop making comments like that? Or I'll be the one puking up chunks. You seem to be feeling better." I ask.

"I told you I was fine," Jessa responds.

"What the hell did you eat? Your puke was black," Margo asks.

Jessa shrugs her shoulders. "Eh, I'm not sure. I saw it. I disposed of it, so now you babies don't have to whine about it anymore."

"How long have you been awake?" I ask.

"A few hours. I took a shower. Your dad told me it was OK."

Leave it to Jessa to make herself right at home here.

"So, are we going to talk about what happened in the forest? That was so cool. So, like, does that make us all witches if this spell worked?" Jessa asks.

I forgot Jessa missed out on our after-forest chat.

"I think so," I respond.

I can't help but smile. If it's true, I have a genuine connection with these girls. A bond that can't be shattered. Real friends, even if Tahlia is a half-breed that can't be trusted. Whatever all that means.

I have a sisterhood.

I belong. These girls need me, and it feels good.

"So, what spell do you want to do next?" Jessa twirls her hair around her finger.

"Hold on a hot second. You missed a lot. Anna was here; she said no more magic," I say with trepidation in my voice. "I do want to try something else, but maybe we should play it safe for a while."

"Oh, you believe that old bag," Jessa responds, not even questioning why Anna was here.

"No, I don't believe her, but how will we know if the curse is broken? I can't just go and let a guy fall in love with me and hope he doesn't die," I respond. "Although it seems that's the path Isobel took. The carnage of her irresponsibility is documented in her curio cabinet—a cabinet full of dead guys."

"Good point. I guess we won't know for sure," Jessa responds. Her lack of sympathy is leaning toward sociopathic right now.

How can I do that to Riley? I can't let him fall in love with me until I know for sure the spell is broken, especially now that I know I'm a bloodline witch and everything is turning out to be true.

What I wouldn't give to hold his hand again. The moment we shared on the couch—he almost kissed me. I could have felt his sweet taste on my soft lips if it weren't for this stupid spell. My knees go weak just thinking about it.

Jessa stomps around my room, smashing through my beautiful image of Riley's lips on mine. "I'm hungry. It's Saturday night. Get your lazy butts out of bed. You want to go out, grab a slice of pizza, and see what everyone is up to tonight?"

"I can't imagine our classmates are doing much. They're probably mourning. Remember?" Tahlia says with sadness in her voice as she shifts her gaze to Margo.

"Oh, crap. That's right. Megan," Jessa says carelessly.

"Jessa, how could you forget that?" Tahlia hisses. "Also, we need to tell you some things."

Margo and Tahlia fill Jessa in on everything she missed during her magic hangover. A story I've heard twice now. So, I let my mind play around with ways to break it to Margo about what we might have done to Megan. Although, it's not entirely my call.

Part of me wants to tell Margo the truth about that night on the road, but part of me is afraid. I don't want to lose this friendship. I wasn't the one driving. Jessa was. Despite that, I feel responsible. I could have forced her to go back to check on the thing moving on the cold, dark road. Even if it's the curse, we might still be responsible. Why didn't we just stop and see what it was? I hate not knowing. It's eating at me.

Jessa's eyes are glossy and vacant as her words slither out of her mouth, "I know we're still mourning Megan, which makes it much worse since Margo was like in love with her, but that doesn't change the fact that I'm hungry. Let's go get a pizza, and then I'll be able to think clearer."

Why is she being so cold? Does she not care about Margo?

"Not cool. Margo is hurting," Tahlia says, her eyes widening.

I know what she's thinking without saying it. *We killed Megan. We feel bad. Have a freaking heart, Jessa.* But Jessa seems unfazed.

I want to leap out of bed, wrap my fingers around her throat, and shake some sense into her, but I don't. I remain under the covers with Margo and Tahlia next to me as Jessa parades herself around my room.

"Pizza. Now. Me hungry," Jessa demands, giggling to herself, finding humor in her odd behavior.

"You're being rude. Plus, you showered; we all look like shit. Izzy has twigs in her hair." Tahlia pulls at the nest of junk in my hair from my time being asleep out in the forest.

"Fine, text me your order. I'll get slices and sticks and come back," Jessa responds.

"Fine," Tahlia says, giving in.

We all reach for our phones and shoot Jessa our order. Cheese and black olives for me, but I'm not hungry. I place my order to appease her. I'm afraid she will order the food anyway and shove it down my throat. I may as well get something I might eat, instead of leaving it to chance. After all, Jessa doesn't know the first thing about me, let alone my eating habits. All she knows is that I'm a witch and I'm cursed, but there is so much more to me than that.

Jessa exits the room, her blonde hair bouncing effortlessly off her back as she closes the bedroom door.

"She seems more rude than usual," I respond.

"She's not herself, that's for sure," Tahlia agrees. The vibrant green in her eyes that appeared this morning slowly recedes in front of my very eyes. Now, her usual moss green doesn't seem so exotic. I'm slightly disappointed.

What happened to us in the forest?

CHAPTER 21
OLD LADY THOUGHTS

When the smell of pizza and breadsticks swarms the room, I can't help myself. I eat everything in front of me. I guess there is always room for pizza, even in a time of crisis and uncertainty—comfort food. The girls leave after our late-night meal. I'm grateful for some time alone—to process.

Now it's Sunday morning and Tim will arrive any minute with coffee and doughnuts. I gaze out my bedroom window, lurking behind the curtain, waiting for his red truck to pull up. Tiny pangs of disappointment punch me in the gut as thoughts of betrayal loom over me. I thought I liked Officer Tim, and we were 'friends', like in an old man, I-think-your-son-is-hot and someday-you-could-be-my-father-in-law kind of way.

He sure puts on a good show when he's here. I never suspected he knew anything about my past. Is he someone I can trust or is he an enemy? Right now, I'm leaning toward enemy. Such a shame. Why did he have to tell Riley about Sondra?

I need to be cautious around him.

I'll have my guard up from now on.

Tim's truck comes to a halt on the street below. He exits the vehicle and places his drink carrier on top of the car as he reaches back inside for the pink box of pastries—his usual routine. My heart thumps hard in my chest as the passenger side door slowly swings open.

Can it be?

Riley's feet hit the pavement before he turns back to help his dad, retrieving the pastry box. Suddenly, I'm not craving my pastry sweets, I'm craving something else—someone else—Riley.

Oh my gosh, he's back. I didn't expect to see Riley in this house again, especially so soon after the awkward incident a few days ago. I squeal with excitement.

I dash out of my room, leaving the door wide open behind me. Then I slowly creep down the steps. I hover over the railing, stretching to listen as my dad answers the door.

"Whoa, am I really to believe what I'm seeing? You can't be Riley?" my dad gushes.

"Hello, Mr. Beswick. Good to see you again. It's been a long time," Riley politely responds.

"Sure has. I hardly recognize you. My, you've gotten tall. Taller than both your dad and I," my dad says.

I'm literally dying of embarrassment, but then again, that's how Tim reacted when he first saw me. What's with dads? So weird sometimes.

"Yes, I suppose so," Riley responds.

"Tim, I'm glad you finally brought your son around, and today's the perfect day. We need three strong men for our task," my dad says with a laugh.

"I was hoping I could chat with Izzy first," Riley states.

"Sure, I think she's upstairs. I will go grab her," Dad suggests.

I take that as my cue to continue down the steps. I'll pretend I didn't hear anything leading up to this moment.

"Oh my goodness, is that Riley Hawkins in my house? My eyes must be playing tricks on me. It's good to finally see you," I stealthily respond, just in case he didn't tell his dad we're in contact. And if his dad knows, well then, I just look stupid, but I don't want to get Riley in trouble.

Riley hands my dad the box of pastries and pushes his hair from off his forehead, giving me a better look at his beautiful face. My entire body quivers at the sight of him. He's so hot. Dang, this stupid curse.

"Hi, Izzy. It's been a long time, hasn't it?" Riley gives me a sideways smirk.

His response makes it clear his dad doesn't know about our meet-ups. I suppose I don't blame him. I'm the big bad city girl with a reputation for pushing people off a cliff, and my Gran-gran is a witch, but whatever.

"Izzy, I was hoping we could chat," Riley says.

"Yes, um," I stutter, glancing around, trying to figure out the best place to take Riley to talk in private. "Um, we can go upstairs to my bedroom," I offer, searching for my dad's reaction, but he doesn't seem bothered. So, I grab Riley by the arm and drag him upstairs behind me before either parent can argue that I'm bringing a boy into my bedroom—alone.

Well, this is shockingly easy. I glance down the hallway to

make sure my dad isn't having a delayed response, but he's not there. I shove Riley into my room and latch the door behind me.

"I'm surprised to see you, Riley." My heart flutters and my knees are weak.

Riley Hawkins is in my bedroom. Oh my God! I'm dying inside.

He takes a seat at the edge of my bed and folds his large hands in his lap. I desperately want to take the spot next to him, but I'm afraid to get too close. What if the curse isn't broken? Plus, we ended things on an awkward note last time.

"I didn't want to come back, but my dad said he needed the help today. I thought we should clear the air since I'm going to be here all day, it sounds like."

Great. He was forced here. Not a good start.

I take a step closer to him, and my hand flickers with heat. I can't tell if these are warning signs or good signs. So far, they've been both—I think. But I'm leaning toward caution, and I redirect my movement to my vanity chair and take a seat.

I glance down, afraid that if I make direct eye contact, he will be able to read my thoughts. I feel raw and exposed. "I want to apologize for the other day. I'm sorry. Things were just moving so fast, and I panicked. See, Riley, I really like you—"

Riley huffs. "You have a funny way of showing it."

I want to toss my hands in the air and tell him I'm keeping him safe, but I remain calm. Riley shifts on the edge of my bed. "It's OK. I get it. We can just be friends. It's easier that way."

Friends! No!

And just like that, my heart cracks right down the middle, bleeding out into my chest cavity. I know I'm dramatic, but it hurts. No one wants to hear the word friend tossed around so easily.

The complexity of our situation is more than I can handle, and the tension in the room is suffocating. I want to scream. I want to shout, and I want to throw myself at Riley. But I don't.

"Sure, friends," I slowly respond. It's the easy response.

He twists his muscular torso, reaching into the back of his shorts for something. The fabric of his baby blue T-shirt clings tightly to his perfectly sculpted muscles. When he twists back around, the sleeve of his shirt folds up, unveiling a fresh half-finished tattoo. It's large and black and covers most of his bicep.

"New tat?" I point at his arm.

He quickly tugs the shirt down, covering his new ink. He doesn't offer any insight into his tattoo, instead, he produces a tiny torn-up notebook.

"I found this at my house."

I raise my brow, giving him a puzzled look.

"It was with my dad's things. I was searching for a permission slip for next week's game. My dad said he left it on the counter, but I couldn't find it, so I searched through his drawers and I found this."

I still don't understand what it has to do with me.

He gets up and crosses the room, setting the item down on my vanity table. "I thought you should have it," he says, retreating to the bed.

The cover of the book is leather, like my spellbook. I pick it up, bringing the item closer to my eyes. *Isobel Beswick* is carved into the leather. The book burns hot in my hands.

"I think it's your Gran's book. I don't know why my dad had it. Maybe he accidentally picked it up with his things when he was here. I don't even know if he knows he has it, but it's not his. It should be here with you."

I let out a gasp. "Did you read it?"

"No, it looks like an old diary or something. I doubt it's anything I'd want to read. An old lady's thoughts, um, no thanks. But I thought you might want it."

I think Officer Tim knew exactly what the book is. He's here searching for evidence of something and telling kids to stay away from my house. But why?

I force a wide smile. "Thank you, Riley. That was very thoughtful of you."

He reaches up and scratches the back of his head. "I guess now that we're cool, I better head downstairs and see what our dads need help with."

Riley gets up to leave, and my heart shatters all over again. I attempt to stand, but my legs won't budge. I can't tell if it's this house and the magic or simply the weight of my sadness.

"OK," is all I can manage to say.

"See you around, Izzy," he says with a heaviness lurking in his eyes. He lingers for a moment before closing the door.

I want to crumble to the floor. I've never been this torn up over a guy before. Sure, I've had crushes, but no one has made me feel this way, like Riley does. I have butterflies, tingles, and palpitations in my heart anytime he's nearby. I feel a pull to him I can't explain. It's like my heart knows we're meant to be together, so how can there possibly be a curse lurking over my love life keeping us apart? I can't end up an old spinster living out my days on wasted dreams in this old house.

I can't.

I won't.

Someday, I hope to test whether the curse is broken, but how will I know for sure without hurting someone I love? Maybe I can find a spell that will show me.

Every fiber inside of me flares with heat. The spellbook calls to me. I reach for Isobel's diary and decide it's best to view it upstairs in my magical space. Thinking about the attic gives me a sense of calmness that I desperately need right now.

All right, Isobel, what are you trying to tell me now?

CHAPTER 22
FADED WORDS

On the third level, I remove the boards and I'm shocked by my sudden realization: We never put the book back, but it's here.

Is Anna the one who put it back? Something tells me she wouldn't leave it for me to find again.

I sift through the dry blood-stained bag. Everything is here, except for the knife. Whoever or whatever returned these items must have put the knife in the kitchen. I hope they cleaned it first. I make a mental note to look for it later.

Either way, I need the key, and I'm glad the book is here.

I loop the bag around my wrist and pull the spellbook out, holding it tight against my chest as I make my way up the three small steps to the attic door. My hands are full as I stumble for the key. I attempt to balance the book in my hand. As I'm doing so, a faint click pulls my attention to the door, directing my gaze to the slowly twisting handle. I press my foot against the door and give it a tiny nudge. To my surprise, it opens.

Once inside, I knock the door back with my hip and it latches.

I watch as the brass knob twists again until it clicks.

"Well, that's a new power." I smirk at the thought of my magic unfolding before my very eyes. I guess I uncorked something inside of me during our time in the forest.

Once inside the circle, I gently place the diary and the spellbook in the middle. I remove the candles from the bag and line them just as they were before. I have the lighter, but I want to test myself—see what I'm capable of without my friends. I mean, I can open and lock a door with my thoughts—I think.

I kneel next to my books, taking several deep breaths, letting my eyes fall heavy, focusing all my thoughts on the black candles surrounding me. I visualize each candle in the room, recalling every single detail I can remember, from the wick to the wax. In my mind, each candle lights one at a time counterclockwise until I'm fully encompassed in a circle of light.

Pulling in a deep breath, I slowly raise my left eye, then my right, and I gasp with delight. The candle directly in front of me sparks with an orangish-red flame.

Poof; one after another.

A giddy laugh escapes from my belly, and a full smile draws across my face. A complete circle of light surrounds me.

I did this on my own.

I'm magic.

"OK, my dear Gran-gran, what do you want to show me today?" I let the question hang in the air, but nothing happens. I pull the notebook close to me and open it.

I peer down at the first page, excited that I have another

item bringing me closer to Gran-gran, but I must remember I can't unsee what's in her diary. Once I read her entries, they will be with me forever. That whole ignorance is bliss thing is very true.

A week ago, I was happily unaware that I was a bloodline witch, and my Gran-gran was just Gran-gran—not a three-century old witch with a horrid curse and a stack of dead husbands.

I'm a witch and I need to know more. I need to understand our history, so I can make things better.

The diary is just as old as her spellbook sitting next to me, and her handwriting is the same. Heat flushes down my arm as I touch the ratty old notebook. Short, simple faded entries run the length of the first page.

Isobel Opal Beswick
Massachusetts Bay Colony 1689-

Seeing that date creates a ripple in my stomach. Even with everything I know about the magic and my family, it's still hard to wrap my head around. It's not logical. But neither is magic, I suppose.

I don't think I'll ever get used to knowing Gran-gran was around in the sixteen hundreds. Parts of me want to tuck that knowledge deep into the back of my mind.

I'm dying to know more about her world in her own words, and I can't help but be curious about how she became a witch. Is she a natural witch or was she taught? I hope I find my answers.

I let my eyes fall back to the diary. I caress the page softly, and just like the spellbook, the ink darkens before my eyes.

January 1689

Mother and Father left the Old World in hopes of a better life. I never knew the Old World, but it seems better than the life I have here now. Mother and Father are long gone. I'm all alone. I take care of the farm and go to church and that's all this life has planned for me.

The Puritan's way is the only way, but I feel deep down in my soul there is something else. A better way to live. I could never say that because it's a sin that would be fiercely punished. However, I'm dammed for even the thought. Even writing it is a sin, but I have no other way to express myself. My diary is all I have, and I must protect it and my words I confess.

July 1689

I hid my diary and the words I confessed. It lived in its safe hiding spot for months and nothing bad happened to me. So, I'm writing again, taking another chance, putting faith into something else. Perhaps, I will elaborate more next time, but things are changing in the colony. The new reverend arrived. I wonder how long he will stay in this contentious colony. They never stay long. I think he can see into my soul, and he knows what lies there. The long glances. The scared look in his eyes. Although he's never said anything, I know it's coming. I feel it stirring.

June 1690

I wasn't sure if I'd keep writing. It's been a while. The Reverend is still here. This Reverend is stern, and we must not disobey, he says. Our sins are the reasons for our hardships. I tried to keep my thoughts and feelings tucked away, but they're strong and pulling me in. We've had native tribes attacking us and many fires in the village. My thoughts and secrets are safe for now, but things have happened that I can't write about in fear of punishment.

April 1691

Constant attacks on our colony. My cow died today in a barn fire. How can I continue this way? I'm destined for a better life than this one can offer. No one suspects the things I know I'm capable of. I can't even write them because they're too disturbing.

June 1691

Life is hard. No good comes. Reverend says the devil is here. I mustn't be trusted with my thoughts. Any sinful thought that isn't pure is the devil's thought.

Disease is spreading fast. My dear friend Mary died of the pox. The Reverend says if we want to cure our village, we must confess all of our sins.

I fear for my life every day. Today I saw someone in the forest, a lady of potions. I didn't listen to her rant; it's the devil's talk. I covered my ears and ran. I can't tell the Reverend. I feel I will be punished for seeing her with my own eyes, but I am like her. I know and feel it inside me. I can't confess my sins, but is there something else I can do?

Goosebumps quilt my body as I flip the page. I remember bits and pieces of the Salem Witch Trials from history class, but we never really touched on life before the trials. Seeing my own flesh and blood suffering and her struggles in her own writing makes my stomach flip.

Did she know she was magical when she wrote in her diary? Is this what she was referencing? I need to know more.

Fire continues to course through my body, heating me to my core, although my body doesn't produce sweat from this heat. It's a strange feeling, but I think it's here to stay.

I flip the page, but the writing doesn't darken this time. I run my fingers over the faded words, but still no luck.

"Gran-gran, it's me. Show me more," I whisper, but the words don't appear.

I strain my eyes, but it's worthless. The book's too old, and the words are too faint. Why did it only work on the first page? It worked for the entire spellbook, but only a measly tiny notebook page this time. I place my entire hand over the book, focusing all my energy on her words. I slowly remove my hands, but the words don't change.

Frustration festers inside of me and I can't help but feel like a failure.

Is my magic gone?

I blow out the candles around me and attempt to light them again with my thoughts, but nothing happens when I imagine the flames.

I'm broken.

My magic is broken.

Did I imagine all of this?

A warm breeze drifts past me, pushing my hair away from my face. "You need your friends," the familiar airy voice whispers into my ear.

My fire inside turns ice cold.

CHAPTER 23
LYING BITCHES

Pieces of a tortured nightmare cling to my subconscious as I stretch my arms above my head. The day Sondra died has been on repeat every time my eyelids fall heavy, but something is different this morning. I press my eyes closed, attempting to pull the new fragments back into focus, but they're all twisted and strung about, teetering on the cusp of my memories.

Is my mind simply filling in the gaps with a new image, or is it playing tricks on me as most memories do as time passes? I shudder at both thoughts, wishing all reminders from that day would fade into the abyss. Sure, there are parts of that moment I can't remember, and I told the truth that I knew to be correct.

But if I'm finally being honest with myself, something is missing—a chink cut out of the chain of recollections. Is my mind trying to mend the broken link? I kinda wish it wouldn't.

I'm just not vibing with you anymore. The sight of you makes me angry, and it's not just because you're poor.

Did you really think we wanted to be your friend, Izzy? Why would we want to be friends with a freak like you? Sondra's words cut through me. Words I don't understand. Words that weren't provoked. Everything was fine until it wasn't. One day, she woke up with a meanness that came out of thin air. Mackenzie and Evelyn followed suit because leaders have that effect on people.

I should never have gone on that hike with them. They already hated me. I don't know why they even invited me.

I was lonely, so I went. People make mistakes when they're lonely and desperate and want to fit in, but Sondra's death isn't my fault. I think.

I shake all thoughts from my head as I reach for my phone. A slew of text messages from the girls floods my home screen.

Jessa: School is back in session if you didn't see.

Tahlia: OK, Jessa. Are you picking us all up?

Jessa: Yes. Izzy, we will swing by to get you too. No more walking for you girlie! We got you! You're one of us now and forever! <3

Margo: OK, pick me up last. I woke up late. I haven't been sleeping well.

I beam with acceptance from my new friends. I'm one of them. I'm not sure how I feel about the forever part, but I'll take the win. I shouldn't keep my new friends waiting.

Izzy: OK. Thank you! See you soon!

I leap out of bed, locking my intrusive thoughts in their secure location in the back of my mind. I toss my phone onto my vanity table and head for the shower.

Letting the hot water rush over me, my thoughts wander to Gran-gran and her diary. I wish school was canceled another day. I want to go back upstairs and try again. Maybe I need to rejuvenate my magic with some sleep and a meal. I doubt that's how it works, but I'm pulling at strings here.

I quickly get ready, letting my hair hang straight with a side part. I pull the longer side back with a cute barrette belonging to Gran-gran. I toss on a black tank and some shorty shorts. I slip into my silver flip flops, the ones with the rhinestones.

My attention is drawn to my vanity as my phone restlessly vibrates against the wood, nearly walking itself off the table. It's blowing up with messages one after another.

The phone is still vibrating when I grab it. What the heck is going on?

Jessa: Change of fucking plans. You guys need to get to my house right now!!!!!!!!!!!!!!!! I mean it!!!!!!! Now!!!!!!!!!!!!!!!!!!!!!

Jessa: Just come. Drive. Uber, cab it, walk. I don't care. Just come now!!!!!!

Jessa: I'm freaking out!!!!!

Jessa: Hello!

Jessa: Answer me!

Tahlia: What's going on??

Jessa: Need you all!!!!

Jessa: NOW! COME!

Tahlia: OK. On my way. My mom left her car today. I'll pick up Izzy and Margo.
Margo: K. C U soon.

What could possibly be so important that she can't pick us up? Can't her drama wait?

Izzy: I'll be waiting.

***

I'm waiting for Tahlia on the top step outside my house, soaking in some morning sunshine, when my phone vibrates in my hand.
What now?
It shakes again before I have time to glance down at the screen.
Seriously, girls, this drama is a little too much this early in the morning.

Unknown number: Two new messages

Not the girls.
And this unknown number isn't Riley. I saved his number with a little heart next to his name. Cautiously, I click on the text bubble from the unknown sender.

Unknown: I found this video of the day Sondra died.

Unknown: Thought you might want to see it.

No, no. This can't be happening. Not right now. Not ever.

My walls are crashing down, crumbling into a massive pile around my silver rhinestone flip flops.

There isn't video of this. Right?

No one else was there.

This has to be a prank.

I need to see it now. I peer down the street, searching for Tahlia, but no cars are in sight. Dad's inside and could step out at any moment. He can't accidentally see what I'm about to click on. I slink over to the side of the house, crouching down behind the yard waste receptacle. I hover over my phone, keeping it close to me in case I need to hide it quickly.

I nervously click on the link.

The video is blurry at first with no sound. I squint to understand what I'm seeing until the image comes fully into focus on its own. Still no sound though.

It's me that day in the forest. I'm chasing after Sondra. A gasp slips past my lips. My hand jolts up, covering my mouth. If my dad catches me over here, he will demand to know what I'm doing.

I keep my eyes locked on the tiny screen as I continue to watch the day that's been on repeat for months in my memories. Although, this doesn't look the same as I remember.

I never chased Sondra.

This never happened.

Did it?

But there it is—on video. It happened, and now Sondra is teetering on the edge of the cliff. This is the moment where things are fuzzy for me—parts of the story that aren't fully developed in my mind.

I'm at least six feet away from Sondra, but my eyes are wildly pinned on her.

Her fiery tendrils blow in the wind as her foot shifts below her a few times, then finally slips, but she catches herself. I'm stationed in the same place, never taking another step toward her.

I extend my hand out. Her eyes widen like I'm right on top of her, but I'm not. I'm still a good six feet away. I push my hand into the air, palm facing out, like I want to push her, but I'm so far away. It's not even possible for me to—

My stomach lurches at the next frame. Sondra is propelled backward in a force I can't even describe. Her body heaves right off the cliff as if she was shoved. Her red tendrils flap in the wind as her mouth opens. I know exactly what she's saying.

My skin burns as she mouths, "Izzy no."

The two words that have found themselves on repeat every day since.

I didn't push her.

But the force in which she flew off the cliff with no one touching her is unexplainable. It wasn't my magic. Was it? I just realized I'm a witch. I only recently got powers, which seem to come and go and do very little.

But no one else was there. It had to be my magic.

I. Killed. Sondra.

Bile rises in my throat. I turn my head to the side and release the sickness within. I'm relieved that it's normal—not black chunks.

Why this text now? And who is it from? Why didn't they give it to the detectives? It couldn't have been the other girls. Evelyn and Mackenzie were so far back. Then again, they said they saw me push her, but they didn't. Lying bitches.

Maybe I'm the lying bitch.

I text the unknown number.

Izzy: Who is this?

The blare of a horn pierces through the air, announcing Tahlia's presence. I stand alert, composing myself. Huffing in a long, deep breath, I shake my hands out at my sides, wishing away all the awfulness that slithered its way into my bones.

I muster up a friendly smile for Tahlia as I rush down the steps. I can't let my new friends know any of this. It will ruin everything. Plus, it's not like I did it intentionally, and I've already been cleared of this situation.

Deep breath. I got this. I can do this. Smile, Izzy. It's game time.

Tahlia's waiting for me in a newish Black Wagoneer SUV, confirming my suspicions that her family is well off. Jealousy slithers under my skin, longing for my old life before things went down the crapper. Sure, we have a nice SUV, but it's older. It doesn't even have touch screen controls. That should be the least of my worries right now, but it's keeping my mind off the video that shouldn't exist.

"Good morning," I greet Tahlia, sliding into the front seat, which is unfortunately vacant.

I secretly hoped Margo would be picked up first, even though she asked to be last—wishful thinking. I would much rather be in the back seat, scheming ways to deal with my random videographer. But that's not the case, and now I'm alone with Tahlia for the first time.

Tahlia and I have a connection I can't ignore after our time in the forest, but Riley's words hiss through my mind, *"Tahlia, she's the worst."* And then Anna's words—*"half breed."*

But neither Riley nor Anna offered any explanations. Does it even matter now? I'm connected to Tahlia through our magical bond, and what's done is done.

"Morning," Tahlia responds with a stony smile.

"What do you think is going on?" I eagerly ask, thankful we have something to chat about, giving myself a reprieve from the video taunting me from beyond my black screen.

"Ugh, knowing Jessa, it's probably an overreaction to self-tanning cream gone wrong or a bug inside the garage. It's probably nothing. She tends to dramatize things. I don't think it's anything we need to worry about."

"Oh," I respond, letting a lick of the built-up tension in my shoulders drop.

With everything going on, I can't help but have my guard up, waiting for the next bombshell to drop.

Bombs away. Another one's dropping. And another one.

Sondra. The magic. Megan. The curse. The video. Jessa's drama.

I replace my thoughts of unease with images of Jessa with uneven tan lines streaking both of her perfectly sculpted legs. An unintentional giggle releases from deep within. I quickly cough to cover my blunder and shift my attention to the window, taking in the scenery.

Tahlia takes the sharp curves a little too fast and tight in her oversized vehicle as she whips through the countryside and away from town. I have to remember she doesn't drive much.

"I don't think I've been down this road before," I say, grabbing onto the *'oh shit'* handles.

"Margo lives more on the outskirts of town. You'd really have no reason to go here unless you were picking her up."

That's a funny thing to say, but I slowly understand what she means as she takes a right down an unpaved road. Rocks and gravel kick up at the vehicle before Tahlia takes the next right down an unmarked dirt path.

When we park, I take inventory of Margo's property, quickly realizing Margo didn't grow up like the rest of us. Her home is nothing like Tahlia's grand historic estate or my beautiful childhood home on the Puget Sound. My decrepit run-down monstrosity that is my current home is a step up from Margo's dwelling and much, much larger. I feel bad for complaining so much about my circumstances because it could be worse.

A beat-up red Honda Civic that looks older than me is parked in the grass next to an overrun field of dying sunflowers. Margo's home is nothing more than a single wide trailer on top of a concrete slab. Bottles of alcohol fill the recycle container outside.

When Margo opens the door, it drops on its broken

hinges. She tugs it back up to secure it and firmly pushes it into place before turning and giving us a friendly wave.

"Is this where Margo lives?" I cautiously question, not wanting to seem rude. Margo mentioned her mom was a black sheep of sorts, but I didn't imagine this.

Tahlia frowns. "Margo's mom is a drunk. That's why she never wants to go home."

I nervously bite at my nails as Tahlia continues. "She'd rather hang out at our houses with our families than go home. She doesn't remember her dad, and there isn't anyone else to take care of her, so she's our responsibility." Tahlia shifts to a smile as Margo approaches the vehicle that's nicer than her home.

My heart yanks for Margo. I guess I know why she thinks booze is the answer to her problems. Poor Margo; no good role model in her life. Her friends are her family.

My connection to Margo is more than just magic. It's a true friendship, and she chose me. She needs me, and I suppose I need her too. Margo is the closest thing to a real friend I've had in a long time. I'll protect her. She's welcome at my house anytime. I don't think my dad could say no once I tell him about her living conditions.

"Hey girls." Margo shoves her bookbag in the back seat, hoisting herself into the SUV. "What's up with Jessa this morning? I hope it's not another spider. I don't think I'm up for spider patrol today," Margo says, wincing at the thought.

Margo doesn't act embarrassed that this is the first time I'm seeing her home. If roles were reversed, I'd make some sort of excuse for living here. She's unapologetic about who she is. She's proud and strong, and I admire that about her.

"Who knows with Jessa. She's so dramatic. She might be falling back into her attention seeking mode, you know, since the attention hasn't been on her lately with Izzy's arrival. Sorry, Izzy. And well, Megan's death. Sorry, Margo. I guess we will find out when we get there," Tahlia responds.

"Speaking of Megan. How are you holding up, Margo? Are you sure you're ready to go back to school? No one would question if you needed another day," I say, letting my head drift to Margo in the back seat. "I'm sure other students are taking more time to grieve."

"Well, I'm not OK. I'm torn apart inside, but I'll be OK. I'd eventually have to go back, plus I'd rather be at school, instead of at home stewing over things. Ya know?"

"I get it," I respond with a sympathetic grin.

Margo scooches into the middle seat, letting her hands rest on both mine and Tahlia's headrests. She leans in, practically hovering over the center console. "Are you two still doing good since the magic?" Margo asks, her breath smelling of cinnamon bubble gum.

I glance at Tahlia, waiting for her to respond first. A sliver of a smile tugs in the corner of her mouth.

"I'm doing great, but it's like a drug that I'm craving. I want to go back to that feeling we had after the forest when everything felt alive and vivid," Tahlia responds.

My insides tingle at the memory of that special feeling. It's one I want to experience again. "Tahlia, I totally understand what you mean. I miss that feeling too. I want to feel it again."

"Maybe we try something small next time. We kinda went

big with a doozy of a spell, and we don't know what we accomplished. I just know I enjoyed the aftermath," Margo says, sliding back in her seat. She rummages through the front pocket of her backpack, pulling out a pair of oversized white sunglasses and slides them onto her face, looking fabulous. "I want—I need to feel that again."

The car falls quiet as we sink our thoughts into Margo's suggestion. I let the idea of finding a small spell fester inside of me until I can't take it anymore.

"I want to try another one!" I ineloquently shout out.

Both girls laugh at my awkwardness, and I join them.

"Let's do it," Tahlia says with giddiness in her voice.

"Yes!" Margo squeals.

Tahlia takes a sharp left off the gravel road, and our ride becomes drastically smoother.

"Hey girls, I don't think Jessa had the same experience as us in the forest. It drained her more than it drained us," Tahlia says. She pauses for a few moments, gathering her thoughts. "I hate to say this, but I don't think she's as special as us, and that's really going to mess with her if she figures it out. We hung out yesterday, and she kept asking me questions about how I felt, hoping it was the same as her. When I began to tell her about the vivid colors, her face went long, and I knew for sure she didn't have the same experience as we did. She agreed with me, but she didn't elaborate. She was faking it. I think she's important, and we need her—she's our fourth—but it took something from her, instead of giving her the gifts we got. So, maybe we shouldn't brag about it in front of her."

Instead of Tahlia's words coming out sincere, they have a hint of superiority to them. I think Tahlia is a smidge happy that Jessa isn't the special one for once. But I hate to break it to her that in our foursome of power, or should I call us a coven now—I'm the top rung. Margo is next, then Tahlia, and as we all assume, Jessa is on the lowest rung. But I guess being third is better than being last. I bet Jessa is never last in anything, so maybe I get where Tahlia is coming from.

I can't help but enjoy the fact that I'm the true bloodline witch. Well, that is, as long as I'm no longer cursed, and my magic didn't really kill Sondra. Those are the burdens of the title. Other than that, I'm the most powerful, and it feels good. I wonder if I should tell the girls that I lit the candles and locked a door with my thoughts.

Nah, I'll keep that to myself for right now. They will eventually see what I'm capable of, but I need them to see the rest of Isobel's diary, so I should probably knock myself down a peg for acting like the all-powerful superior high priestess, when I have things I can't do without my coven. Look at me using witchy words now.

"I know. She's been acting strange since it happened and if she really knew our experience, she'd be so jealous," Margo adds. "And Jessa doesn't handle jealousy well."

CHAPTER 24
LYING WITCHES

When we finally arrive at Jessa's, her home is luxurious. Tahlia pulls through a gated entryway and down a steep, long, windy driveway. Decorative lights line the entire path, making it appear more like a runway. When we reach her house, I realize it's a newer build, unlike most of the homes in our historic town. It seems out of place nestled amongst the old maple trees. A large aboveground pool juts off the left side of the house.

We get out of the car and step toward three carriage-style wooden garage doors. I follow the girls to the slightly raised one at the end. Tahlia crouches down and crab walks under the door in her little black sundress. Margo and I both slink under at the same time.

When my body is fully upright, I immediately spot Jessa curled up in a ball near the far-right corner of her immaculately organized garage. She shifts her body until she's facing us, quickly pulling herself to her feet.

"What's going on? Why so cryptic? It better not be another bug fiasco," Tahlia jeers as she approaches the front of the garage.

"Look!" Jessa demands, pointing at her car, her hand shaking, almost vibrating. Her face is splotchy, and her nose is bright red, like she's been crying.

Tahlia walks around to the front of the white Jeep. Her mouth drops with her mossy green eyes widening in shock.

"What did you do?" Tahlia shrieks.

"Nothing. I came straight home after your house yesterday," Jessa says with a grave look, her voice high and strained.

"Do you think—" Tahlia begins.

Jessa cuts her off. "There is no way. But—"

"No, that's insane—" Tahlia responds.

My eyes bounce between the two girls, trying to play catch up to their quick banter. Margo's brows tighten, conveying her confusion as well.

"I know, but I don't know what else to think." Jessa tugs at her stick straight hair as fat tears fall down her splotchy cheeks.

I cautiously walk to the front of her Jeep, finally seeing what Jessa and Tahlia are going on about.

I let out a long-winded gasp as my eyes land on a smashed in front end. The passenger side headlight dangles loose with brownish streaks I can only assume is blood. Chunks of flesh are embedded into the metal, along with long strands of blondish-brown colored fibers—hair.

"What the fuck?" I scream, tripping backward into the wall. "What the actual fuck?"

"You swear you didn't hit anything on your way home yesterday, Jessa?" Tahlia presses.

"I swear to you. I came straight home, and my car was

fine. T, you saw it yesterday. It didn't look like this. The only thing I hit—well, I *thought* we hit—was that deer or small animal. But that was five days ago. What the hell is happening?" Jessa paces the length of her bloodstained Jeep. "What if we were wrong, and we did hit—you know?"

"No, that's just not possible. The Jeep was fine," Tahlia says.

I think back to the moving figure of darkness in the road and the voice that whispered, *"run."* I swallow hard, pushing down the lump making its way up my throat. "Do you guys think it's the magic? What if it was protecting us from seeing what we did?"

"What on earth are you guys talking about? Will someone please tell me what's going on now!" Margo demands, stomping her foot on the ground.

Jessa rocks restlessly on her heels, nervously biting at her fingernails, ignoring Margo's question.

I keep my eyes pinned on Jessa, waiting for our secret to slip off her perfectly glossed lips. My heart drops as images of Megan fighting for her life on the cold, dark pavement flicker in the back of my mind. I blink a few times, trying to dislodge my thoughts.

"I didn't kill Megan! My car was fine. I didn't kill her. We hit a small animal. We didn't hit Megan," Jessa spits out, keeping up her rocking and anxious biting. "No, no. That's not right," she shouts.

Her delivery isn't well-timed. She's lost her cool and is coming unhinged. This isn't how Margo should find out our ill kept secret.

Margo's eyes darken as she angrily lunges toward Jessa, grabbing her by the wrist, pulling her close to her body. "What did you say? Tell me what you just said. I don't think I heard you correctly." Her voice is low and powerful.

"Margo, I didn't mean to. I don't know what we hit."

"You're telling me *you* hit my girlfriend like some kind of wild animal and left her for dead in the middle of nowhere? That's what I'm understanding."

Her head twists to Tahlia and me, searching for answers that she's not getting from Jessa.

This isn't how I thought this would go.

"Margo," I say softly, reaching out.

I gently grab her by the arm, but she doesn't budge. Her feet are cemented firmly in place. I reposition myself in front of her and her darker than night eyes cut through me like a sword. The rage that's inside of her transfers to me in the form of fire that zips up my left arm, almost knocking me off my feet.

"Margo, Jessa hit something that night. We thought it was a deer or a small animal, but when we got back to my house, there was no damage, so we thought we were fine," I softly explain.

"You mean to tell me you didn't stop to see what you hit? That you're uncertain about who or what you killed that night?"

"Yes. You were passed out and Tahlia and Jessa had been drinking. It wasn't safe for us to stay there any longer."

"So what? You just left with the possibility that you hit someone, and you felt better once you got home and saw no damage? Then the next day Megan's body was found, and you didn't think to say something, even to me?" Margo drops Jessa's wrist and shakes herself free from my grip, releasing me from her rage.

Margo steps backward until her body is flush up against the garage wall.

"There was no damage that night, so no crime done," Jessa insists.

"What's wrong with you?" Margo continues to shout, spittle flying from her mouth. "What's wrong with all of you?"

"There was no damage, Margo. I don't know how to explain what's going on and why we're seeing this now. It makes zero sense. We saw this Jeep for the past five days, and it was completely fine. Plus, I'm sure the police have been scouring the streets, searching for a car with notable damage. None of this makes any sense," I respond.

"Well, right now the car is suggesting otherwise," Margo cries. "Megan is dead. I loved her, and you killed her," she hisses, pointing at Jessa. "You—take a look at what you did. That's her hair, her flesh, and her blood. I don't know how it got there, but it's there now. Look at it!"

Jessa bursts into loud uncontrollable sobbing.

"And you, Izzy. I thought we were going to be great friends. I didn't think you were a secret-keeping, lying witch. What do you have to say for yourself?" Margo says, seething, cutting my heart in half.

I can't lose Margo, and did she just call me a witch? It's not in my head. Things are so out of control. None of this makes any sense. How is this happening?

All three girls stare at me, waiting for me to respond. My breath escalates. The words won't come out.

Sondra.

Megan.

Two dead girls.

The magic.

The video.

I can't breathe.

"Shit!" Tahlia exclaims, taking the attention off me.

"What is it?" Jessa asks.

I pull in a few choppy breaths, waiting for Tahlia to answer.

"My brother is blowing up my phone. Apparently, my mom left the car for Callen to take to work. He's going to kill me if he's late for his shift. OK, we need to go now."

"But what about Jessa's car?" I manage to say. "What about all of this?"

"Leave it. We can't deal with this now. Jessa, your parents never come in your part of the garage. The car should be fine here until we can figure out what to do with it. Maybe we can find a spell to undo the damage. We'll figure this out as a group. So, grab your backpack and let's go. My brother will have to drop us off on his way to work. We need to hurry; we're already late. Although I feel like the school will let it slide since we're grieving," Tahlia says.

"I don't think I'm going. I need some time," Jessa says, giving us no time to change her mind before she exits the rear of the garage, letting the door slam shut behind her.

"OK. I guess it's just the three of us today," Tahlia says.

"Make that two. I'm going to walk home. I can't go to

school knowing what I know now. I can't look at either of you," Margo adds angrily.

"Let me drive you home, at least," she pleads, but Margo is already sliding under the garage door, leaving me alone once again with Tahlia.

CHAPTER 25
CREEPER VIBES

The ride to Tahlia's house is silent, except for the air whipping through our open windows. There are no words for the horrific sight in Jessa's garage. The newly damaged vehicle that appeared normal all week is now clinging with pieces of a crime scene. This can't be possible. But nothing makes rational sense since arriving in East Gate. The only thing I can think of is that somehow it's connected to the magic. It has to be.

I have so many questions sloshing around my brain, like a wave rushing back and forth, and I'm on a boat in the middle getting nowhere.

And to top things off, now I have to deal with a mysterious texter. That video can't exist. Am I really responsible? We were alone that day in the forest. Who would take such a video and not rush to help the poor girl who fell off a cliff? None of this makes sense.

If Tahlia wasn't sitting so quietly next to me, I would scream. What's happening around me? I feel lost and out of control. And we're hella late for school. My dad is going to kill me if he finds out.

I should be a normal new kid, keeping my head down and pushing through the year until college. But instead, I'm dodging one bullet after another. What the hell else can this day throw at me?

When we arrive at Tahlia's house, her brother is waiting at the end of the driveway with a bright yellow to-go coffee tumbler in hand. He's dressed in slacks and a white-collared button up. His foot's tapping in an insistent rhythm, seemingly frustrated with his younger sister. I didn't even know Tahlia had an older brother. There are so many things I don't know about my new friends.

I squint to get a closer look at him, but his features aren't coming into focus due to the blinding sun, and I don't have my sunglasses. Chalk that up to another fail of the day.

Tahlia gets out of the car to greet her brother, but I remain inside, unsure what to do, keeping my distance. I don't want to get in the middle of any family business. I don't have a sibling, so I don't understand the drama that comes with it. Being an only child has its perks, but it also comes with a lot of loneliness.

I yank my phone out of my pocket and click the text message icon. I need to replay the video, study it, search for clues.

Wait! Where is it?

It should be the first one on my screen. I flick my finger down, searching for the mysterious message.

It's fucking gone!

My insides tremble, vibrating with anxiety.

Am I losing my mind?

Is the magic playing with my head? Is it like Jessa's Jeep? What the hell is going on?

I jab my fist into the door, letting out a controlled, muffled shriek.

"Mom's pissed, T," Tahlia's brother says sharply, his voice carrying through the open windows, bringing me back to Tahlia's driveway and away from questioning my sanity, which seems like a new part-time hobby of mine.

"T?" her brother says again, waiting for her response.

Apparently, Jessa and her brother get to call her T. I wonder if I'll earn the privilege. Although have I ever heard Margo call her that? I don't think so. What gives Jessa special treatment over Margo? If Tahlia and Jessa are so close, then maybe Margo and I can be just as close. I wonder if she's felt like a third wheel this whole time until I came along—her back seat buddy.

The thought of a blossoming friendship excites me, but I'm also terrified about the existence of our friendship after today. Why am I cursed in the friend department? After all, I did have horrible judgement with Sondra, Evelyn, and Mackenzie. The three worst people in the world. They're still finding ways of getting under my skin, and one of them is dead. Bitches.

Tahlia's voice invades the car, bringing me back to my current reality. "Sorry, I thought it would be OK. The car was just sitting in the garage and Mom wasn't home, so I thought it was fine."

"T, that's the problem with you. You're so self-absorbed you never know what's going on if it doesn't directly involve you. My car is in the shop and Mom said I could borrow hers. It's been there since last week. You haven't noticed or bothered to ask me where my car has been?"

"I'm sorry, Callen, it's been a crazy week. Do you even care that one of my classmates died? Talk about self-absorbed. You never cared to ask how I'm doing."

"You weren't even friends with Megan, so don't jump onto grief by proxy just because it's convenient."

"Ugh! You drive me mad sometimes," Tahlia shouts.

"Ditto."

"Whatever, Callen."

"So, I assume you're still in need of a ride to school," Callen asks with annoyance coating his voice. "Where are the girls? In the car?"

"Well, it's just me and my new friend, Izzy. Jessa and Margo decided to stay home another day. You know, grief by proxy or whatever you called it," Tahlia hisses.

"Izzy?" her brother questions.

It's strange the way my name rolls off his tongue—almost familiar.

"She's new here. You wouldn't know her. And don't get any ideas in your head. She's off-limits."

"Oh, off-limits, huh?"

There's that phrase again. Riley was off-limits, and now I'm off-limits. Tahlia is a little possessive, isn't she?

"Well, where is this friend of yours? Don't be rude, T. Introduce me."

I slowly hop out of the SUV. Cautiously, I make my way over to the two of them. I uncomfortably wave at her brother, acknowledging him, when I'm struck with the realization that I've met him before.

"Izzy, this is my older brother, Callen."

"It's nice to meet you, Izzy." Callen reaches out to grab my hand.

"Nice to meet you too," I carefully respond, twisting my head, trying to make sure I have Callen pinned correctly.

I'm not mistaken. We've met before.

His dark eyes securely lock on mine, drawing me in, and I know it's him—Mr. Barista—the Mr. Whip Cream and chocolate sprinkles creep from The Perk. He doesn't acknowledge our meeting, so I don't bring it up. Maybe he doesn't remember me, but the way his velvety black, hauntingly beautiful eyes are fixed on mine tells me he remembers.

Too much time has passed, and our greeting should end, but instead, Callen squeezes my hand tighter.

Is he pulling me closer? Or am I imagining things? My not-so-new-anymore fiery feeling flames hot in my veins, zipping up into my shoulder. I want to drop his grip, but Callen doesn't loosen his.

He grins, twisting his head ever so slightly.

Does he know the effect he's having on me?

No, he can't.

"OK, Callen, you can let her go now," Tahlia says. "You're being a weirdo."

Callen lets my hand drop, and with it, the force that was making its way up my arm evaporates like mist in the sun. Whoa, that was intense. Callen flashes me a quick, mysterious grin—one that makes me uncomfortable. I still can't tell if he's flirting with me or just strange.

I already have one guy I need to keep safe from the curse. I can't go adding another one to the list. Callen is a fine specimen of a man, even if he gives off creeper vibes.

Everything is off right now. I'm not sure how to act. I shift on my feet, rocking on my heels, waiting for direction from one of the Latham-Hart siblings, who I suddenly feel inadequate around. Tahlia and Callen hit the gene pool lottery. I'm afraid to meet their parents—the people who created these gorgeous human beings. I was finally getting used to Tahlia's beauty. Her crudeness tones it down some, but seeing her with her older brother is like seeing two models on a runway. Callen is tall and toned, with tight curly black hair like his sister. His face is long and narrow with the same high cheekbones too. I should have realized he's related to Tahlia when we met. Now, being with both of them, it's undeniable that they're related.

"All right, high-schoolers let's get this show on the road. You're already late, and I'm even later. Thanks, T," Callen says, finally giving us some direction.

OK, maybe the flirting is all in my head. He called me a high-schooler—which, of course, I am—but the way he says it makes me feel bad about my age. Hell, I'm nearly eighteen. He can't be a day over nineteen. I'll have to ask Tahlia when I have the chance. Although, why do I care?

This guy is getting under my skin, and I don't like it one bit.

CHAPTER 26
TRUTH, MAGIC, AND INSANITY

On our short drive, I study the siblings from the back seat. An unease creeps into my tummy, watching the two of them bicker about Tahlia's selfishness.

I can't pinpoint the source of my strained feelings, but something doesn't sit right. There's something off with the Latham-Hart siblings. This is one family that's hard to read. I find it odd that Callen doesn't ask me any questions, not even the usual: where are you from, or why did you move here? His curiosity vaporizes quicker than it came about.

Callen drops us off at the front entrance of our school, and I'm relieved when the ride is over. I wish things turned out differently this morning. I even wish Jessa was with us right now.

"Well, it looks like we missed first period," I inform Tahlia, glancing at the time on my phone. "And second period just started."

"Time for some damage control. I'll swing by Mrs. Jamison's class and give her an excuse for us." Tahlia offers a flat smile.

I rummage through my bag, searching for my English Lit. book, which it appears I don't have. "Great, thanks. Looks like I have to swing by my locker," I respond, but Tahlia's already down the hallway when I glance up.

I really hate being late, mostly because I hate the attention it brings. I don't need any unwanted scrutiny right now. I'd rather fly far under the radar these days.

Ooh, I wonder if I can fly. Add that to things to look into later. My mind is like a frickin' squirrel right now, all over the place. I can't help but wonder if witches can fly, or is that just in the movies? It seems like that's a Hollywood thing. I'm no Sarah Sanderson. I'm just Izzy Beswick.

Thoughts of zipping around on a broom weave in and out of my thoughts as I rush down the empty hallway.

Shoot. Principal Miller's door is wide open.

I don't need him asking questions. Taking a quiet long stride past his doorway nearly works, but I'm stunned, frozen in place mid-stride by the sight of Officer Tim standing next to Miller's desk.

I guiltily wave. Busted.

But he doesn't wave back.

That's strange.

I tuck my head and truck it to class, leaving thoughts of my magical broom outing in my dust, along with my cold encounter.

***

"Oh, Miss Beswick. So kind of you to join us," Mrs. Schneider says, embarrassing me as I attempt to sneak in unnoticed.

I think quick on my feet, coming up with my unplanned excuse. "Sorry, I was consoling a student and thought it would be rude to leave her in her time of grief." It's only a partial lie. Truth is, I was consoling Jessa and Margo this morning, but for very different reasons that don't concern Mrs. Schneider.

"Well, take your seat, won't you? I will let it slide because we are all dealing with things our own way right now," Mrs. Schneider replies.

I nod and drop into my assigned seat, letting my booty hit the metal chair a little too hard. I crinkle my nose at the slight nuisance of pain, but quickly direct my attention to the chalkboard, trying to catch up.

My sudden burst of studiousness stalls by the sight of the purple and white home game jerseys sprinkled throughout the room. There seem to be a lot of football players in this class. However, it's not that realization that nearly knocks me out of my seat, but what's on the jerseys.

Calhoun—Calhoun—Calhoun—Calhoun.

The sight of Megan's last name taped across the back of all their jerseys causes my body to tremble. The blood, the flesh, and the hair from this morning. Megan's gone. I nearly choke each time my breath catches in my throat.

I try to look past all the jerseys toward Mrs. Schneider, but it's impossible. One catches my eye through my peripherals and my stomach lurches.

I can't do this.

I wish I knew the truth.

"What did you do?" a soft voice whispers in my ear.

I gasp, quickly tossing a shy glance over my right shoulder. Who said that?

Billy Drake? The scrawny nerd with Elvis Costello glasses that's directly behind me?

I flash him a confused grin, and he responds with an annoyed, "What?"

"Nothing," I whisper, turning around, recoiling into my embarrassment.

I'm just losing my mind. No big deal. I've done a lot of things lately, like being an accomplice in a hit and run, playing with magic, ruining my friend's life, and, of course, Sondra. So, my little ghost witch friend is going to have to be more specific.

I wait, but nothing else happens.

When the bell rings, I leap off my chair and run for the door. I burst into the hallway, letting a long puff of air release from my belly.

I was suffocating in there with all the jerseys, but the hallway doesn't prove to be any sort of relief as purple and white blast me from every direction: Calhoun-Calhoun-Calhoun. Megan's memory is everywhere. It's a good thing Margo isn't at school today.

I direct my gaze to the ground, beelining down the hallway. Once at my locker, I spin the dial and twist in my four-digit combo. With that simple movement, the tension releases in the lock, and it gives me a sense of calmness. I yank the door open, sticking my head inside. Not sure what good this will do, but I hope to drown out all insanity, even if just for a moment. I pull in a long breath, hold it for ten full Mississippi's, and then exhale. I repeat several times until a group of juniors take up residence three lockers down from mine. Normally, their loitering between classes doesn't bother me, but today I need the peace.

"Did you see Riley's dad is here with a few other cops?"

My curiosity is piqued at the mention of Riley's dad. I let my eye wander to the crack in the door between the hinges, lending an ear to their gossip.

"I heard they pulled Sam Hornsby out of first period," a tall kid with wild blond hair shares.

Sam? Why him?

"I think he's still in the principal's office," a spunky brunette adds.

That must be why Tim ignored me. He was interviewing Sam.

"What do you think they want with pizza face Sam?" a skinny red-headed girl with freckles asks.

"I wonder if it's about Megan," the spunky one questions.

"Do you think Sam killed her?" another one asks, although I can't see who the voice belongs to.

Their group seems to be multiplying by the second, and my view is the same.

These juniors have no business spreading rumors like that—dragging Sam's name in the mud.

"No, there's no way that kid has it in him, although it could have been—" the blond guy says with his last words cut off by the one-minute warning bell ringing intrusively above my head.

I grab my books for my next two classes, shoving them

into my backpack, pondering the gossipy juniors' words. Why would the police think Sam Hornsby is at fault? Sure, it was his party, but he didn't run Megan over.

We did.

I think.

The lines between truth, magic, and insanity are growing thinner by the minute.

Add Sam being a person of interest to my increasing list of things to feel guilty about.

CHAPTER 27
SPELL IT OUT

A crumpled up piece of paper whips past my head, landing on my open trigonometry book. I quickly check, making sure Mr. Roland's eyes aren't on me. I quietly unfold the paper under my desk, coughing a few times to cover up the rustling sound on my lap.

Check your phone. Now!!!! The note demands.

Assuming Tahlia is the author of the note, I toss my head over my left shoulder. Her chin is sticking out and her mouth is pursed tightly, pulling all her features close together, confirming my suspicions—the note is from her. She nods to my backpack, where my phone is nestled deep into the side pocket.

I bend down, quietly pulling it from its resting place. Discreetly, I unlock my phone. A message banner displays across my home screen: *One new message from Margo*

Margo: I'm so sorry. I overreacted this morning. I can't believe the news. I knew it couldn't have been you girls. XOXO

What the heck is she talking about? What news?

I glance to Tahlia again. She shrugs her shoulders, appearing just as confused.

A burst of chatter erupts from the girls in the front of the classroom, turning louder by the second, with more students joining in.

"Would someone like to tell me what's so important to interrupt our study time?" Mr. Roland questions.

No one responds. More students grab their phones, and whatever news Margo was talking about is spreading like wildfire through our classroom.

"Holy shit!" Trevor Nolan, a football player, shouts.

"Language, Mr. Nolan. And can you please tell me what on earth is causing this eruption?" Mr. Roland demands.

"Um," Trevor stutters, "It's Sam Hornsby. He's um, getting arrested."

"What on earth for?" Mr. Roland curiously questions.

Olivia, the artsy looking girl in the front row spouts out, "Drugs."

Drugs? But what does that have to do with Margo forgiving us?

"All right, all right. I need you to settle down. We shouldn't gossip. Let's all set our phones down and get back to our lesson," Mr. Roland says calmly.

No one listens, instead, everyone scrambles over to the three large windows facing the parking lot, Mr. Roland included. Curiosity gets the best of everyone in times of uncertainty. But my own reaction is delayed as I'm shocked by this revelation. I don't know Sam well, but I kind of like the guy. He was nice to me at the party.

"Sam killed Megan!" Trevor brutishly shouts, looking up from his phone. "Alicia Foley just sent me a text; she was in the hallway when the officers were searching his locker. They found roofies, which the officers said were in Megan's system when she died and were her cause of death. Something about 4000 nanograms in her body. Whatever that means. But she wasn't hit by a car. She was merely found on the side of the road. She wandered off and died from an overdose, and too much alcohol mixed with the drugs," he says, without stopping for a breath.

Trevor's words stun me, and a tingle tousles under my skin, followed by a long sigh of relief.

Is it true?

When the shock levels out, I realize I'm the only one seated. I will my legs to move, meeting Tahlia at the farthest window, away from all the other students gathered in a flock, gossiping and hugging each other as they gaze out the large windows together in solidarity.

Without saying a word, we both direct our focus to the sidewalk down below. I'm cautious as I peer outside, half worried what I see isn't real. After all, I've been imagining things. But the gasps releasing from the other students ensure that what I see is indeed real. Four officers, including Tim Hawkins, are escorting Sam outside. He's in handcuffs.

Turning into Tahlia, pressing my body into her side, I whisper into her ear, "So, if we didn't kill Megan, then what's going on with Jessa's Jeep? This doesn't make sense."

Just saying the words sends a shiver down my spine.

Is the magic playing tricks on us?

I don't know what's real anymore.

My wrinkled reality is all sorts of fucked up.

"We need to see the Jeep again. Are we going crazy? We saw it damaged, didn't we?" Tahlia responds.

I nod, keeping a close proximity to Tahlia, afraid that if I move, the whole room will hear our secrets.

"OK, we'll get to the bottom of this mess as soon as the bell rings. We only have fifteen minutes of school left. We need to act normal. Text Margo. Tell her we'll pick her up after school."

"Tahlia, you don't have a car, remember?"

"Oh crap. That's right," Tahlia says with a frown. "Callen will still be at work, and so will my dad."

"My dad is at work too."

"I guess we're walking." Tahlia frowns. "We'll meet Margo later. We can't ask her to walk a second time today."

"You girls need a ride home?" Trevor eagerly offers.

Oh crap. How long has he been standing near us? Did he hear anything? We're trying to be careful.

"No, we're fine," Tahlia responds, biting off each word.

"We don't need any more people in our business," she mouths to me.

I nod in understanding. We can't have any of this getting out. Jessa's car, the magic, the spellbook, Margo and Megan, and, of course, my past full of unknowns. We have too many secrets to play friendly with our classmates right now.

When the bell rings, Tahlia and I hurry to the door, cutting everyone off in the process. We successfully ignore the groups gathered in the hallway; we don't have time to get sucked into their gossip. We need solid answers.

My plans for an easy escape are derailed by the sight of Riley leaning against the railing on the stairwell. My entire body freezes at the sight of him. A sense of shock rocks his features; his friend is being accused of murder.

I want to rush over to him and pull him into my embrace. I want to help ease his pain, but I know I can't, for his own safety. Plus, I have my guard dog, Tahlia, latched to my side.

Tahlia leads me down the other side of the stairs, away from Riley, but the world seems to pause around me, like in the movies where everything turns to slow motion. My head rotates at the exact time his chin rises, meeting me in direct eye contact. It's almost electrifying as we lock eyes. I nod as he smiles. This time the heat that flushes my body isn't the magic, it's attraction. It's fireworks. I know it. There's a spark between us still. He feels it too.

But this can't happen, at least not right now.

I quickly twist my head. Out of the corner of my eye, I catch Riley's face fall flat in rejection, just like on my couch, and my heart breaks all over again.

Tahlia yanks me out the door, and the world is once again chaotic with students bustling around me.

I'm disoriented as I haven't taken much time to get my bearings in my newish town. I've really only walked from my house to school and downtown. The rest of the time I've been in a car, so walking has me all turned around and confused.

I wait for Tahlia to guide the way. She takes the first left on Maple Street.

"It's only a twenty-minute walk to Jessa's house. The hill" —she nods to a boisterous bluff of trees ahead of us—"is a bitch, but it's the fastest way there."

When we're a good block from school, I finally dare to ask, "Do you think it's true that Sam Hornsby really drugged Megan? I obviously didn't know him well, but he seemed really nice and not like that."

Tahlia shrugs her shoulders, keeping a quick pace. "You think you know someone. But that could explain why I always got drunker at his parties than anywhere else. He could have been drugging everyone's drinks, for all we know. Plus, as sad as it sounds, this is a good thing. We're off the hook. I think."

I can't help but think of Margo passed out on the porch swing after a couple of drinks. So, maybe Sam is guilty, and that's one thing I can check off my list of things to feel bad about. This wasn't our fault. But what really happened?

A black vehicle slows to match our pace, catching me off guard. My heart bangs in my chest as my pace quickens to walk faster than the car. That whole stranger danger thing is engrained behavior, I suppose.

Tahlia grabs my hand, tugging me back.

"Dude, it's just Callen. You're on high alert, aren't you?" Tahlia responds lightheartedly.

Truth is, I am, but for some reason, knowing it's Callen still has my perception meter in full freak-out mode. We don't need anyone in our business right now; that's what Tahlia just said. And that's including her brother, whom I just met hours ago and don't trust yet.

The car comes to a complete stop, with the passenger window sliding down. Tahlia yanks me to the curb.

Callen stares wide-eyed at us, his velvety glare piercing through me, making my heart pump faster. "You two need a ride home?"

Just tell him no and let him be on his way.

"Yes, that'd be great, but we need to stop by Jessa's house. We want to check on her. Can you swing by there?" Tahlia responds.

"We should walk. Come on Tahlia," I whisper, yanking on her hand.

Say goodbye. Let's go.

Tahlia shakes my hand away, ignoring my request.

"I suppose I can do that. I really shouldn't because of this morning, but I guess I'm feeling generous," Callen says with a hint of deviance, making me uncomfortable.

"Wait. Shouldn't you still be at work?" Tahlia nods for me to get into the back seat.

"Yes, and that's another reason I'm being way too generous with the two of you. My boss said since I was so late today, I got cut first. He said I clearly didn't care about my hours, or I would have been on time," Callen snarls at Tahlia as she slams the door closed.

"I already said I'm sorry, Callen. You don't have to give us a ride. We can walk." Tahlia reaches for the door handle, but he steps on the gas, pulling back into the lane of traffic, causing Tahlia to rock backward into her seat.

"Geez, Callen," Tahlia says, irked.

He turns up the music, tuning out his sister.

Sitting quietly in the back. I notice Callen changed his clothes since this morning. He's now wearing a black hoodie and jeans. I thought he came from work. Plus, it's hot as hell for his attire. This family is so strange. Will I ever be able to figure them out?

My phone jostles in my bag. I reach down and pull it out.

Tahlia: Hey, Callen can be nosey. Stay in the car with him. I'll check on Jessa and the Jeep. We'll play this by ear.

"I heard some shit went down today at school. Sam Hornsby, huh?" Callen pumps the volume down on his stereo.

"Innocent until proven guilty," I respond. "Man, gossip spreads fast in this small town."

Callen turns his head slightly over his right shoulder, giving me a flat, unreadable, classic Latham-Hart stare before returning his eyes back to the road.

"Oh, he's guilty. I'm sure of it," he responds.

"You think?" Tahlia questions.

"Duh, T. He's such a creep. He can't get a girl on his own, so he resorts to drugging girls to sleep with him."

I don't know why I keep wanting to defend Sam. Maybe because no one gave me the benefit of the doubt with Sondra. It benefits me and my friends greatly if he's guilty, but for some reason, I can't help but feel in my gut that he's innocent.

I glance down at my phone vibrating in my hand.

Tahlia: Hello?

Izzy: OK, fine. But I thought we didn't want anyone in our business?

Tahlia: Sorry, I really didn't want to huff it up that hill. It will be fine. Don't stress, just keep him busy. Jessa annoys him, so I doubt he'll want to come in anyway.

Izzy: Should we text Margo the plan?

Tahlia: We will once we ditch Callen and I assess the Jeep.

A discomfort nestles inside of me. Alone with Callen. That seems worse than being alone with Tahlia.

A couple of minutes later, Callen pulls down Jessa's long driveway.

Tahlia hops out. "I'm just going to be a few minutes. Izzy is going to wait in the car with you, so you don't leave us."

"Good." Callen's lips curl into a mischievous grin.

Tahlia slams the door shut, leaving me stirring in my seat, wondering what Callen's deal is. Tahlia wouldn't leave me alone with her brother if he were dangerous. Would she?

I stare out the window, willing Tahlia to come back, but it seems we aren't that connected. Instead, she tucks herself under the garage door that's ajar, just as we left it hours ago.

Now I'm all alone with Callen.

"You should move up front with me," Callen suggests.

I shift around in my seat, uncomfortable by his request. Nervously, I tuck my hair behind my ears as I debate how to answer him. I'd rather stay in the back seat, but I don't want to be rude.

"Um, sure. I guess I could do that," I faintly respond.

As I slip into the front seat, Callen twists his head to face me. His expression is one I can finally read: serious. He stares at me for a few moments before speaking. "So, you're Isobel's great-granddaughter." He lays it out there like it's more of a fact than a question.

My stomach twists. "I never told you that," I say, jumping into defense mode.

"You didn't have to."

"Oh, I know everyone in town thinks—"

Callen cuts me off. "No, it's not that."

I gulp, buying time, afraid to ask. "Then how did you know?"

A smirk floats across his face. "Let me show you."

I'm stunned as he so freely grabs my hands. I'm surprised at how soft and smooth they are as they fully cup mine. He pauses briefly, closes his eyes, and pulls in a long, deep breath.

My hands vibrate within his grip. It's like a surge of energy is encompassing my cells, zipping back and forth at a pace too quick to be humanly possible.

Callen's face hardens like he's concentrating so hard it hurts. His brows pinch as his face scrunches. I'm jostled back into my seat by a wave of heat forcing its way up my left arm. It moves across my back, down my right arm, then vacates my body through my fingertips.

I don't move.

I stay still, afraid to admit anything happened.

Is he trying to prove I'm a witch? Is he messing with me? Trying to out me? But why?

I attempt to slide closer to the door, but he grabs both my wrists with one hand, locking me in his grip, pulling me closer; now just inches away from my face.

"Did you feel that?" he asks, his breath warm on my skin.

"Of course I felt that. How could I not?" The words fly out of my mouth as I yank my hands back, this time freeing myself.

Shoot.

I shouldn't have said that.

Now he knows.

I want to reel the words back in. I want to leap out of the car and run away and never look back. I let my hand find the door handle while keeping my eyes locked on Callen's velvety stare.

"I'm like you, Izzy."

Curiosity wraps its little hands around me, but I keep my fingers clutched on the handle, ready to run. "Like me, like how?"

The corner of Callen's mouth tugs upward, like it's being yanked up with a string. "I can sense my own kind, if you know what I'm saying."

"No, I don't know what you're saying."

He leans in, tucks the hair that's fallen loose behind my left ear and whispers, "Do you need me to spell it out for you?"

I pull back, confused by his words.

He tilts his head, leaning back in, his breath hot on my neck as he slowly murmurs in my ear. "I'm a W-I-T-C-H."

CHAPTER 28
TRUST NO ONE

I'm frozen in my seat, afraid to move.

Did he say what I think he said? The hairs on my arms stand erect like little soldiers obeying orders.

"Izzy, do you understand what I'm confessing to you?" Callen asks.

There is no way he's a witch. I can't breathe. This is all too much. I have enough to worry about. I can't deal with this.

"I'm a witch, Izzy. Well, actually, I'm a warlock—a male witch—but I'm just like you."

The color drains from my face.

"I'm not a witch," I respond. Denying it seems like the proper thing to do. That's what you're supposed to do when accused of being a witch, right?

"You don't have to do that with me, Izzy."

"Do what, Callen?"

"You can't argue with facts. You said you felt it too."

"I lied."

"Stop playing. We don't have much time before Tahlia gets back."

Oh, Tahlia. I forgot she's alone with Jessa and that's the situation I expected to be handling right now. Not this. I need to go check on them. I need to get out of this car now.

"Stop trying to think of ways to get out of this conversation," Callen says confidently, like he's reading my mind.

I flash him a frustrated expression. "You aren't a witch. That can't be possible. You're messing with me."

"Why not? You're a witch, so why can't I be one too? Let's stop this song and dance. I admitted to you I'm a witch, and for the rest of this conversation, we're going to pretend that for all intents and purposes, you are too. OK? Just humor me."

My fingers loosen around the door handle and drop to my side. "Well, if we're going to pretend"—I pause, taking a deep breath through my nose—"how many fucking witches are there in this town? It's not like we're in Salem, Massachusetts in 1692."

Callen laughs. "We may as well be."

I give him a puzzled look.

"East Gate may as well be the new Salem," he responds. "And we need to be careful."

All the air feels like it's being pulled from my lungs. This isn't what I expected today. I've been naïve to think only my family and clique were tuned into this world. The world where magic, curses, and witches exist.

I swallow hard, preparing to ask my next question. I need to know. "Is Tahlia a witch?"

"That's a tricky question, with a really long answer that we don't have time for right now. It's complicated."

"Half-breed," the words slither off my tongue.

"I guess that's one way to put it. Where did you hear that?"

"My grandma, Anna Beswick."

"Fucking Anna!" He rubs his temples.

"You know her?"

"You could say that."

"You need to tell me what's going on now!" I demand.

"Fine, but the second my sister comes back, you shut up and don't mention anything to her. You got it?"

I nod.

"So, T doesn't know about our family. She has strong feelings and urges she can't explain. I also had them. Why do you think she's so bitchy all the time? It's not just teenage hormones rushing through her body."

"So, she's a witch?"

"Keep listening, Beswick."

"I am—I was a half-breed, as you call it. I was half witch and half"—he glances out the window, pulling in a long breath before returning his gaze to me—"half hunter."

"Hunter?" I shakily question.

The spell. A hunter must fall. *Kill all the hunters, Izzy.*

"My mom is a witch hunter, and my dad is a witch."

"Well, that's got to make things difficult. How the hell does that work?" I question, but as I'm saying the words, I realize the severity of them. A hunter hunts witches—hunts me.

"We don't have time for that story right now. It's not important. What's important is that their offspring—me and my sister—we were born with half witch and half hunter blood. Both sides pretty much lying dormant until we turn eighteen. On a hybrid's eighteenth birthday, one side will prevail as the dominant side."

"And your dominant side is a witch?"

"Yes. I don't even feel the hunter side of myself anymore."

I stare dumbfounded at Callen. I'm at a loss for words. Witches—hunters—what else is real?

"When does Tahlia turn eighteen?"

"November first."

"So, what if the hunter side takes over? I'm so confused. I have so many questions about hunters and your family."

"We'll deal with that when the time comes, but I need you to understand. Izzy, there is so much more we must talk about, and I'll tell you everything, but Tahlia could be back any minute now. You need to know that I could feel your presence since you arrived. So, that means others can feel you too, and they'll be looking for you."

I give Callen a puzzled look.

"I sensed you were here, but I didn't know who you were, if that makes sense. When you walked into The Perk a few days ago, I felt an electric charge in the air. You immediately piqued my curiosity, but I didn't know for sure until we touched. Then it was unmistakable."

"Wow, that's intense. But what others, and why me?"

"Hunters and other witches. See, a witch's bloodline weakens over time—watered down through the generations, but you, Izzy, you're almost as pure as they come. You're fourth generation, which is nearly impossible considering it's the twenty-first century, and the most powerful witches lived in the seventeenth century. Your ancestor, Isobel, hung out in hiding for so long, keeping her bloodline the closest to pure there is."

"Oh," I respond, swallowing the lump that's made its way up my throat. "You sure know a lot."

"I eavesdrop a lot and I'm a witch, so I have my ways of getting info. I'm nosey, like my sister said."

"How?" I think back to our private text message moments ago. There is no way he could have seen the screen.

"I have my ways, and now that you're here, my magic is more powerful. The moment you arrived, everything changed for me. I felt it in the air, just as others are probably feeling it too."

Margo. She felt it. I don't let her name slip. Callen is from a family of hunters, so I don't know how much I can trust him. I need to keep Margo safe. Maybe even from one of her best friends—Tahlia, the possible hunter.

"You'll have to forgive me, but all of this sounds so crazy. A few months ago, I had no idea witches were real, I mean, for all intents and purposes."

Callen laughs, and for the first time, I'm really seeing him. His laugh lingers in the air, cutting through the tension, and I can't help but giggle.

"Yes, for all intents and purposes. Witches and hunters are very real," I respond, agreeing with Callen. "So, I need more history on the hunters. Who's the original hunter? How did all of this start?"

"All I can say is you need to be careful who you trust. You need to be just as suspicious of everyone around you as you were of me a few moments ago. Don't let your guard down so quickly next time. It could mean your life if you do."

My phone vibrates in my lap, annoying me, because for once I'm getting some answers. I need to keep this conversation going. I have a million questions.

Who should I not trust? What else does he know about Anna and Isobel? Is my dad safe? Who are the hunters? Does he know about the bloodline curse? Am I in danger? Are my friends in danger? What about Tim Hawkins?

My phone vibrates again. I can't forget about Jessa's Jeep and our situation.

"Sorry, this could be important."

Tahlia: Ditch Callen and Hurry!
Tahlia: Now! IZZY!

"Looks like you need to go?" Callen says.

"How?" I question, but I know it's useless. He has his ways. . .

"Just be careful, and like I said, trust no one."

"So, I shouldn't trust you?" I joke.

Callen gives me a smirk. "Beswick, you're going to be a pain in my ass, I can feel it. Now go. My sister needs you."

CHAPTER 29
MAKE IT RIGHT

I press my fingers into my eyes, pushing hard, swirling them around a few times. I blink rapidly before letting my gaze rest on Jessa's Jeep a second time.

It's fucking normal.

How?

I catch myself about to release a laugh. Because of course nothing is as it seems lately. I need to stop asking how because I'm pretty sure I know my answer—magic.

Maybe I should ask why instead.

So, why was Jessa's Jeep a tangled mess of Megan's hair, flesh, and blood? And now, absolutely nothing? There is no way Jessa had time to get it fixed.

Wait! Where are the girls?

I assumed they'd be in the garage.

"Hello," I call out, but no response.

I exit out the rear door, the one I saw Jessa leave through this morning, crossing over some lush grass that's greener than Tahlia's eyes, even on magic. I knock on the sliding glass door, but my impatience gets the best of me.

"Hello," I yell, entering a three seasons room that looks like something Martha Stewart decorated herself. "Jessa. Tahlia. Mr. and Mrs. Dewitt. Is anyone home?"

I cautiously step into the next room. "Hello!" I shout louder, hoping I don't have to go room by room until I find someone. "It's me, Izzy. Where are you?"

"Upstairs," Tahlia's voice calls. But something sounds off about her tone.

"I'm coming," I shout, leaping up the steps, taking them two at a time.

The first door at the top of the elaborate wooden staircase is cracked open with a dim light leaking onto the oak flooring.

"Tahlia?" I slowly push the door open.

Oh my, what's that smell? It's rancid. I yank my shirt over my nose, but it doesn't help. I take a deep breath and step into the room.

First, I spot Tahlia sitting up against the farthest wall, her knees pulled tight to her chest. Her mossy green eyes are wide and fear ridden as tears swim down her cheeks. Panic sets in as I follow her line of sight. Jessa's body is curled up on the floor with her blonde hair fanned around her head, nearly blending in with the porcelain tiles.

"Jessa," I say, stepping over her. She doesn't respond.

My shirt slips below my nose, and I gag.

"What the hell is that smell?"

"Look," Tahlia says, her hand extended toward the toilet.

I hold my breath and reluctantly peer down into the bowl. Black chunks, just like a couple nights ago, float in the water that's turning darker by the second. "What the hell?" I lean over the toilet reaching toward the lever, ready to flush it down to extricate the putrid smell.

"Don't." Tahlia shrieks. "We need to figure out what it is and why she keeps throwing it up."

"She needs a doctor," I respond, pushing down on the lever, ignoring her request.

I step back, this time plugging my nose with my fingers until all the black chunks are whooshed away. I release my fingers and gag again, as the smell hasn't quite dissipated. The air is thick and stagnate.

"It's like her magic hangover," Tahlia says.

"I know, I was there," I snap, but immediately regret my tone. "Sorry, I didn't mean for it to come out like that. I'm just scared."

Tahlia nods. "I know, me too."

"Jessa, sweetie. What's going on? You need to talk to us," I coax her.

She garbles something incoherent and tries to leverage her body up but doesn't get very far before falling flat.

"Izzy, I found her like this," Tahlia says, her eyes reddened from the swarm of tears streaming down her face.

I can't help but think about what her brother said. Soon, she could be a hunter. This friendship could be over when it's just beginning, and now I want to cry. I can't lose Jessa and Tahlia.

I wipe the tear that's attempting to escape my eye. "I don't know what those chunks are, but she's probably severely dehydrated if she's been puking like this for a while. I doubt she will be able to keep anything down, but we should try. We have to do something."

I spot a glass sitting by the sink and fill it with water, while Tahlia tries to move Jessa to a sitting position. She can hardly keep her head up as I coax the cup to her chapped and cracked lips. She takes a few tiny sips and slinks back down to the floor.

"When do her parents get home?" I ask.

"They're workaholics. Probably late, like always," Tahlia responds.

"Should we call them?"

"No," Jessa mumbles.

"We can't just let you die here," I respond. "What do you suggest we do? This isn't normal."

Jessa slurs out a few incoherent syllables.

"Jessa, please. Let me call a doctor," I plead.

"Magic," Jessa spits out. "The book," she puffs.

"Is she asking us to do a spell?" Tahlia asks.

Jessa moves her head slowly up and down.

"I think that's a yes," I respond. "But I don't think magic is the answer. It's what got us into this mess in the first place. It has to be."

"Please." Jessa pulls on the fabric of my shirt. Her face is pale, and her eyes are dull.

"No, this isn't a good idea. You need a medical professional. I can't do this."

I hold the cup to her mouth again, and Jessa lets a few more drops of water slide into her mouth.

"Tahlia, did you see the Jeep is fine now?" I ask.

"Yes, I was shocked, but maybe what we saw earlier wasn't real and it was punishment for doing the spell wrong. Maybe we need to try again—make it right. Plus, what are we going to say to a doctor?"

She's right. What would we say? *We did magic, and our friend is suffering the consequences. We didn't have a hunter's blood, and I'm not a high priestess.* The doctor would take one look at us and send us for a psych evaluation. I don't think modern medicine has a cure for witchcraft gone wrong.

"OK, so if I decide to go along with your idea, how are we going to make it right? We're running out of time by the looks of it," I reply.

"I think we need to go back to your house. Get the book and figure it out."

"We can't take her like this. She can't even stand up."

"Well, good thing we're getting used to dragging people. This isn't our first time," Tahlia responds with a small smile.

"Sad but true."

"Text Margo that we're picking her up. We can take the Jeep since it's fine. You did tell Callen to go, right?"

"I think it was assumed," I respond.

The wheels are in motion now, leaving me no time to question our decision further.

We pull Jessa up, swinging her arms around our shoulders. Her head hangs limp, letting her straight hair cascade down, dangling toward her feet.

"Jessa, you need to help us if we're going to get you down the steps," Tahlia says.

I'm huffing by the time we make it the few feet to the

staircase. Going down the stairs won't be easy. We begin our descent, letting Jessa's feet drag, hitting each step harder than the last as we rush down the steps, not letting our momentum be stopped, or we will all fall. Jessa is going to have a few bruises, that's for sure. Sorry for that, Jessa.

We drag her out the door and across the patch of grass and into the garage. We shove her body into the back seat. I don't do it with grace because I'm too exhausted, and I know I'm going to have to do it again when we get to my house. At least we will have Margo to help us.

I send Margo a text.

Izzy: URGENT: Coming to get you. NOW.

Three little dots flash on my screen.

Margo: OK. I'll be waiting.

CHAPTER 30
MAGICAL ILLUSIONS

We make it through the back roads to Margo's house in record time. I mean, what do I expect with Tahlia driving? She's a wild woman behind the wheel.

As expected, Margo is waiting for us when we pull up. I want to jump out of the car to prepare Margo for what she's about to see, but there isn't time.

"What the hell?" Margo screams, opening the door to the sight of Jessa curled up in the back, with her head lying in the middle seat.

"Eh, as you can see, the Jeep is fine now and well, Jessa, she's. . . not. The chunks are back," I respond.

"Where are we taking her?" Margo questions. "You better say the E.R."

"Not exactly. She won't let us. She wants to try a spell, and what the hell would we tell a doctor?" Tahlia responds.

"Have the two of you lost your minds?" Margo squeals.

Maybe we have.

"Izzy and I think maybe that's the answer. We played with magic and there are consequences. We need to fix what we did. We need to make it right," Tahlia adds.

"And what spell exactly are we going to do to help her?" Margo snarls.

"I haven't thought that far ahead. I'm sure the right spell will appear. The book will sense we're in trouble, and it will show us the way," Tahlia responds with certainty in her voice.

"Yes, but the spell might be the reason she's in trouble. Remember, she's not like us," Margo says, nodding to Jessa.

"We're strong together. We can fix her. We have to try," Tahlia says. "You guys, what should I do? The turn for the hospital is coming up. Do I turn or keep going straight to Izzy's house?"

"Straight," Jessa wails.

"Turn!" Margo shouts. "Turn now!"

Jessa moans and crunches her body tighter until she's coiled into a smaller ball.

"Jessa, this can't be what you want," Margo says, running her hand over Jessa's head.

"Izzy's house," she says quietly between moans.

"Fine, go straight, but if she doesn't get better within five minutes of doing a stupid spell, we're taking her to a professional," Margo says.

Even when Jessa's incapacitated, we still take orders from our leader.

I glance back and offer Margo a smile, trying to give her some comfort. "It's going to be OK," I say, but I have no clue if that's the case.

"So, Sam Hornsby?" Tahlia says, drastically shifting the conversation in the car.

"I'm sorry about this morning. Accusing you girls of murdering Megan," Margo replies. "I should have listened to you."

"No, Margo, we're sorry. We shouldn't have kept that secret from you. It was horrible of us. If it makes you feel any better, it was eating me alive inside," I respond.

"Good, it should have," Margo says, her voice cracking.

I frown, feeling the pangs of disappointment creeping in. "I'm sorry for all of this. Megan shouldn't have died. I really hate to say this because Sam killing Megan lets us off the hook, but I don't think he did it."

"Izzy, that hurts. Why would you say that? I finally have some closure, no matter how horrible it is. I know Sam killed Megan, and it wasn't this fucking Jeep that ran her over. She had drugs in her system when she died, the same ones that were found in his locker. I can't think of any other possibilities right now," Margo says.

"I'm sorry for upsetting you, but I feel Sam is innocent. It's hard to explain, but the more I think about it, the more an awful feeling weaves through my stomach. It wasn't him."

"Drop it, Izzy. Please," Margo pleads.

"Sure, Margo. I'm sorry," I respond.

"So, I hate to add to this, but why do you think the car changed? I'm sorry Margo, but we have to discuss this."

"I don't know. It's so confusing. All of this is so God darn confusing. It's like a magical illusion. Fine one minute and wrecked the next, then back to fine. Kinda like Jessa. She was fine for a while too," I respond.

"I think our clock is ticking. We need to figure this mystery out before things change again," Tahlia says, speeding through town.

When we arrive at my house, I'm relieved to see it's only four o'clock and my dad's not home yet, but he should be soon. So, we need to hurry.

"We need a plan of attack," Margo says.

"I wonder if we should go into the forest. That's where all this started. Plus, if my dad sees Jessa, he will take her to the hospital. You two can start getting Jessa back there, and I'll meet you. I need to grab the book and the other items," I tell the girls.

"OK. I think you're right. But how are we going to get her into the forest? She's getting weaker by the second," Tahlia asks.

Tahlia's right. This will be a grueling task. I scan my yard for anything to help us get Jessa there quicker. An old wheelbarrow leaning up against the house seems like the most convenient option.

"Use the wheelbarrow over there, and I'll meet you at the back door."

I don't offer to help the girls get Jessa up the steps; I've done that task enough times to last a lifetime.

"Hurry," Tahlia calls to me as I leap up the front steps.

I toss my key in the door, quickly turning it. I let my bag fall to the floor. I know time is precious, and I need to act with haste.

On the third level, I retrieve my book and the other items. Now I need to find our knife. Let's hope whatever brought our items back inside left the knife in a place I can find it.

In the kitchen, I open the drawer nearest the stove where I found it the first time. It's not there. I open the next two drawers. It's not there either.

Where's that knife?

The floor groans above me.

"Hello. Dad, is that you?"

No response.

I don't know if I'll ever get used to this creepy old house and all its noises. I don't have time for this.

I continue searching each drawer for our knife. I know any knife will do, but I want that knife. It should be here.

The floor groans again, this time with unmistakable heavy footsteps. The sound ceases near the back stairwell, the one that leads from Dad's wing into the kitchen.

I pause, letting all my motions come to a halt. I try to quiet my breath.

I'm not imagining things. Someone is in the house.

Panic surges through my veins.

The movement shifts to the wooden staircase as a creak indicates someone is coming.

Fire burns in my hand, and fear takes over every cell of my body. I slowly reach to the counter, grabbing the second largest knife from the knife block.

I need to run. I know it. I feel it.

The wood creaks again, getting closer. I take a step toward the screen door, leading out to my friends, who should be arriving any second now.

I take another cautious step to the door.

The creak is getting closer.

"Are you looking for this?" a familiar voice asks. The missing kitchen knife shines in his hands as he brandishes it in front of himself.

CHAPTER 31
SURPRISE

All the blood leaves my face as I stumble backward. My hand searches for the counter to keep me steady. My body stiffens as I freeze in shock.

"Let me repeat myself. Is this what you're looking for, Izzy?"

Tim Hawkins is standing at the bottom of the stairwell holding the knife—our knife. He's deviously twisting it in his hand, taunting me.

"How?" is all I can spit out.

"Oh, Izzy. Don't think for a second I didn't know what was going on here. I sensed you the moment you pulled up to this shithole of a house," Tim sneers.

Callen said I have to keep my guard up. I must play dumb. I can't trust anyone—even Tim Hawkins.

"What are you talking about?"

"Cut the bullshit. I know what you are, and I have to protect this town. It's my job," Tim says, tapping at his badge.

"I don't think your Sergeant would appreciate you terrorizing teenagers. I highly doubt that's your job," I quip.

Tim lets out a maniacal laugh, shaking me to my core. "Funny thing about that, Izzy; I'm not talking about the law here, and you know that too, don't you?"

"No, I have no idea what you're talking about."

Tim nods to my spellbook with a devilish grin.

"Oh, that silly thing. I found it. There's a lot of interesting stuff in this old house. You should know that. You're here all the time."

"So, you mean to tell me there isn't witches' blood on this knife?" Tim flaunts the knife in front of me.

In the back of my mind, the pieces slowly weave themselves together. Tim was the first to respond to our call about the intruder. He's been here watching us, pretending to be my dad's friend. He warned Riley about me and maybe not just because of Sondra. He stole Isobel's diary. The diary that's currently sticking out of his back pocket. He came back for it. What does he want with it? It's hardly readable to a normal person. Was he watching us in the forest too? How else would he know what we did with that knife?

The sound of rusty hinges causes me to divert my attention to the back door.

Tahlia's voice calls out, "Izzy, hurry! Jessa's fading."

"Jessa," I gasp, nearly forgetting about my mission to save my friend.

Tim doesn't waste any time, taking my momentary distraction as a sign of weakness and lunging toward me. He pulls me tight, twisting my right arm behind my body.

"Tim, you're hurting me!"

He ignores my cries for sympathy as he scoops up the

book and my bag of items, pushing me out the door.

Tahlia and Margo's eyes widen. This isn't the view they were expecting. But as Tim walks past them, the girls don't move; instead, their glare stays focused behind me. I keep my head twisted behind as Tim pushes me forward.

My mouth involuntarily falls open.

"Riley!" My voice catches as I shout. A glimmer of hope flutters inside of me. "Riley, please help us! Your dad has lost his mind."

Riley drops his gaze as he reaches around the door and pulls out several long zip-ties. The kind police officers use when they don't have enough handcuffs.

"Tie them up," Tim directs his son.

"No!" I scream. "Riley, you don't have to do this," I plead.

Riley keeps his head down, avoiding eye contact with all of us as he ties up my friends.

I kick at Tim, trying to free myself, but he twists my arm harder, pressing it into my back.

"Keep your mouth shut, or this is going to get a whole lot worse for all of you," Tim hisses.

Tears race down my cheeks as Tim forces us into the forest.

"Walk," he directs me.

Tahlia and Margo are sniffling behind, one on each side of Riley, who's pushing Jessa. Her face is gray and sickly. We need to do something, or she's going to die, but neither Hawkins seems to care about the poor girl.

Tears snake down my cheek. I can't believe this is happening. Why are they doing this to us?

A soft whimper comes from behind.

Is that Riley?

I slowly twist my head, and for a moment, Riley's eyes crease in pain. He's suffering. I don't think he wants to hurt us.

"Keep your eyes forward. I have a surprise for you," Tim says.

"Oh, great. I love surprises," I say sarcastically.

Rushing water and the familiar scent of the mossy trees flood my senses. My stomach twists because I know where he's taking us. But why does he want to go to our circle?

Tim pushes me into the clearing. Our magical space is just as we left it.

Except now, there's something in the middle.

I squint my eyes, trying to focus on the object in the center. The sun shines brightly through the trees, obstructing my view.

Riley leads the girls into the circle. He picks up Jessa and gently lays her down outside the ring. I find hope in the kindness he shows Jessa.

Tim, however, shoves me inside my sacred place and pushes my face into the grass. He grabs a zip-tie from his pocket and ties me up. I struggle as I try to face the object in the center.

Tahlia shrieks and I jerk my head up, but Tim presses it back down. I can't see a thing.

"Anna! Izzy, it's your grandma!" Tahlia squeals.

"No, she said she was leaving," I cry out.

"Surprise!" Tim shouts. "I sensed she was here, so I snuck over to your house on Saturday, and to my delight, Anna was cleaning up your mess. I found her on the third floor, stuffing your items in your hide-a-hole, and I just couldn't resist," Tim says, letting go of his grip on me. He stealthily moves to Anna, who's slumped over, placing the knife on her shoulder.

Anna doesn't move.

"So, I thought how fun would it be to kill two witches with one blade? Izzy, did you know killing a witch with her own blood actually hurts worse? You wouldn't think so, but it does. It stings longer and draws out the pain and prolongs the death. And since your bloodline is connected, Anna is going to feel the pain too," Tim sadistically says.

How does he know this?

"Please, don't! You don't have to do this," I beg.

Tim ignores me. He snickers to himself and repositions the knife above Anna's chest. "Killing a second-generation witch is going to be pure bliss, but killing a fourth-generation witch at the same time is going to be icing on the cake. Too bad you two weren't here when I killed Isobel, but either way, I'm killing off a dynasty one by one. Keeping this town safe."

His words hit me harder than a blow to the stomach. That's not true. Isobel died of old age. Didn't she? This can't be true.

"What about my dad? Are you going to hurt him too?" I ask.

"Oh, Izzy. Don't you see? Your dad has never responded to the dark magic calling him. I've been keeping an eye on him for years. He will be safe as long as he doesn't respond. I can't act unless he shows signs of magic. You, however, opened yourself up to receive their calling. So, this is all your fault. If you wouldn't have been so eager to fall into the darkness, I wouldn't have to kill you."

"You can't kill us. That's murder!" I shout.

"Like I said before, it's my job. It's what I, or should I say we"—Tim nods to Riley—"do. We're hunters and we must extricate all witches by any means necessary. Fun fact, Izzy. Did you know that when a hunter kills a witch, they actually get stronger? Imagine how strong I'm going to be after killing two bloodline witches. Well, maybe three." Tim nods to Margo.

"We'll see what comes of you. I might need you later," Tim says to Tahlia. An eager smile beams across his face.

Tahlia's expression shifts from fear to confusion, but I know what he's referencing. Tahlia might be a hunter too. I can't imagine her like Tim—a thirst to kill. But that won't matter if I'm dead.

Margo gasps. "A hunter's blood. A hunter must fall," she whispers, but I think Tahlia and I are the only ones who hear her. She's recalling our spell.

If only we could take down Tim before he takes us down.

"Izzy, I have no choice. It's what a hunter does. He hunts, and he kills witches. It's not murder if it's for survival and the greater good." Tim pushes the tip of the blade into Anna's pale, wrinkly skin.

"Dad. Don't!" Riley hollers, his voice catching in his throat.

"Riley, we talked about this. You don't have a choice. This is our responsibility. You'll understand soon enough. You can't fight it. It will take over and control you. It's in our blood. Once that tattoo is fully formed on your eighteenth birthday, then you'll understand. You'll feel it too. You're so close now. Just five more days."

The tattoo I saw in my bedroom. It was a hunter's tattoo. Did he know what was happening to him? Was he keeping me at bay for my protection?

"I'm begging you, Dad. Please don't kill Anna. I'll never speak to you again."

"Riley, I have to," Tim says with conviction.

Anna doesn't fight. She doesn't even flinch.

My fire burns hot inside of me. "Anna, wake up! Please, Anna. Just fight," I plead.

Tim's expression shifts to a predatory grin as he slides the blade downward, piercing Anna's skin. Blood trickles from the incision as he pushes further into her chest and down toward her heart.

"No!" I scream. "Anna, no!"

CHAPTER 32
IT WAS YOU

My body convulses as a hum of vibrations strum through my head. I desperately tug at my hands to cover my ears, but they're tied.

Make it stop.

The humming escalates until I can't hear anything else.

"What's happening?" I shout, but no one answers.

I press my eyes closed with tears fighting to escape. When I raise my eyelids, I'm standing, gazing down at the forest floor, seeing my body tied up. It's just like my strange dream in the foyer on my first day in East Gate.

Everyone is frantic, but I can't hear their words.

Flashes of light flare around me, coming at me from every direction. Visions race through my mind. But these visions don't belong to me.

They're not my memories—they're Anna's.

Her life is flashing before my eyes.

An angelic voice purrs next to me, and the humming stops, ceasing all other movement, pausing the world. "We don't have much time."

Anna extends her hand, and I grab it. She squeezes it tightly, and our fire forges together, burning hotter than anything I've ever felt.

"Watch," she says.

Just like my movie reel of nightmares from the day in the forest, her life plays out in front of us.

Quick flashes of Anna as a little girl with Isobel light up my reel. Then it shifts to Anna and my dad as a baby. He giggles as Anna tickles his fat belly.

Anna caresses the hair away from my face, tucking it behind my ear. She leans in and whispers, "Find Jonathan Kent." She pulls back and smiles.

I lock that name into my memory. I nod and the reel continues.

The next scenes flash rapidly, firing one after another, making me almost dizzy.

Anna, Isobel, and my dad in Isobel's house.

Anna and Isobel fighting.

Anna holding me as a baby.

Anna and my mother.

Isobel's funeral.

My mom's funeral.

I'm lightheaded by the sudden bursts when something shifts.

I'm no longer seeing Anna's memories. I'm seeing my own. It's the forest. The day Sondra died.

But something isn't right. Something feels off.

Wait, it isn't my memory.

"Look behind you," Anna says, turning my head.

Anna is on the trail behind us on that horrible day. But how? Her long gray hair blows wildly in the wind as she extends her hand, palm forward, and pushes. This time, the energy changes around us. The colors of the forest grow deeper as the magic swirls, building a force that keeps growing until it hits Sondra.

"Izzy, no!" Sondra calls out.

I gasp, pulling in a puff of breath that nearly chokes me, catching the entire way down my throat.

"It wasn't me; it was you," I whimper. "She didn't see you. I didn't see you."

"I always protect my family," Anna says, with tears flowing down her pale cheeks.

"Why did you do it?"

"She was going to hurt you."

"That's not possible. She wasn't capable of hurting me. Emotionally, yes. But physically, no," I cry.

"You need to think back. You were close to those girls until one day you weren't. You did nothing wrong, child, but you saw a shift in her feelings toward you. Didn't you?"

I nod.

"Sondra is a hunter."

"Sondra," I gasp. "No, that's not true."

"She was turning fast, changing, and almost eighteen."

Thoughts of Riley and Tahlia tug on my heart. If my friend Sondra changed so quickly, then they can too.

"Her thirst to kill was growing stronger every day. You needed me. I felt it and I came."

"Why couldn't I remember?"

"Your mind blocked out what it couldn't understand. Once you moved here and knew who you were—a witch—I tried helping you remember."

"The video. It was you?"

Anna nods.

"Where did the video go?"

"It never existed. It was magic. An illusion to help you understand it wasn't your fault."

"What if you got it wrong with Sondra?"

"You need to trust me. I saved your life. I'm always with you, Izzy."

She finally called me Izzy.

"Why were you so mean to me all this time? I thought you hated me."

"I never hated you. I pushed you away to protect you from all of this, but my mother called, and you answered. I was mad at her mostly, but it's in our blood. It's hard to deny the calling. Please keep my son safe. Never tell him any of this. It's for his own good, Izzy."

"I'll keep my dad safe. I promise."

"It's my time to go. I'm tired and I'm ready."

"I'm not ready for you to go."

"You need to find the truth. Not all Isobel's magic is good. She didn't care about all the men she hurt trying to undo that horrid curse. I don't have a father because of her."

"Robert Tucker," I whisper.

Anna nods. "Trust me when I say, she has other intentions in mind. Please, be careful with your calling. Watch out for the darkness," she says, her voice growing distant. "I've always loved you, child. The future of our bloodline is in your hands."

Her image slowly fades right before me, like she's evaporating in the wind.

"Anna, don't go. Don't leave me. I need you."

"Off-limits," her voice calls out, nearly inaudible. Her faint image winks as she completely disappears into thin air.

Off-limits. Anna must have been in Tahlia's ear, keeping things in line, watching out for me. It breaks my heart that I can't be with Riley, and Anna knew all along. It wasn't so I could protect Riley; it was so Riley didn't kill me. Anna was there, whispering magic into Tahlia's ear because she was open to receive it. Maybe there's hope for Tahlia becoming a witch, after all.

Tears flood down my cheeks, and I can't believe how emotional I am. I had no idea Anna loved me. She protected me, and I couldn't save her. Tim needs to pay for what he's done.

I cough, nearly choking on my uncontrollable sobs that keep catching in my throat. I'm coming back to the me that's on the forest floor.

I shift my eyes open, letting out a shrill scream.

The bloody knife is barreling toward my chest.

Tim's going to kill me.

Oh, hell no, this isn't how I'm going out.

I close my eyes tight, mustering up all my strength, pulling my feet into my chest, ready to kick Tim with all my force. The ground vibrates under me, channeling the earth below, pulling from the elements.

I propel my feet outward with a powerful force toward his stomach, but my feet fall hard, hitting the ground at an insanely painful speed.

I missed.

I flip my eyes open, searching for him. Where did he go?

A loud thud echoes through the trees, pulling my attention to a ball rolling near me.

No, it's not a ball.

It's Tim and Riley.

Riley propels Tim to the ground with a thunderous sound, pinning him underneath his body.

I rock myself forward to my feet, with no help from my tied hands.

"You can't hurt her. I have feelings for her," Riley cries, punching Tim in the jaw.

Feelings? He does care about me.

"Silly boy. Trust me when I say you'll have a different kind of feeling for her in five days," Tim taunts.

"Dad, you fucking killed Isobel—an old lady—now Anna. You've lost your mind. You monster," Riley roars, slugging his dad in the mouth.

Tim turns his head, spitting red. Blood.

"Riley, you don't know what you're doing," Tim says.

"Yes, I do," Riley responds, reacting by clocking his dad in the nose.

Thank goodness Riley is strong. While he's holding Tim at bay, I pivot my body, searching for the girls. They're huddled close together over Jessa. Tahlia's eyes are searching, almost looking through me.

I part my lips to speak, but Tahlia speaks first. "Callen?" she questions.

"What?" I quickly whip my head around, nearly making

myself dizzy. What's he doing here?

Callen rushes at us in a full sprint, reaching our circle quicker than I can process that he's here. He flashes me a quick charming smile before slamming into Riley, knocking him off Tim.

"I got this; trust me, you don't want to be the one who hurts him," Callen insists. He drops onto Tim's stomach, using both of his fists, alternating punches until he's fully knocked out. Blood spatters every which way.

Callen gets up, nursing his hands.

"Callen, how did you know?" Tahlia shouts.

"It's a long story." Callen winks at me.

CHAPTER 33
SO SHALL IT BE

Callen gives me a hero's grin as he saunters in my direction, leaving Riley kneeling next to Tim. "I told you I could sense you. We're connected," he says.

I childishly hold out my tied arms, hoping for a rescue. He reaches into his pocket, pulling out a pocketknife. As he cuts me free, he whispers, "I'm glad you're OK, Beswick."

Tahlia curiously eyes us but doesn't ask any questions. I know she will have a million of them. She and Margo anxiously hold out their arms as Callen makes his way to them with his knife.

"Well, this is a mess." Callen studies our circle of carnage.

"What do we do now?" Margo asks. "Jessa needs us, but we have to deal with them." Margo nods to the Hawkins men. "With the hunters," she hisses.

"And Anna," I add, with tears building in my eyes.

My heart drops, plummeting to my stomach, seeing her body slumped over, lifeless. All she wanted to do was protect me. I curl over, wincing in emotional pain, letting out an animalistic cry.

A warm, gentle hand caresses my back, soothing me. It's Margo. I turn to flash her a tender smile.

"I'm glad we're friends," I softly say, knowing her touch is absorbing and feeling my pain too.

"Me too," she says with her kind eyes, giving me the reassurance I desire.

"Girls, we don't have much time. I don't know how long Tim will be knocked out. I'll be right back. I have to make a call," Callen says, stepping away.

"OK. Back to Jessa," Tahlia says, directing our attention back to our first priority.

"They messed everything up," Margo says, seething.

"But maybe they didn't." I smile, pulling myself upright. "We need to stick to our plan and redo the spell. We have a real hunter's blood, and our hunter has fallen. Look, he's even in our damn circle. That's got to be bonus points. Our spell must work now," I say excitedly. "I feel it in my bones. We can help Jessa by undoing our damage. We were being punished, and this is our chance to fix it."

"OK, let's do it," Tahlia says.

"Start getting the circle prepped," I order the girls, catching Riley making his way over to me. I don't have any words for this—for what just happened—for him—the hunter.

"Riley… I'm… I'm so— I attempt to say, but he cuts me off.

"Izzy, I'm so sorry for my dad. I didn't think things would get this out of control. I had no idea. You must believe me." Riley gazes up at me with sorrowful eyes.

"I didn't want to help him. You must know that. He made me do it. I had no idea about our lineage. I just found out a few days ago. The day this stupid thing began to appear on my arm. I thought I was dying." Riley releases an uncomfortable laugh.

"I didn't fully understand, and I still don't. I can't be like him," he says, grabbing my hand that's zipping wildly with fire. "I'm falling hard for you, Izzy. I only wish you felt the same."

"Oh, Riley. I do feel the same," I say, letting my heart speak instead of my mind.

"Can I kiss you now?" he asks, leaning in.

I put my free hand up to his soft lips. "Not yet."

Riley pulls back, confused.

"I have something I need to take care of first. I have a three-century old curse that needs to be broken," I tell him.

"You know, a week ago I would have thought you were crazy saying that, but now I think anything's possible. What can I do to help?" he asks.

"Just watch your dad. Make sure he doesn't get up."

"All right, I can do that."

"I think we have everything we need to truly break the bloodline curse and save Jessa. Let's get started," I say to the group, who's almost done preparing our space with Jessa in the middle.

"I don't know if this will work. We don't have our fourth. Jessa's incapacitated—and a normie. Not special," Margo whispers as if Jessa can hear her. "We didn't think that through."

"I can be your fourth," Callen says, walking back into our circle.

Tahlia tosses him questioning eyes.

"Now isn't the time for questions," Callen says before Tahlia can even ask.

She nods, knowing our time is limited.

The four of us come together, huddling around Jessa. We each take our turn slicing our hand, letting our blood come together with the hunter's blood. I take the knife that's now coated with hunter's blood, our blood, and Anna's blood and forcefully drive the knife into the ground, feeling vibrations as it slides into the earth.

The four of us move closer into the perfect position, each extending our hands outward, letting the others grip them tightly.

Our circle is complete.

An energy that feels nothing like the first time electrifies me, causing all the hairs on my arm to stand erect. The energy whips through me, leaving my body and surging into Margo's body. It fully makes its way through each of us, returning to me in perfect harmony.

I can't help but know this is right. Callen is our fourth. We're all witches—at least for now. Tahlia is a half-breed, but it works. I feel it.

Tahlia begins our chant, calling out, "Earth."

Margo boisterously shouts, "Air."

I continue the spell. "Fire."

Callen says, "Water."

Together, now chanting, "Earth, air, fire, water."

The energy swirls through the middle of the circle, twisting up dust and twigs, bringing out the vibrant colors around us.

I recite the spell to undo the curse. This time, the clouds don't darken. Instead, the sun shines brighter. There isn't thunder or lightning. Instead, the birds sing songs, and the frogs croak to their harmony. A beautiful swarm of butterflies dance through our circle. We're fully connected to the elements.

As I open my mouth to say the final words, Jessa coughs and shifts on the ground. It's working.

One final question for thee.
Let this spell bring no curse or harm by spree.
By our coven, this spell is cast.
By the will of Hera, it will be fast.

So shall it be.

Color begins to restore in Jessa's face. Callen slowly lets his grip drop, bending down to Jessa. Margo and I join him, staying connected. As we approach her, her hair begins to shine, coming back to its full vibrancy.

We did it right. We broke the curse. We healed our friend.

"We did it," Tahlia says, crying.

"What's going on?" Jessa questions. "Did you do magic without me?"

The four of us break out into a joyous laugh. Typical Jessa. Never wanting to be left out, even when she's near death.

"Oh, sweetie, we have so much to tell you," Tahlia says, caressing her hair. "But first, you need to finish healing." She practically scoops her up like a baby, pulling her tight against her body.

A smile involuntarily spans across my face at the sight of them.

A long airy voice whispers, "You broke the curse."

This time, I know it's Anna's voice and not Isobel's. I can trust that we did it. Anna's still with me. I find comfort in that.

My stomach twists with the good kind of butterflies. My friends—or should I say, my coven—we did it. We broke the bloodline curse.

With that reassurance, I rush to Riley, who's staring in awe. I don't blame him. This stuff is weird. But I can't waste time explaining. We're on borrowed time. At any moment, his switch will flip, and he will have a new desire for me—a desire to kill me. A thirst to hunt. Sondra started to change before she turned eighteen. So, I know this moment could be my only chance.

I place both of my hands on his face, pulling him close. Riley locks his baby blue eyes on mine as he closes in on the space between us. He wraps his arm around my back, pulling me tightly against his chest. His heart pounds against mine.

He turns his head ever so slightly. "So, I can kiss you now?"

I eagerly nod.

Riley parts his lips as he inches closer. My heart is pumping hard against his chest, in sync with his. When our lips finally meet, his kiss is delicate, and he tastes sweet. Fire surges through my entire body, warning me, but I ignore the warning because I know, in this moment, Riley won't hurt me.

I tug him closer, kissing him harder as he glides his hand up my back.

"OK, get a room," Tahlia shouts.

Riley pulls away, moving his lips up, giving me a soft kiss on my forehead, letting our moment linger just a second longer. When I finally allow my attention to return to the group, because for a second in time, it was just me and him, I catch a glimpse of Callen's eyes falling to the ground.

Was he watching us?

I shake the thought and pull Riley back into my gaze. "Now, we need to figure out what to do with you being a hunter and your inevitable desire to kill me."

"About that," he says, letting that thought linger in the air.

"So, I hate to break up your moment, Izzy, but what should we do about Anna and Tim? Should we call the police?" Margo asks.

"I've taken care of that. My parents are on their way. They're trained for stuff like this," Callen says.

"What the. . ." Tahlia shouts.

"Like I said earlier, T. I have a lot to explain, but now isn't the time. Please trust me," Callen replies.

"Yes, you have a lot to explain," Tahlia says, with her hands resting on her hips.

"Hey, Tahlia," Riley calls out, summoning her to us. "Is this whole ordeal the reason you told me to stay away from Izzy at Sam's party? That she was off-limits and not to even think about it. You said she was too good for me."

Tahlia shrugs her shoulders, seemingly confused by his accusation. But I know there was someone whispering in her ear, keeping me safe, directing her, even if she didn't understand. I can't help but wonder if Riley was feeling other things for our friend. A hatred that he can't control about his half-breed buddy.

"I was so mad at you girls," Riley says, laughing. "I thought you were being snobby, and I'm sorry for that."

"Hey Izzy, can I talk to you for a second?" Callen says, pulling me away from Riley and Tahlia. He leads me far enough away that no one can hear us. What's so important right now that he can't share with the group?

"I have one more thing I need to tell you. You were right about Sam Hornsby," he says.

My mouth drops open, with no words escaping.

"He didn't drug Megan. I knew you girls were in trouble. Jessa really did hit Megan with her Jeep. I saw the whole thing when we touched this morning. The image of Megan moving around on the ground, and Isobel in your ear, telling you to run."

I'm frozen in place, afraid to move, wishing this was all just a dream. We had an out, but now I'm back to where I was hours ago—feeling guilty.

Callen takes a deep breath, gathering his thoughts. "I couldn't have you and my sister getting in trouble for that. The second I knew you were a bloodline witch, I knew I had to protect you and keep you safe. So, I forced some solo magic and planted the drugs in Sam's locker this morning after I dropped you off."

I'm at a loss for words, so I let my expression speak for me, giving him questioning eyes.

"I did a spell. I honestly had no idea if it would work. I've never tried anything so big before. I willed the toxicology report to come back with the same drugs I planted in Sam's locker. I'm so sorry, but I had to do it."

"Callen, how could you do that to Sam?"

"He's still not as innocent as you think. Where do you think I got the drugs? They were his. They might not have killed Megan, but they could have killed someone. You can't tell the others, though; this has to stay between us."

"Callen, how am I supposed to keep that from them? The first time nearly killed me keeping that from Margo."

"You have to, or we'll all be found out. It's not just about you girls now. It's about the magic, and if anyone else finds out, you could be killed."

"OK, I understand. I'll keep the secret. But how can I hide my visions from them? You saw everything when we touched. Why hasn't Margo seen the secrets I kept from her?"

"I'm not certain, but you're a strong witch. Stronger than any of us. You had your guard up around Margo. You were protecting that secret and those visions. Since I'm a stranger, you had no reason to have your blocker up."

"I guess I just need to keep those thoughts guarded."

"Yes, you have to try," Callen agrees. "We can only hope that's the case."

"So, do you know why the Jeep wasn't damaged, and then was, and then wasn't?"

"Well, the second time it was me. I glamoured it. I saw it was damaged in the vision after we touched. I had a busy morning, Izzy. I was keeping you safe, and you had no idea. The first time, I'm not sure."

"What? Glamoured?" I shake my head in confusion.

"It's a spell to make things appear different."

"Oh," I respond, shocked.

"But the glamour wears off, as you've already witnessed. So, we need to deal with her Jeep. We need to get rid of it. Just in case."

"Jessa's going to be so pissed."

"I'll deal with it."

"So, what about the first time? Right after we hit Megan? The Jeep was fine by the time we got home," I say.

"I'm not sure. It could have been your ghost witch granny, Isobel. She's been in your ear, so it must have been her. She told you to run. She's probably been directing you toward your truth this whole time. Remember, she's powerful," he responds.

"So, if that's true… How is it possible when she's dead?" I ask, sensing I already know the answer—they never leave us.

"Witches are special beings, and they never fully move on. They live in limbo between worlds. Most never reach out, but Isobel is different," Callen says with a smirk.

He sounds insane, but it makes perfect sense. I was in that world with Anna just moments ago. I think. But I'm not ready to share that experience with anyone.

"OK. So, what are your parents going to do with Tim and Anna?"

"I'm not sure, but they said they would handle it."

"OK. I trust you know what you're doing."

"I appreciate your vote of confidence. We have to stick together. Everything I do is for the good of our kind. But, Izzy, now we have to figure out what to do about Riley. And

Tahlia, if she turns."

"All right. Let's do this, Callen. Let's break the hunter's curse."

The End

ACKNOWLEDGMENTS

Writing a novel can be a lonely experience. Thankfully, the publishing side is not, and I'm blessed to have so many incredible, encouraging, and talented people on my side.

First, I must thank my wonderfully supportive husband, Jeremy. My writing career wouldn't be possible without your love, encouragement, and support. I seriously couldn't do this without you!

A huge thank you to my editor, Nichole Heydenburg, at Poisoned Ink Press. I'm beyond thrilled that you agreed to work with me on this series! Your attention to detail and keen eye helped make this book what it is today. I'm grateful for you and I'm so glad we crossed paths.

Natasha MacKenzie, thank you for another brilliant cover. You outdid yourself with this one. The illustrations are gorgeous! Seriously, I can't thank you enough! You're truly the best at what you do!

For my loving family and friends who let me vent, talk shop, and pump me up on the regular. To my mom for your love, daily encouragement, reading the final draft, and a million other things. Dad, for your enthusiastic support and being my biggest fan. Emily, for our book chats and giving me notes on the final version. Sarah, for loving my characters as much as I do, and for pushing me to finish the story so you could find out their fate. Rachel for being you and letting me download all my crazy. Pam, for your encouragement and reading the final copy. To Tess for reading the early chapters and encouraging me to continue. To the rest of my family and friends who support me by sharing my posts, buying my books, attending events, and helping me get my name out there. Thank you!

Thanks to my critique/accountability partner, Stacey Spangler. I couldn't have finished the first draft without you!

Mariëtte Whitcomb for all your advice and for being the glue!

To the amazing Bookstagrammers I've met on this journey.

The Thriller Babes. Your expertise, guidance, and support is always appreciated.

To my beta readers and ARC team.

A huge thank you to everyone who helped me promote this book!

And last, to you, the reader. The reason I keep writing. Thank you from the bottom of my heart.

ABOUT THE AUTHOR

Jamie Lee Fry is an Oregon-based author with Iowa roots who enjoys creating dark, captivating, and fast-paced stories. When Jamie's not hunched over her desk plotting her next thrilling novel, she's hiking in the mountains with her husband Jeremy and their two dogs. Jamie never says no to a good adventure as long as mountains and waterfalls are involved. Jamie loves documenting life with her camera. She also enjoys stand-up paddleboarding, kayaking, cross-country skiing, baking, and consuming copious amounts of coffee.

CONNECT WITH JAMIE:

@Author_JamieLeeFry

www.authorjamieleefry.com